THE LOST LUGGAGE PORTER

A Novel of Murder, Mystery and Steam

Andrew Martin

faber and faber

First published in 2006
by Faber and Faber Limited
3 Queen Square London WC1N 3AU
This paperback edition first published in 2007

Typeset by Faber and Faber Limited
Printed in England by Mackays of Chatham plc

A CIP record for this book
is available from the British Library

ISBN 978–0–571–21904–9

ISBN 0–571–21904–7

2 4 6 8 10 9 7 5 3 1

Acknowledgements

I would like to thank PC Kevin Gordon of the British Transport Police (who would certainly not approve of some of the police behaviour here described); Mike Ellison of the North Eastern Railway Association; Nick Wellings, Marine Steward of The Brighton Circle; Michael Sanders; James Freedman 'The Man of Steal' (stage pickpocket); Peter Cox of the UK Immigration Service; Andy Hart of the SNCF Society; the left luggage staff at York station; Steve Earl; Dr P. Nockles of the Methodist Archive Centre at the University of Manchester; Mr M. G. Stewart; Ron Johnson and Clive Groome, train drivers.

All departures from historical fact are my responsibility.

PART ONE

The Twinkling Wanderer

Author's Note

This book is a work of imagination. No reference is intended to anyone who worked on the North Eastern Railway in 1906, or who lived in York or Paris at that time or any other.

Chapter One

In York Station, the gas lamps were all lit.

It was a wide, grand place. Birds would fly right through under the mighty span, and that roof kept most of the rain out too, apart from the odd little waterfall coming down through gaps in the glass.

I was on the main through platform on the 'up' side – number four, although it was the number one in importance, and crowded now, as ever, and with a dark shine to all the polished brass and the black enamel signs, pointing outwards like signals as you walked along: 'Gentlemen's Waiting Rooms First Class', 'Ladies' Waiting Rooms First Class', 'Refreshment Rooms', 'Left Luggage', 'Station Hotel' and 'Teas'.

No *lost*-luggage place in sight, however, although I knew that York, as the head station of its territory, did boast one, and that practically any article left on any train in the county came through it.

Wondering whether it was on the 'down' side, I stepped on to the footbridge, into the confusion of a hundred fast-moving railway clerks, all racing home towards supper and a glass of ale. A goods train was rumbling along beneath. It was a run-through: dirty, four-coupled engine with all sorts pulled behind. I leaned out from the footbridge to take the heat and the smoke and steam from the chimney: the soft heat, and the sharpness of the smell . . . I'd heard of blokes who gave up the cigarette habit but one whiff of the smoke and they were back at it . . .

Half a dozen banana vans came towards the end, the rain-water still rolling off them, and finally the guard, leaning out of his van like a man on a boat. A telegraph boy came trotting over the bridge, and I put a hand out to stop him, thinking he'd know me as a Company man like himself but of course he didn't, for I was in ordinary clothes. The kid pulled up sharpish all the same.

'Any idea where Lost Luggage is, mate?' I asked.

'Down there, chief,' he said.

But he was pointing to *Left* Luggage – the one on Platform Four.

'No,' I said. '*Lost* . . . *Lost* Luggage.'

The lad took a step back, surprised.

'Lost Luggage is out of the station, chief,' he said.

'Not too far, I hope,' I said, mindful of the teeming rain.

'Over yonder,' he said, putting his arm out straight in a south-easterly direction. 'Out the main exit and turn right. What have you lost, chief? I'll keep my eyes skinned.'

'Oh, nothing to speak of.'

'Right you are,' said the kid, who was now eyeing me as if I was crackers, so I said:

'Fact is, I'm down a quantity of *Railway Magazines* . . . Brought 'em in on a train from Halifax, then left the buggers on the platform, I think.'

'*Railway Magazines*?' said the lad, 'Blimey! I should think you *do* want 'em back!'

Evidently the kid is a train-watcher, I decided, not just an employee of the railways, but keen on 'em too. I nodded to him, then walked out of the station and turned right, going up Station Road, which went over the lines that had run into the *old* station, the trains proceeding through the arch that had been cut into the city walls. The building of those lines had been like a raid on the city made forty years since, but York was a tourist ground, an *Illustrated Guide* sort of place; jam-packed with the finest relics of old times. It had its looks to consider, and had fought back against the dirty iron monsters, with the upshot that the new station had been made to stand outside the city walls, with its fourteen platforms, its three hundred and fifty-odd trains a day, the great hotel with its two hundred rooms hard by.

From the highest part of Station Road, I looked at the miles of railway lines coming out of the station to north and south, spreading octopus-like. For a moment there in the rain blur, the scene looked just like a photograph, but then one goods engine out of dozens began crawling through the yard to the south, proving it was not. The engine rolled for ten seconds, then came to a stand. It had been like a move in a chess game, and now the rain came down and everybody on the North Eastern Railway fell to thinking out the next one.

The Lost Luggage Office was on Queen Street, which was half under the bridge made by Station Road. Before it, came a part of the mighty South End goods yard, which lapped up to Queen Street like a railway flood, and before *that* came the Institute, from which came a beer smell that decided me to put off my enquiry for a moment. I turned into the Institute, where I passed by the reading room – where the fire looked restless and the sole occupant slept – and walked through the long billiard hall towards the bar at the far end, reaching into my coat pocket as I did so.

'How do, love?' said the barmaid, reading the warrant card in my hand: 'Be it remembered that we the undersigned, two of His Majesty's Justices of the Peace in and for the City of York have this day, upon the application of the

3

North Eastern Railway, appointed James Harrison Stringer to be a Detective with and upon the railway stations and the Works of the North Eastern Company.'

'That's smashing,' she said, when she'd left off reading.

Only railwaymen could get a look-in at the Institute, and I was a railwayman of sorts, though not the *right* sort.

I put the card back in my pocketbook, and ordered a pint of John Smith's. Outside, the raindrops hitting the tops of the windows had a long way to fall. There was electric light in a green shade over each of the tables, darkness in between, and only one game in progress. The blokes playing looked a proper pair of vagabonds.

A copy of the *Yorkshire Evening Press* lay on the bar, and the barmaid passed it over to me. It was open at an inside page, from which one article had been neatly snipped. The barmaid saw me staring down at this hole, and she pointed to the glass cabinet, where the article had been pinned. It was headed 'The Twinkling Wanderer', and gave the news that the planet Mercury would be visible from York between 7.16 and 8.57 that evening, just as if it had been timetabled by Bradshaw. 'No difficulty should be found in picking out the planet,' I read, 'as no other object in the sky has sufficient lightness at that hour . . .'

I turned forward a page, then found the front page and read: 'Hotel Porter Found with his Throat Cut'. The article ran on: 'Late last night when the hotel night porter at the Station Hotel at York was called to go on duty, he was found in his bedroom with his throat cut. The unfortunate man, named Mr Richard Mariner, aged about 50, was found quite dead, and a razor with which the wound had been inflicted was also found in the bedroom.' That might turn out a matter for the Railway Police, I thought – the Pantomime Police, as I already knew they were called throughout the Company.

4

I looked again at the words 'throat cut'. The average man could read that and give it the go-by. Not if you were a copper, though.

The date at the top of the page was Friday 26 January. On Tuesday the 30th, I would report to the Railway Police Office on York Station for the commencement of my duties. I'd been sworn the week before at the York Police Court, and collected my suit as provided for in the clothing regulations. Detectives were allowed a plain suit and they could choose it themselves, providing the cost didn't overtop sixteen bob. I'd gone with the wife to the tailoring department of one of the big York stores for a fitting, and the design that we – by which I mean the wife – had settled on was a slate-blue mix twill; pilot cloth, 27 ounces to the yard, with Italian silk lining. I was now wearing it in . . . and it was sodden from the day's rain.

Next to the bar were notices in a glass cabinet. The minutes of the North Eastern Railway's Clerks' Amateur Swimming Club were posted up there. Membership was not up to its usual standard, the locomotive department having for some reason dropped out. I wondered whether it was to do with the strike: some York enginemen had been on strike for the best part of a month.

I looked above the bar: 5.45 p.m.

I would drink my pint before asking after my magazines, and I would have ten minutes' study. So I left the *Evening Press* and, taking from my side coat pocket my *Railway Police Manual*, I sauntered over to one of the long wooden benches lining the room.

The book was set out like a police work dictionary, and I began at 'Accomplice' while supping at my pint. But the queer talk of the two snooker players kept breaking in. They were both weird-looking: something wild about them, but something half dead too. One had his black hair kept down by Brilliantine (or a superior sort of engine grease); the other's hair sprang up. But they had about the same *quantity* of hair, so I guessed they were brothers, and pretty close in age, too: middle-twenties or so. Brilliantine was making all the shots, although he wasn't a great hand at potting. Curly hair was just looking on.

'I like the red balls,' curly hair said, and a lot of spittle came with the words. 'I like them to stay up.'

'You're in luck then, en't you?' said Brilliantine, taking aim, and making another poor shot.

'Will I get a turn soon, our kid?' asked curly, who was evidently a bit cracked.

'You'll get what you're given.'

No sound but that of missed shots for a while.

'I have a glass of beer but no cigarette,' said the crackpot.

Brilliantine moved around the table, looking at the balls.

'Will I have a cigarette soon, our kid?' said the crackpot.

'How do I fucking know?' said Brilliantine, still pacing the table. 'It's nowt to do wi' me.'

The crackpot caught me eyeballing him.

'You all right?' he said, fast.

'Aye,' I said, colouring up a little at being found out spying.

'Keeping all right?' this funny fellow said, in the same rushed way.

'Topping,' I said.

'Still raining out?'

'It is that.'

Brilliantine looked up from the table, saying:

'Don't mind him. Lad's a bit simple.'

I nodded, made a show of going back to my reading. Brilliantine made a few more shots in the game he was playing against himself, then took out a tin of cigarettes and lit one, grinning fit to bust. He handed a cigarette to the younger one, and struck a light.

'I like you, our kid,' said the crackpot in his gurgling voice. 'Nice, wide smile . . .'

Brilliantine played on for a while, and the idiot brother smoked. At last Brilliantine struck a red ball sweetly, and it went away straight towards an end pocket, or would have done but for the brother, who stepped forward, put his hand down over the hole and blocked it.

Brilliantine looked up sharply, saying, 'What are you playing at, you soft bugger?'

He walked the length of the table, and lammed out at his brother. As the lad went down, I stood up.

'Hold on,' I said to Brilliantine. 'That's an offence you've just committed.'

'Who are you . . . Talking like a fucking copy book?'

'I'm detective with the railway force,' I said, only half believing it myself.

'Give over,' said the bloke. After a space, he added: 'Prove it.'

I held up the warrant card.

'Means nowt to me,' he said. 'I don't know me letters.' He nodded towards the cracked kid, saying, 'How will he ever learn if *I* don't learn him? Smart table, this is – slate bed, best green baize. *She'll* not thank me for letting him put his grapplers all over it.'

He pointed along the hall towards the barmaid, who was looking on from the far end.

'It does not justify blows,' I said.

Nothing was said for a moment; then the bloke piped up with:

'Reckon you're going to nick me, then?'

I didn't know whether I was or not.

'Or would you let us off with a caution?'

That was a good idea.

I looked back at the nutty one.

'How's that cut?'

'Champion,' he said. There was a bright, brimming red line at his eye. 'You all right?' the boy then called out to me, 'Keeping all right?'

His affliction took him in such a way that he never uttered the first of those two questions without adding the second. At any rate, I ignored him.

A caution would meet the case, I decided.

'You are to be cautioned,' I said to Brilliantine, wishing I'd reached up to 'C' in my *Railway Police Manual*.

The bloke was chalking his cue.

I took out my notebook.

'Name?'

'Cameron,' he said, blowing loose chalk off the cue tip. 'John Cameron.'

'What's your brother's name?'

'Duncan,' he said.

I set down the date and then: 'I, John Cameron, having committed the affray of assault, have been cautioned by Detective Stringer of the Railway Force.'

'Sign here,' I said, passing over the pencil and the notebook, which came back with a great cross over the entire page, and most of what I'd set down obliterated.

'There's no need to look like that,' he said, 'I told you I didn't know me letters.'

I put the notebook away.

'Work for the Company, do you?' I said.

But he must have done, otherwise he wouldn't have been drinking in the Institute.

He nodded.

'Department?' I asked.

'Goods station,' he said, with the greatest reluctance. 'Outdoor porter.'

'And what about the lad?'

'Not up to working.'

'Well, if I see you scrapping in here again, you're for it,' I said.

I turned away and an arm was at my throat, squeezing hard. It wasn't Brilliantine. He was standing before me like a soldier at ease, with snooker cue in lieu of rifle, and seeming to grow smaller, to be shooting backwards in a straight line along the gangway between the tables. It was crazy, but the thing that was amiss was of the order of a disaster: I could not breathe. The snooker hall was being shut off by a blackness coming from left and right above and below. But in the light that remained the man before my eyes was moving. He was cuffing the idiot once again, inches away from me, and miles away too.

'Now do you take my meaning?' said Brilliantine, as the air rushed into my mouth, and my lungs rose faster still. The idiot was back where he'd started from, on the bench, giving me a strange, sideways look.

'He's round the twist,' said Brilliantine.

'I'll bloody say,' I said, as I set my collar and tie to rights.

'Usually it's me that cops it. He ought not to take a drink. In and out of the nutty house like a fiddler's elbow, that bugger is.'

'Under the doctor, is he?'

Brilliantine nodded.

'Bootham,' he said, meaning the York asylum.

He then went back to his snooker, with the idiot in position as before, holding his cue, waiting for the shot that never came.

As I saw off my first drink, and bought a second – to unstring my nerves – I couldn't help thinking that I'd been bested twice over by the pair. I sat back down, and carried on with my reading; or at least picked up my book and looked at the entry after 'Accomplice' which was 'Aiding and Abetting', but I had to keep a corner of one eye on the nearby loony, and couldn't concentrate. The brothers carried on their one-sided game until half-past six, when they walked out. By then I was looking at – but not reading – the entry for 'Arrest'.

I finished my pint, pocketed my book, and walked out of the Institute, skirting around the shadowy wagons in the goods yard that lay between the Institute and the Lost Luggage Office (which scrap of railway territory was called the Rhubarb Sidings, I knew), only to see a notice propped in the door of the latter office: CLOSED. Looking beneath, I read the advertised office hours: 6.30 a.m. to 6.30 p.m. I stood in the rain before that notice, and cursed the bloody Camerons.

Chapter Two

The following Monday, I was back in the Institute after another day of dangling about in York. It was a quarter after five, and this time I planned to be at the Lost Luggage Office in good time for half-past. It was still raining, and the Institute was just as empty as before, only with two quiet, reasonable-looking blokes in place of the Camerons. The day's *Evening Press* was on the bar, just as it had been on Friday last. I glanced at the front-page advertisements, turned to the sport at the back: 'York v. Brighouse,' I read, 'another defeat for the City team.' The barmaid was looking on.

'Try page two,' she said.

So I turned to it, and saw what must have been a good six paragraphs running down the middle of the page like a scar: 'York Murder' I read at the top, followed by 'Horrible Find at Goods Yard'. 'Last night,' began the article proper, 'Duncan and John Cameron, believed to be brothers, were found shot to death on the cinder path by York goods yard . . .'

The rest was just meaningless words to me, about how the York police were enquiring into the matter, appealing for witnesses to make themselves known. I couldn't take any of it in, such was the knock I'd received. Friday last there'd been the cut throat in the Station Hotel, and now this.

The paragraphs . . .

My eye ran up and down them again.

The barmaid was watching me narrowly.

'Surprised you didn't know about that,' she was saying, '. . . you being a policeman.'

'I'm sworn, but I haven't started in the job yet,' I said, turning to her with no colour in my face. 'Who were this pair, exactly?'

'Well, one was a railway man, on and off. That was John. And his brother was . . . well, I hardly know how to put it nicely . . .'

She thought the matter over for a while.

'He was soft in the head,' she said, eventually, 'as you found out last week.'

'Often caused trouble in here, did they?'

'Often enough.'

She moved away to serve one of the quiet blokes who'd walked up to the bar with the tread of a cat.

The York police were investigating – that meant the regular constabulary, not the railway police. I reached into my inside coat pocket and took out my Police Manual (with the page folded down at the point I had reached in my reading: 'Embezzlement') and hunted through it for 'M' and 'Murder'. But it didn't run to murder. Instead I saw 'Misappropriation', 'Misdemeanour', and 'Money Found on Prisoner'. Small stuff – lawyer's talk. Murder was out of the common. How many times would it come up in the working life of a copper? I shoved the book into the side pocket of my new coat, giving a nod to the barmaid, and quitting the snooker hall. On my way out, I glanced into the reading room. There was one man in there again, and this time he was awake all right, hunting through the Yorkshire papers on the big table, looking for more news of the Camerons, I was quite sure of it.

The same wagons stood in the Rhubarb Sidings, and now there was a light burning in the lost-luggage place beyond. I clanged through the door and there was an old fellow at a long counter guarding heaps of umbrellas. They were laid flat on a wide shelf ten feet behind him, in a room that smelt of wood and old rain. The walls were whitewashed brick. There was an overhead gas ring, with the light turned too low, and the white shades half blackened with soot, like bad teeth. This shone down on the old man, but its rays didn't quite reach a kid who was sitting on a stool in the shadows between racks of goods running at right angles to the counter. There were many of these, and what they contained I couldn't see, but all the ones parallel to the counter and facing out contained umbrellas.

'How do?' I said to the superintendent of the office.

He gave a grunt.

'What's that?' I said, giving him the chance to try again.

But he just grunted once more – it was the best he could do.

It was hard to say what was greyest about him: his hair, his beard, his eyes, his skin. He was like the old sailors in Baytown, only they had light in their eyes. I reckoned he must've been with the Company a good half-century, all the while being pushed further and further towards the edge of the show.

'I'm missing a quantity of *Railway Magazines*,' I said to this dead-ender, 'bundled into dozens, and stowed in a blue portmanteau.'

'Date of loss?' said the old man, with hardly energy enough to make a question of it. He had a telegraph instrument at his elbow, and a ledger set in front of him; beside this was a copy of the *Press*. Otherwise the counter was empty. The kid in the shadows at the back had only the stool he was sitting on.

I told the bloke the date, and the man started turning the pages of the ledger back towards it: 7 January, that stormy

13

Sunday when the wife and me had had our first tiff, a real set-to on the platforms of Halifax Joint station as we took our leave of the town for good. There was the wife, angry and in the family way – not a good combination – and there was I, still mourning the job I'd lost, and all around us the four bags we'd not entrusted to the guard's van.

When we'd got to York, I'd attempted to carry those four but, looking back, I only picked up three. When we discovered the loss, the wife had said: 'We'd have had no bother if you'd not been too mean to fetch a porter', and it hadn't sounded like the wife speaking at all but like something read from a book called *Familiar Sayings of Long-Married Women*.

'No,' the old clerk said after a while. 'I can turn nothing up in that line.'

'All right then,' I said. 'I'm much obliged to you.'

I turned towards the door, and I heard a scrape of boots from the shelves. The kid in the shadows was standing up.

He called out: 'They were marked down as "Books: miscellaneous", Mr Parkinson. I have 'em just here.'

The kid had a high, cracked voice, as if rusty from want of use.

Parkinson, the lost-property superintendent, looked at my belt buckle for a good long time, evidently annoyed that I should have struck lucky. Then he rose to his feet, saying: 'It is long past my booking-off time.'

He drew a line in the book and signed his initials against it.

'If the porter can be of any assistance you are free to consult him,' he went on, 'but I can spend no more time on the matter.'

Parkinson walked to the wall where his waterproof hung on the same peg as a dinty bowler. He put them both on, and walked towards the umbrellas, looking at them all for a moment, quite spoiled for choice, before finally giving a heave on a bone-handled one. He said nothing to the porter but walked to the doorway where he opened the door and shook the brolly furiously for a while, making a good deal of racket about it. When at last the brolly was up and over his head, it was like the moment when a kite takes off, and he walked away fast under the rain. Then the telegraph bell began to ring. After four of the slow dings, I looked towards the porter who was still standing in the shadows, now with a pasteboard box under his arm.

'Will you answer that,' I said, 'now that the governor's gone home?'

'He's not gone home,' said the porter.

'Where's he gone then?'

'Institute.'

That was rum. The superintendent had launched himself out into the rain with the look of a man at the start of a long walk.

The bell was still ringing.

'But will you answer it?'

He shook his head.

'Not passed to do it, mister.'

'But it could be a pressing matter,' I said.

'Such as what?' he said.

I couldn't think.

We listened until the bell stopped, and then we were left with just the sound of the rain. There was one mighty crash from the goods yard outside, and the kid said:

'I have your magazines here, mister, if you'd like to step through.'

There was a part of the counter that was hinged. I lifted it up, and walked towards the shelves, the lair of the lost-luggage porter.

'You a policeman?' he said.

'Sworn as a detective with the Railway force. How do you know?'

He pointed at the book that was sticking out of my side pocket: I put my hand to it, and saw that the words 'Police Manual', written in gold, could be made out.

As I closed on the porter, I could see that there wasn't much difference in width between his head and his neck. It was as though his neck just kept going up through his stand-up collar until it met his fair hair. My guess was that he had had some disease, and been growing in the wrong way ever since; he looked like a sort of ghostly worm. He wore the uniform of a platform porter, with the same low cap, but there was no company badge. Even the telegraph boy in the station had sported a badge, but they couldn't run to one for Lost-Luggage Porter.

The porter showed me the box. Looking inside, I read the familiar words: 'The *Railway Magazine*, 6d'. On the topmost one, there was a picture of an express inside a little circle as if seen through the wrong end of a telescope. I was glad to have them back, though they brought back sad memories – which was why I'd put off collecting them. Over the years since schooldays I'd supposed the purchase of each one to be a milestone on the way to the job of engine driver, but it would be a miracle if I ever attained that goal, after what had happened at the back end of 1905, in the Sowerby Bridge engine shed at Halifax.

'Miscellaneous, eh?' I said, looking down at the magazines.

The lost-luggage porter nodded, or shook his head; I couldn't really tell.

'All items are entered by Mr Parkinson,' he said presently, 'and he is very fond of that word.'

'Do you have the portmanteau they came in?' I asked.

'Reckon so,' said the porter, and he moved deeper into the maze of shelves, giving me a clearer view of the one containing the books. Each volume was inside its own little tin coffin, with a number chalked on the side. I looked into the first of the tins: *A History of Hampton Court Palace*. The second one I saw held *Every Man his Own Cattle Doctor*.

I began drifting along the lines of shelves. As far as most of it went, 'miscellaneous' was pretty near the mark: a ball of string, a stethoscope, a fan, a muff, some sort of automatic machine, a pair of field-glasses, a length of lace, sundry pictures, hair brush, shovel, leather hatbox, tin ditto, scent bottle, whistle, a pair of scissors, a clock, a lamp, a china figure, a box of collars, a pair of braces, a knife, a thermometer, a birdcage, a pail, a fishing rod. Sometimes like met like: one shelf contained only good cloaks, wrapped in brown paper – against moth, as I supposed. All the top shelves contained nothing but ticketed hats. Walking sticks and travelling rugs had shelves to themselves while another was for gloves by the hundred. And there were more umbrellas at the back, too.

The porter returned, dustier than before, with my blue portmanteau in his hand, and began loading my magazines from several of the metal tins back into it.

I said: 'A charge is made for collection, I suppose.'

'Thruppence,' said the porter.

I fished out the coin from my pocket, and handed it over.

'You've to sign the ledger,' he said, 'and put down your address.' So we went over to the counter again.

'You've a lot of umbrellas in here,' I said.

No reply from the porter.

'I daresay everyone says that,' I said, setting down my name and address in the ledger.

'The brollies ought by rights to be stood up,' I said, look-ing up from the book. The porter had unwrapped his buffet from brown paper. He was sitting on the high stool formerly occupied by Parkinson, and starting to eat bread.

'. . . If they were stood up, they wouldn't rot,' I said.

The porter just chewed at his bread, and looked at me.

'The worst weather for you blokes must be rain,' I said. 'You must be head over ears in work whenever there's a downpour.'

'Folk don't forget umbrellas when it's chucking down,' he said. 'They forget 'em when it stops.'

'I see. Because then the brollies are not like . . . first thing on their minds.'

I looked at the clock that ticked above the staff coat hooks: it was nigh on half-past five.

'You must want it pouring all the time then,' I said.

After a longish pause, the porter said:

'It can do just what it likes.'

Behind me, I heard the sound of the rain increasing.

I spied a shelf containing nothing but leathern purses and pocketbooks. I went close and saw that they were all empty.

'What's become of the money that was in these?' I asked the porter. 'Pinched,' he said, still eating.

'So you reckon the finders lift the money before bringing in the pocketbooks?'

'No,' said the porter.

'How do you account for it then?'

I waited quite a while but there was no answer from the strange kid.

'Well, thanks for turning these up,' I said, tucking the port-manteau under my arm.

He might have said something to that, and he might not. I turned towards the door and the rain; I opened the door.

'Items lost across all the North Eastern territories are forwarded here under a special advice if not called for after a week,' the porter said, and I stopped. He was climbing down from the high stool, and for some reason – maybe the thought of being left alone in that dismal room – was suddenly minded to chat.

'Why are some brollies kept at the front, and some at the back?' I said, letting the door close behind me.

'Paragons and silks at the rear,' he said, 'cotton brollies at the front. They would be stood up, only where would the water drain off to?'

'I never thought about that.'

'I have. All hats are kept high so as to reduce damage by pressure.'

'Eh?' I said.

'Many curious articles do come to hand,' he said, crumpling up the brown paper in which his bread had been wrapped. 'We had a banana in last week.'

'Where from, mate? Africa?'

'Leeds. Well, Leeds *train*, any road.'

'What happened to it?'

'Mr Parkinson entered it in the ledger.'

'As what?'

'A banana.'

'What happened then?'

'It turned black, and I asked Mr Parkinson for leave to pitch it into the stove.'

'Waste of good grub,' I said. 'If somebody had tried to claim it would you have required them to furnish a full description?'

He seemed to hesitate on the point of utterance, but in the end simply looked at the black window.

I opened the door again.

19

'Well, I'm much obliged to you, mate!' I said, stepping out into the rain with my bag.

I was skirting around the wagons again, when he called after me:

'Where you off to?'

'Home,' I called back.

'Can you get over to the station in one hour from now?'

'Why?'

He coughed a little.

'. . . See summat,' he said, after a while.

'Where exactly in the station?'

'Down side!' he called back with the rain sliding down his bent, white face. 'I've to lock up first, but I'll see you at half six!'

'Aye,' I said, 'all right; half six, then.'

It would mean biking back to Thorpe-on-Ouse an hour later. The wife would be put out, but she couldn't expect me always home directly in my new line of work. I wondered why the queer stick wanted to see me, and then it hit me: I was a policeman.

Chapter Three

I lugged the magazines with me through Micklegate Bar – the grandest of the city-wall gates – and on into the city. At the Little Coach in Micklegate, I took another drink, putting the peg in after a couple of glasses, and when I stepped out the rain had eased off, though the streets were still empty.

I knew York a little, having grown up nearby at Baytown. (I'd also had an earlier spell of working for the North Eastern Company, my railway start having been a lad porter out at Grosmont.) But I couldn't think of where to go, so I pursued an aimless way about the centre of the city, where the streets were narrow and ancient, the houses all overhanging, falling slowly towards the pavements. I turned into Stonegate, where a solitary horse was turning on the cobbles, too big for the street.

I walked on through those ancient streets: cobbles, shadows, funny little smoke-blowing chimneys on powdery-faced, sagging houses; old buildings put to new uses: bakeries, drug stores, tea rooms – newly established or selling off, the shopkeepers came and went at a great rate but the old houses carried on, even though some of them looked as though they could barely support the gas brackets that sprouted from them. I turned and turned, and presently I struck the Minster, the great black Cathedral; the Minotaur of the labyrinth, as I thought of it, with its two mighty West towers, sharp-pointed and horn-like.

I doubled back across Lendal Bridge, looking along the river at the coal merchants, sand merchants, gravel merchants. They all became one at night: so many shouting men, so many cranes, so many dark barges, which were like the goods trains – meaning that they seemed to shift only when you turned your back.

In Railway Street, on the approach to the station, I passed by two dark, dripping trees with *Evening Press* posters pasted on to the trunks. The first read 'York Brothers Slain'; the second made do with '*Yorkshire Evening Press* – The People's Paper'. A constable was coming towards me. I'd seen him before about the station, but he was not with the railway police. Of all the lot from Tower Street – which was the main copper shop of the York Constabulary – he was the one whose patrol took him nearest to the railway station. He was a smooth, dark, good-looking fellow with a waxed moustache; he looked like a toff who'd dressed up as a policeman for a lark, and he passed me by without a glance or any hint that we were in a way confederates.

A two-horse van nearly knocked me over as I wandered under the arches into the station forecourt, and another came charging close behind. I walked past the booking halls, and struck the bookstall, and here were *Evening Press* posters by the dozen, loosely attached to placards and pillars, and this time every one of them reading, 'York Brothers Slain'. The posters moved in the cold breeze that blew through the station, and I thought of each one as soaked in blood, so to speak, like pieces of newspaper stuck on to shaving cuts. The whole bookstall was blood-soaked, now that I came to think of it: the shilling novels full of murders; the periodicals with their own mystery killings, moving towards their solutions in their weekly parts, and each tale with its own detective hero – a sleuth hound with peculiar habits but a mighty brain. The man who stood in the centre of all this sensation – the stout party who kept the bookstall, who was nearly but not quite to be counted a railwayman . . . he stared out at me with no flicker of recognition in his piggy eyes. Did he not see in me the invincible detective type?

I moved in on to Platform Four. The station was alive even if the city was not, and it was ablaze with gaslight. 'Down side,' the lost-luggage porter had said. That meant crossing the footbridge, and, as I put my boot on the first step, the telegraph lad came skipping down towards me with telegraph forms in his hands.

'You found it then, chief?'

He was looking at the portmanteau.

'Aye,' I said, grinning at him, 'office and bag both.'

'Champion,' he said, before haring along Platform Four to the telegraph office, where he would doubtless have a couple of minutes' rest before being shot out again like a bagatelle ball.

'Down' side . . .

Well, half the platforms were on the 'down'.

With the portmanteau seeming to grow heavier by the minute I walked over the bridge to Platform Five, where a train was about due. A dozen folk stood waiting, and there was a big fellow lying on a luggage trolley smoking: a station lounger, waiting for a 'carry'. I walked west of the platform, through an arch in the station wall to Platform Fourteen. It was a wooden platform – a new addition – but this was where the Scotch expresses called, and there must have been one due, for thirty or so people waited, including the platform guard with his silver whistle strung about his neck, and his little army of porters, all talking in short bursts, as if nervous.

The clock on Platform Fourteen showed 6.40 when I saw

the engine come swerving through Holgate Junction, steam flowing from the chimney like a witch's hair, the line of lights behind bulging to the left, then to the right. I heard a cough behind me, and it was the lost-luggage porter, sopping wet and with a small valise over his shoulder. He said nothing but just gave me a half-nod as the engine came up, the handles on its smoke box making the shape of half-past four.

The engine pulled up alongside us, and it was another thing again close to, with the leaking steam, and the rain on the boiler like sweat. Hard to credit that it needed the permission of signals or the help of men to get to its destination.

'What's going off then?' I asked, just as the engine came to a stand alongside us.

'*Summat* is,' said the porter. 'The Blocker's pitched up, so the Brains'll be here presently.' He was looking vexed, staring along the length of the platform, observing all the give-and-take of train arrival.

'What's your name?' I said.

'Edwin Lund.'

He said it fast, without putting out his hand; he didn't seem over-keen to learn mine but I gave it him:

'Stringer,' I said. 'Detective James Stringer.'

No; still didn't sound right.

A man came up, half running half walking through the arch that led to Platform Five.

'The Brains, I call him' said Lund in an under-breath nodding in the direction of the man. As he spoke, Lund was shifting along towards the north end of the platform, looking away from the man he'd just identified.

The man was too tall for his coat, and his long hands were held out to the side, so that he settled like a bird onto the platform. He began looking about. Then the really big fellow, the lounger from Platform Five, was with him.

'You'll have your bob's worth now, mister,' said Lund, who'd taken up position on the opposite side of a porter's cabin from the two blokes we were watching.

The Blocker was straight into a party of ladies boarding at a door somewhere about the middle of the train. He seemed set on doing the job of a porter, and was offering to help a lady with her basket, but she was shaking her head, and so he only added to a mix-up of cloaks, bags, and over-sized bonnets. The Brains stood looking on. A porter was coming up the crowd now. The Brains stopped him in his tracks, and started trying to chat with him, but the porter would have none. He was after the tips from that scrimmage of train-boarding women.

At the front end of the train, the north end, the fireman was down on the tracks, wrestling with the coupling and the vacuum pipe. The engine he'd helped bring in belonged to the Great Northern Company. It would now be replaced, and the train taken onward by one of the North Eastern's locomotives. The fireman was right below my boots. The fellow was sodden from the rain that had blown into the cab on the trip; he was clarted with oil and coal dust, and his oilcloth cap had a great burn hole in its middle. I was jealous of him all the same . . . I was jealous of every engine man that stepped.

I moved to try and make out the number of the engine, which was an Ivatt Atlantic.

'Look out,' said Lund.

The confused ladies had been abandoned. The Blocker was walking fast along the platform in our direction, and the other was following behind, but he was the one you noticed, and what you noticed most particularly were his long hands. The Ivatt Atlantic was now pulling away from the front carriage, leaving a great gap in the air. It always looked wrong when an engine uncoupled, like a head being chopped from a body. You half expected blood.

But I should have been looking south, as Lund was.

'Wham!' he cried, and his thin voice cracked at the word, just as the Blocker clattered straight into a man who'd lately climbed down from a carriage, and was fishing in his waistcoat for his watch.

And now the Brains was on the scene, also assisting the gent who'd been knocked down. The Great Northern engine was off and away, leaving the train beheaded. The knocked-over gent was set back on his feet, helped into the train, and Lund was saying quietly, half to me, half to himself: 'They have it now, I'm certain they do.'

Brains now had his back to us; after a second, a small black object twirled away from him and landed under the carriage of the train into which the toff had stepped. Almost before it had landed, he was walking away, his hands held out and down, like something precious, and the Blocker was at his side.

Then they were running, as they went through the arch leading to Platform Five.

'Watch that,' I said to Lund, pointing at my bagful of magazines, and I scarpered after them. 'I am a detective, and I shall arrest you on a charge of theft.' The words ran through my head as I came onto Platform Five, where there was a man leaning against a pillar . . . and *another* man leaning against a pillar. They were not the Brains or the Blocker; they had similar weird looks to the fighting Camerons of the Institute. All of a sudden, the station seemed full of loungers – fellows who could not be relied on to come and go with the trains.

I dashed onto the footbridge. I was the arresting officer, and I would bring the charge; I would be in the Police Court, and in the *Yorkshire Evening Press*, too: 'Detective James Stringer, of the North Eastern Railway force, who is stationed at York, took the stand . . .'

The thing was not to fret about the job. Get in deep. Then I again couldn't see the Blocker and the Brains even from the centre of the footbridge, which gave views of the whole station. I looked about for a constable, and gave a glance over in the direction of the Police Office, which was also on Platform Four. My view was blocked by the signal box that overhung the bookstall on that platform, and I couldn't even make out if light burned in the Police Office.

I gave it up, walked back to Platform Fourteen.

The 'down' express had gone, carried by its new North Eastern engine off to Newcastle, Berwick, Edinburgh. Lund, the lost-luggage porter, stood on the platform coughing. The pocketbook was in his hand, caught up from the tracks.

'Did you tell the gent that his pocketbook had been lifted?' I said.

He shook his head.

'Why ever not?'

'Train pulled out in double quick time,' he said, and he began coughing again – a real workhouse cough.

'You all right, mate?' I asked him.

He nodded. His uniform gave him a schoolboy look, but it was impossible to make out his age.

'I'd have thought you'd take an umbrella with you on evenings like this.'

'Why?'

'Well you've about three thousand to hand in your place of work.'

'It's against regulations to take 'em out.'

'But your governor, Parkinson, does it.'

No answer to that.

'Why did you not tell the police before – about those two, I mean?'

I gestured along the empty platform.

No reply.

'What'll you do?' he said after a while.

I thought hard for a second.

'I'll make a report,' I said.

He looked at me and then looked away. He'd been galvanised by the activities of two vagabonds, but now he'd gone back to his silent ways.

'You'll be a witness, won't you?' I said. 'You'll stand to all we've just seen?'

He might've nodded; hard to tell. I picked up my bag, just as an S class 4-6-0 rumbled up to the place recently left by the Scotch Express. More steam, more rain-sweat. It was a mighty green beast, hard to ignore, but Edwin Lund managed, standing there on Platform Fourteen with his cap in his hand and his long, twisted face turned away from the engine.

As I made to walk off, he suddenly called: 'Garden Gate!'

'You what?' I said, stopping in my tracks.

'Garden Gate,' he repeated. 'Public house. You'll be able to put your hands on those chaps in there.'

'How do you know?' I said.

He shrugged.

'They're regulars there. Never fail.'

'But *how* do you know?'

'I live close by, Ward Street, and I've seen 'em in there,' he said. 'Well . . . *going* in, any road.'

'You didn't follow 'em in?'

He shook his head.

'Taken the pledge, like.'

'Well,' I said, 'I might get across there tomorrow . . . That's my starting day on the force.'

'Garden Gate, Carmelite Street,' said Lund, before being overtaken once again by his cough.

Chapter Four

I walked over the footbridge, heading for the bike stand at the front of the station. My way took me near to the Police Office and sure enough it was shut for the night. A notice on the door asked any passenger in distress to contact the night station manager. I'd been in the Police Office once before, very briefly, on the day I was sworn.

At the bicycle stand, the Humber was waiting. I took the lamp out of the saddle bag. There was water in the top all right but I was rather low on carbide. I pulled the little handle that set the water dripping on to the powder, opened the front of the lamp, lighted a match and put it in. The rain in front of the lamp now fell through white light. I fixed the lamp to the front fork and set off for home.

I cycled up Railway Street with a trace of acetylene smell coming to me from the lamp. It had been a twenty-third birthday present from the wife, and at five bob was worth more than the bicycle. I was glad of it, of course, but while beforehand I'd thought of every subject going during my cycle rides, I now thought of only one: the bloody lamp. It would keep going out, and it *would* keep falling off the bracket.

Along Thorpe-on-Ouse Road new, white-brick houses were going up. In the ones already occupied, light burned brightly, as if for swank: look at us, nicely settled with electric light, running water upstairs and all modern conveniences laid on. I thought of the Camerons, and then I thought of Edwin Lund. He had a down on the pickpockets of York station . . . But why were they any concern of his?

Beyond the building line, I was flying past the racecourse when the gas gave out in the lamp, and so I went on just as fast, but with a little nervousness. I came along by St Andrew's Church. The field in front was like the night stretched out and laid flat on the ground. One minute later I was skirting the gates of the Archbishop's Palace and skidding into Thorpe-on-Ouse Main Street, which was really the *only* street, separating the two rows of trim cottages set in nearly straight lines. Johnson, the bootmaker, faced Scholes, family butcher; Lazenby's post office faced Daffy, newsagents; the Grey Mare public house faced the Fortune of War public house, and if one shop or business should close down, it was like a tooth knocked out of a mouth. And so it had long been.

No man in Thorpe-on-Ouse supped in both the Grey Mare and the Fortune of War. It would be like bigamy. The Mare had *its* lot and the Fortune its own. I was for the Fortune of War, but I couldn't have said why. I looked across to the front bar. No noise from there and no movement behind the lace curtains. I could hear a horse shifting in the stables behind, but that didn't mean it wasn't asleep and dreaming.

I stood under the street's one gas lamp, listening to the River Ouse rolling on out of sight past the eastern edge of the village. You could hear the river at any time in Thorpe, but you needed to work at it. It came to you if you paid attention. I looked up at the sky, trying to make out the planet Mercury – the Twinkling Wanderer, the *Yorkshire Evening Press* had called him. There were a few stars staring straight back. Nothing twinkling. Over the road and along, I saw an *Evening Press* placard propped outside Daffy's newsagent and seeming to glow somewhat. I could not make out the words, but I knew they would be 'York Brothers Slain', the news blaring out though the shop was long since shut. Would the placard be there the next day? For John and Duncan Cameron would still be dead then.

I opened our garden gate. The cottage we'd taken at five bob a week was just over from the Fortune of War, cut away from the road with a long garden in front and another behind. It was number 16A, as though squeezed in at the last minute between numbers 16 and 17. The people who'd had it before had risen to pig keeping, and there were makeshift sties to front and back. It was only as I approached the front door that it struck me I was without the portmanteau and its magazines. 'Buggeration!' I said out loud. Where had I left the bag: on Platform Fourteen or at the bike stand?

I opened the door, which gave directly on to the parlour, and there was the wife, sitting at the strong table by the fire, and going at her typewriter as usual – fairly racing at it. Whereas some women took in dress-making, the wife took in typewriting from an agency in York, and that by the armful.

'How do?' I said, kissing her.

'Did you get your magazines then, our Jim,' she said, not stopping typewriting.

'I got 'em, but then I lost 'em again,' I said.

'You 'aporth,' said the wife, clouting the lever that slid the typewriter carriage. We had the machine on hire; it was a Standard, and the wife said it was worn to pieces but it seemed to serve pretty well.

'I collected it from Lost Luggage all right, but then I left it near the bike stand, what with all the palaver of . . .'

It was unfair to blame the lamp, so I stopped there. I fettled up the fire a bit, saying: 'How's t' babby today?' and giving a grin. The wife didn't like these Yorkshire speaks.

31

Between her and the typewriter was her belly under the maternity gown. She had all on to reach the keys.

'I'm too busy to be thinking about that,' she said, and I looked across at the page in the machine: 'Thank you for yours of 14th inst . . .'

'That kid's going to be born writing letters,' I said, walking through to the kitchen where I found a bottle of beer in the pantry.

'Oh I was forgetting. There's a telegram for you!' the wife called.

I hurried back into the living room with the bottle unopened – news of a telegram could make you do that.

The wife was pointing at the mantle shelf, at an envelope addressed: 'Detective Stringer, 16A, Main Street, Thorpe-on-Ouse, York'. It was a shock to see myself called a detective in print. The form read: 'REPORT TO POLICE OFFICE 6 A.M. TOMORROW'. My instructions had been to book on for my first day's duty at eight, so this was a turn-up. But it was the name at the bottom that really knocked me: Chief Inspector Saul Weatherill.

It had to be concerning the Camerons. What police business in York could *not* be just at that time?

The wife had stopped typewriting, and was looking at me.

'It's from the Chief Inspector,' I said to the wife. '. . . Top brass.'

'What's he say?'

'He wants me in at six.'

'In where?'

'The police station.'

'Where *is* that, exactly?' said the wife, going back to her typewriting, only more slowly.

'It's at the railway station.'

The wife frowned over the keys, saying:

'So you're stationed at the station?'

Was she the one person in the vicinity of York who knew nothing of the murder? Ought I to tell her? She'd pushed me towards police work, and she ought to see what it meant in practice . . . But she was not in the condition to receive shocks.

'There must be something on,' I said, dropping the telegram into the firewood basket.

'We had a letter as well,' said the wife. 'Your dad . . . He's coming here on Sunday.'

No smile came with these words. My dad and the wife did not get on. Dad had turned out in all weathers to listen to the Conservative chap in the late election, and the wife . . . Well, the wife was a suffragist.

'If he's coming, he's coming,' I said, sitting down on the sofa.

'Yes,' said the wife, still typewriting. 'The train service between Baytown and York is unfortunately excellent.'

'On the day,' I said, 'you are to make a big tea.'

The wife was like a cat on hot bricks whenever the subject turned to cooking. Cheese, bread, cocoa, yes: anything more, a fellow had to fight for it.

'I will make a *tea*,' she said carefully.

We had many more hot dinners out than other couples similarly placed, and ate a sight more from tins than was probably good for us. Then again, the wife earned money typewriting, and a good deal of that went on the housekeeping.

'When he comes,' I said, standing up and walking over to the fire, 'will you try to avoid a set-to?'

'How am I to do that?'

'Just don't bring up the subject of votes for women as soon as he steps through the bloody door.'

33

I crushed a speck of coal that had flown out on to the linoleum. I could not sit down when having these discussions with the wife.

'Is it my fault if your dad suffers from sex prejudice?' said the wife.

'He's sixty-five,' I said. 'He didn't know what sex prejudice was until you showed up.'

'Well then,' she said, 'I'm only too happy to have been of assistance to him.'

I looked about the room.

'Where's the sewing machine?' I said.

'It's in a safe place, where it will not get in the way.'

Or used, I thought.

Dad had bought the wife a sewing machine, sent together with a note suggesting that she might make a layette for the baby. But the wife meant to *buy* a layette for the bairn, and that was all about it. He'd also taken to sending her "The Ladies' Column", snipped out from the *Whitby Gazette*. It was all recipes and household hints. The wife had read the first one only. 'I don't believe it's written by a woman at all,' she'd said, before pitching it into the fire.

'We must put the sewing machine out again when Dad comes,' I said.

'Very well,' said the wife.

'He's trying to make you a wife more like his own,' I said. 'She loved cooking, you know, my mother . . .'

'The poor soul,' said the wife, typewriting away.

But it was best not to dwell on this subject, for Dad's wife, my mother, had died in childbirth (with me the child in question).

I sat down, thinking once again of the Camerons, but saying:

'. . . Chased some pickpockets today at York station.'

'Arrested them, did you?'

I shook my head.

'They ran off.'

'What're you going to do about it, then?'

'Make out a report,' I said.

'That'll settle 'em,' said the wife, grinning.

She might tease me but the wife was pleased that I'd joined the police. It was one of the few things she had in common with my dad: they both wanted me to get on. Dad, of course, was an out-and-out snob with about as many aspirations as any comfortably retired butcher could run to, while the wife . . . Well, she was something of a snob too, for all her belief in the woman's cause and Co-operation.

I had suffered alone after being stood down from my job on the Lancashire and Yorkshire Railway. To the wife, it was simply a great thing that the tin tub was not now needed every night. Then again, she came from money herself in a modest way. Her mysterious, lonely-looking father had owned several properties in and about the viaducts of Waterloo, and the wife had come into a bit when he'd died, with the result that she was plotting the purchase of a house to replace the one we'd lately sold in Halifax. This, she said, would be equipped with a thirty-shilling walnut bureau 'for our correspondence' and a five-pound pianoforte for 'musical evenings' which I had spent hours trying, and failing, to imagine. (Neither of us could play a note, to begin with.) These were the fixed aims of her domestic life, and housework could go hang in the meantime.

I had supper of boiled bacon, pickles and tea, and read a little more of my *Police Manual*, telling myself I would keep at it until the biggest log on the fire burnt away, but it didn't seem to burn, only to turn black. There was a lot of it left by the time I got up to 'Fraud' and quit the book.

I went up to bed with the wife at a little after ten. Before pulling the lace curtain of the bedroom to, I peered past the fern that stood on the window ledge. Nobody about in Thorpe. I thought for some reason of the Archbishop sleeping in his Palace, the river flowing slowly by; and it was impossible not to imagine him looking like one of those statues found on church tombs. The Palace would bring a few trippers to Thorpe in summer (I'd been told) but it was a sleepy spot, all right. After Halifax, it was like being left behind by the world. Yet, two weeks before we'd arrived there'd been a windrush through the village – not occurring anywhere else – and forty-nine objects, according to the vicar, had been overturned, including the oak next to the Old Church, which stood marooned by the river.

The wife came into the room carrying her raspberry tea, recommended for those in her condition. Her nightdress hung about one foot higher than usual, because of the baby bulge beneath, and her travel around the bed put me in mind of the orbit of the planet Mercury. Her due date was two months away. If the idea bothered her, it didn't stop her sleeping, and she was quickly off.

I wanted a boy – tell him about engines. Except that I was done with them myself. I could hardly think about locomotives now, without going back in my mind's eye to Sowerby Bridge Shed, 12 November 1905. To think that at the start of that day, I'd still been able to see my way clear to a life on the footplate. What with memories of that calamity, and wondering whether I'd be put to chasing murderers come six o'clock in the morning I couldn't sleep, so walked down to the kitchen for a bottle of beer. But we were all out.

PART TWO

The Garden Gate

Chapter Five

It was 5.55 a.m and raining hard when I pedalled up to the bike stand just outside the forecourt of the station and dashed inside. I raced past the bookstall, where the placards of the *Yorkshire Post* (a morning paper) read 'York Horror', but also 'Terrific February Gales at Coast'. The bookstall was long and narrow like a carriage that never moved, and I didn't care for it. The stout party in charge was laying out his murder library. As a kid, I'd been warned off light literature by my dad, with the result that I read little in the way of fiction at all, having no real liking for the heavier stuff. I had read always of the railways, and railwaymen were the ones I'd looked up to, not detectives, but it would be something to settle the Cameron business, and for the first time in weeks I was entering railway premises with some of the excitement, and some of the fear, of my engine-firing days. I felt lean, forward-thinking, useful again as I strode towards the Police Office.

One man stood at the ticket gate. He was jumping to keep warm. I showed him my warrant card, and he said, 'OK,' still jumping. I turned left at the ticket gate thinking about Chief Inspector Weatherill. It wouldn't just be me and him. There'd be others present no doubt: Shillito, the Detective Sergeant, who was to be my governor – I'd met him shortly after being taken on. Langborne was the Charge Sergeant, and then there was Wright the Chief Clerk . . . I'd yet to meet this pair.

I hurried along under the clock on Platform Four, with the Police Office now in sight. It had two main frontages in the station: one looked westerly, facing out onto Platform Four; the other faced south, and overlooked the buffers of a bay platform, number three. The door (set into the southerly façade) was unlocked, which it hadn't been the evening before; so somebody had pitched up. I walked in. The gas was lit, but not the stove. The big desks and cabinets were like islands, and no two faced the same way.

A few feet from the cold stove stood the cold fireplace: two chances for heat spurned, making me feel colder still. Above the mantel, instead of a painting, there was 'By-Laws and Regulations of the North Eastern Railway Company', and on the mantelshelf below stood a photograph: 'Grimsby Dock Police Football Team 1905'. I thought I recognised one of the players: Shillito, the DS. It was him all right, for the names were written along the bottom. He must have transferred from Grimsby.

Grimsby was in the Eastern Division of the Company force, whereas York was the headquarters of the Southern Division, and Chief Inspector Weatherill was the governor of the Southern Division. The only man senior to him was Superintendent somebody or other, who was quartered at Newcastle, and boss of the whole show.

Opposite me was a solid blue door. This led to the holding cells, I knew, of which they were two. Nobody was kept in overnight. If charged and remanded they were taken over to the regular copper shop at Tower Street, in a station hansom if need be. At the far end of the office was another blue door: Chief Inspector Weatherill's office. I walked up to it, and yanked it open just to make sure that the fellow wasn't in there.

But he was.

Salute? Yes, no. Yes.

I saluted but might as well not've. Weatherill was sitting side on to me, looking up at *his* cold mantelshelf. He seemed to be gazing at a little silver cup, and I could make out the words 'TUG OF WAR' engraved on it. They were nuts on sport, this lot.

Chief Inspector Weatherill was a big, untidy man who looked as though he'd done a lot in life. He wore a long green coat – of decent cloth but none too clean – buttoned right up to his head. He had only scraps of hair; they were of an orangey colour, and swirled about his big head like a dog chasing its tail. His nose wandered down from his eyes to his mouth by a very winding route, which made me think he might've been a prize fighter in his day. He'd been through it all right.

'It's a good suit,' he said, turning slowly about to face me, 'nicely damped and pressed, 'n' all.'

He stood up, walked around the desk towards me. He had his hands in his pockets, which somehow gave him a look of being about to do absolutely anything. He took his hands out of his pockets and pulled open my coat, looking at the lining. Steam came from his mouth, and a sharp smell. There was all sorts wrong with his face when seen close-to: scars, lumps, burn marks maybe. His nose seemed to have tried out lots of shapes, and settled on none in particular. His one perfect feature was his moustache, which was darker than his hair, and stretched out widely like a spirit level or the governor of a steam engine. It was there for balance.

'You put in for the allowance?'

'I did, sir,' I said.

What was all this blather? When would he come to the Camerons? I could hear his breaths as they came and went through the 'tache. He was still looking at the lining of my coat – he seemed easily entranced by little things.

41

'Best Italian silk, sir,' I said.

'Where's your Derbies?'

I took the handcuffs out of the side coat pocket where I kept them, and he put his hand in where they'd been.

'Too small,' he said. 'Suit coat should be extra long in the skirt pocket to stow the Derbies. You see, a detective should have plain suiting but not *ordinary* suiting . . . But it's a good rig-out.'

The room smelt of carbolic and old ash. Weatherill took a cigar out of his desk, lit it.

'. . . But you're going to have to put it away for a while.'

I didn't like the way he kept saying 'but'.

'Why, sir?' I said.

'We have some bad lads in York just at present,' he said, through smoke. 'Some shocking bad ones, but we've no notion of who they are, or where they are, or *what* . . .'

He broke off to stare again at the little trophy; he didn't seem able to bring to mind the third thing he didn't know. He put his hand through the remainders of his hair, pulled at his collar.

'Sit down,' he said suddenly, 'sit down.'

I sat down. At last we were to start talking murder . . . But nothing at all happened for a moment, except for Weatherill taking a few pulls on his cigar.

'You've heard of a put-up job, I take it?' he said, presently.

'I've heard the expression, sir,' I said.

'What do you understand by it?'

'Well . . .' I said. 'It's something arranged beforehand, like.'

'No,' said Weatherill. 'I mean, *most* things are arranged beforehand, wouldn't you say?'

'Most things are on the *railway*, sir.'

He thought about this bit of philosophy for a long while, or maybe he just looked as though he was thinking about it.

'A put-up job,' he said slowly, 'is an *inside* job. It depends on information that can only be got from inside a locked bureau of a railway office.'

'Is this matter touching the Cameron brothers?' I asked, at which the Chief Inspector frowned while shaking his head slightly. He looked at me narrowly, and I directed my gaze away from his face and towards the wide cabinet behind his desk. The top drawer was marked 'PLANS'.

'I want you to go out into York,' he said, holding his hands suddenly very wide. 'And I want you to trace out the bad lads in the Company who are putting up the jobs, and the bad lads outside who they're putting 'em up *to*.'

Silence in the room, clock marching on loudly.

'*How?*' I said at last.

The Chief Inspector fell to smoking, and looking at the top of his desk, and after a bit of this it struck me that I was most likely not going to get an answer. So I spoke up again, as I slowly tried to get to grips with this unexpected task I'd been given.

'You want me to wear a different suit for the work?' I said.

'I do that. Something in cloth of a lower grade, and I want you to stay out of the city when you're not on the job. You live at a fair distance, don't you?'

'Three miles on the bicycle . . . well, three miles *anyhow*.'

'You're not known in York, are you? I mean, it's not yet widely known that you're on the force?'

As he spoke, the Chief Inspector was producing papers from his desk, and looking at them as if he'd never seen them before.

'You are to search in all directions,' he continued, 'and once you have found these fellows, you are to become their confederate.'

'You mean give out that I'm crooked myself?'

He nodded, saying:

'You are to play a double game.'

I was not chasing killers, but it struck me that there was danger in this business too, and some of my earlier excitement came back, and some of the fear.

The Chief pushed the papers over to me. There were two piles. Pointing to the first, he said, 'These are cases that have been occurring along the lines I've mentioned.' Pointing to the second bundle, he said: 'These papers are quite blank.'

I picked these last mentioned up and looked at them. They were *not* quite blank. At the top of the pages were the words 'North Eastern Railway Police', neatly printed. The Chief Inspector folded his arms. I looked back at him, and he nodded at me for a while. The question why I'd been given the almost-blank sheets was on my lips, but I felt I'd asked a sight too many already.

'You're to write down the progress of your investigation on those,' he said after a while. 'At the top of each page, put "Special Report", then write "Subject" and, next to that, "Persons Wanted". Write up the report at the end of every day and send it in to me.'

'How?' I said again.

The Chief looked down at his boots; I heard the air moving in and out across the moustache again.

'In the post,' he said, looking up at last.

'In the *post*?'

'Reason being you are not to be seen about this office in daylight hours. Oh, and put your hands on some carbons, so you can keep a copy of each sheet for yourself.'

'What should I do if the matter is urgent?'

He sat back, quite amazed at the question.

'There are four postal collections a day in this city, you know,' he said.

'How many hours do I give to the job, sir?' I said.

44

'How many hours? You can't be clocked to this kind of business with a patent time clock, lad. Do you have any notion of where you might start?'

'Yes,' I said. 'The Garden Gate.'

The Chief Inspector gave a puzzled smile up towards the Tug of War cup, then turned his gaze my way.

'Wanted!' he suddenly exclaimed. 'Nice cottage, with orchard!'

'The Garden Gate is a public house, sir' I said. 'The haunt of some low characters so I've heard. It's in Carmelite Street.'

'Layerthorpe way,' Weatherill said, nodding, the smile quite gone now. 'The York constables go down there two at a time, you know.'

Nice, I thought.

I was on the point of telling Weatherill about Edwin Lund, about the Brains and the Blocker, but it had all come to naught, after all. Instead, I finally brought up the matter of the Camerons, although again leaving myself out of the picture: 'I've read that a Company workman and his brother were shot on,' I said. 'It happened in the goods yard – bodies turned up on Sunday.'

'Wrong,' said the Chief, loudly. 'It happened on the track *outside* the goods yard, and that is the most important fact in the case.'

'Is that right, sir? Why?'

'Because it means we don't have to bloody solve it. That track is York, not the railway; therefore what happened happened in *York*. Therefore Tower Street can try their luck.'

Tower Street – the main copper shop of the York Constabulary.

The Chief Inspector stood up once again, and opened the door that led from his office to the main one.

'I'm stepping over to the hotel for a spot of breakfast,' he

45

said, and I took this as the signal that I should stand up, too.

'The Hull fish special comes in to Platform Three at 6.45 every weekday,' said Weatherill. 'You can't miss hearing it, because it thunders up as if it's about to crash through the bloody door. Now, if you need to use this office, I want you out of it by then. He took a draw on his cigar and the smoke came out in rolling chaos as he said: 'You were a footplate man yourself, weren't you, over on the Lanky?'

'Aye,' I said.

'What happened?'

'They say I wrecked a locomotive, and a ten-bay engine shed.'

The Chief looked at me.

'It wasn't my fault,' I said.

'How come?'

'The steam brake wasn't warmed, and I was told it had been.'

'You're blinding me with science now, kidder. But I can credit it.'

He continued to look at me, nearly smiling, but expressions were hard to make out from his face. What might've started out as a smile could have easily got lost on the way.

'Let's say a fortnight's observations and becoming familiar, Detective Stringer,' he said. 'Your wages will be sent out to you by special post. Light the stove if you want, but remember: out by quarter to.'

I saluted again, although I wanted to ask: 'If something should go amiss with my investigation, how do I give the alarm?' I watched the Chief Inspector walk through the door of his own office, and the door of the main office, leaving them both open, and rocking in the freezing draught.

Then he came back. Putting his head around the main door, he said, 'Never go home straight to your village while

46

you're on this duty – always by a roundabout route,' which set me thinking of the wife at home, typewriting alone in the cottage cut away from the street.

I nodded, and he was gone again.

Chapter Six

There was a pail next to the stove with kindling and coal in it. A billy stood on top of the stove, and I found a tea caddy, pot and cups on a window ledge. It was strange to be at large in that empty office, to hear my boots rattle on the boards, to brew up with other blokes' tea. It was as though I was the fugitive, not to be glimpsed in daylight. Beyond the door the station was coming to life, like a slow explosion of growing power. I could hear engines coming in . . . the stopcocks released, giving that great sigh of steam as if the engines' only task was to bring steam into the station, and empty it out directly. It was gone six when I'd done lighting the stove, and as I turned to the papers I'd been given, I felt I'd spent too long on the job.

The first bundle was a heap of criminal record papers, all tied together with string. There were photographic portraits and I thought: all this lot are my enemies now. Most of the subjects had queer-looking eyes like the Camerons: broken glass eyes. And you tried to read the story in the eyes – match it with what was set down in print.

The details began with 'Correct name', 'Aliases', 'Nickname', 'Marks'. Most didn't have an alias or a nickname, but most had marks. 'Lady Godiva tattoo on shoulder', 'Tattoo of a dagger on upper arm'. The 'Last Known Address' of most of them was York or villages roundabout. 'Places Frequented' . . . that was all pubs. Criminals didn't frequent anywhere except pubs. The category 'MO' interested me. In the timetables of Bradshaw that meant 'Mondays Only'. Here it meant . . . what? Manner of operation? Method of operation? It was not explained. Entries under this heading were diverse: 'Smooth character'; 'Impersonates carter'; 'Card sharp knocks on doors'. I put the papers to one side, reckoning that I would need not only a different suit but a different name for the fortnight ahead. Looking down at the top board was a man whose face was tipped forwards – his face pointed down, and his hair pointed up. His offence was marked down as 'Stations, Setting Fire To' and his name was Allan Clough, which seemed about right as far as the name. Allan, any road.

I would need a profession: Thief.

And an 'MO'.

Steals anything, anytime.

No, I wouldn't need that. Criminals did not exchange record cards like the gentry with their calling cards. Very likely, most didn't know they *had* an 'MO' but just went about being themselves. I looked through the stack of cards again, and struck a man who had 'Nuisance' written as the entry for 'Offence'. He was the only one of the whole lot pictured smiling, so he was evidently a loony as well as a nuisance. This was the world I was entering: the world of nuts and double crossers.

Well, I was in queer all right.

I sat back on my chair, pictured myself on the high footplate of one of the Lanky's Atlantic engines, the Highflyers, and how, up there, you just soared, receiving the most wonderful return for expenditure of coal that I could think of.

The next bundle on the table before me was stuffed into an envelope that had the words 'Occurrences – Large Theft'

49

scrawled across it. There was another word underneath, but I couldn't make it out. Inside were not more than half a dozen sheets of paper, each one fastened behind a bit of pink pasteboard. At the top of each sheet were the words, 'North Eastern Railway', 'Division', 'Station', 'Date', and 'Log'. It was all written in a quite shocking hand, and I had all on to read the entries. The first recorded 'Attempted (possible actual) burglary at office of Goods Superintendent, York Yard South. Mr Cambridge (Goods Super) will endeavour to ascertain losses. No losses reported at present.' The date given was 1 December 1905. The second concerned the South Yard again: two vans had been entered by persons unauthorised and unknown. Lindsey and Jones, wine and spirit importers of Liverpool, were down three crates of whisky and a quantity I could not make out of claret. The van was not locked, but had been sealed. The seal appeared undisturbed, and yet the goods were gone. So it must have been broken, and replaced by somebody who could put their hands on the Company's seals. On the same night, 14 December 1905, a lock had been smashed on a Company van containing items belonging to the Acetylene Illuminating Company of South Lambeth. Nothing was taken, as far as could be seen.

The next gave details of a robbery at the York Station Hotel, the very spot where Chief Inspector Weatherill was putting away his eggs and bacon at just that moment – the very spot where Mariner, the night porter, had been slashed in the throat, or slashed himself. The robbery had happened on 16 December. A safe had been opened in the housekeeper's office. One hundred and fifty-five pounds, two shillings and ninepence had been removed, and a mysterious 'personal article' belonging to a Mr Davenport, a guest, together with one golden wristwatch belonging to same, and something I couldn't read.

Then came a final piece of pasteboard and a final clip, but no paper. I fretted over this for a moment, then gave it up, tied the two bundles as I'd found them, and put them back on Weatherill's desk. The only thing on the desk was a blotter, and I could read some of the words where the ink had come through. 'Firing catapults from trains,' I read, before the words broke up and faded away. I walked over to the little trophy above the blank mantelpiece, and read the inscription: 'Presented to York Division, Runners-up in Tug of War, Malton Field, 1902'. It bothered me that he should've given pride of place to a runners-up trophy.

I walked back into the main office, set the stove for slow burn, gave my tea cup a wipe and walked out of the Police Office, closing the door firmly behind me just as the Hull fish special rolled in to Platform Three dead on time. I'd heard of this train, which was famous for not being what it was supposed to be. It was mainly a passenger service, but half a dozen boxes of fish – special fish – would come down every morning from the guard's van, and be taken into the hotel. Little local deliveries of goods such as this could sometimes avoid being sent round the houses into the York goods station.

It was one of the new eight coupled engines that had brought it in, and the driver was leaning down looking along the platform. He moved slowly, with a tea bottle in his hands; that was his privilege after all he'd done since Hull. But the porters attending the train moved fast, rolling back the tall doors on the guard's van, taking down the fish boxes consigned for York. There was much shouting, and spilling of ice on to the platform, and mixing up of fish boxes, portmanteaus, and passengers.

The train gave off coldness; the engine heat. I stood next to the engine, and the driver gazed down at me with a look of curiosity – it was quite clear who he was, but who was I? He took off his cap, as if to scratch his head over the matter and it was just as though the hair went with it: he was quite bald, but that did not signify. I watched and waited, thinking about my last days in Halifax, as he ran round his train, then pulled it away south again, tender end first. A hundred yards beyond the station one high signal among dozens moved for his train, while a single porter remained on Platform Four, kicking ice down on to the tracks.

I would have given fortunes to be that driver.

Chapter Seven

It was bitter cold, and still raining as I walked over to the bike stand with my head down, revolving a new thought about the Camerons. I'd had a run-in with them, and been seen about it. The barmaid at the Institute was a watchful sort, and knew my name. It might come up in the investigation. A thought checked me: I might be suspected of having done it. That would be about right, for in becoming a policeman I wasn't really doing a job so much as working out a punishment.

I walked on, thinking that if the Camerons were all they'd seemed, there'd likely be a long queue of suspects ahead of me. One had worked in the goods yard, and there'd been crimes in the goods yard. He was the second Company man to meet a violent end. The first had been Mariner, the night porter at the hotel, whose throat had been slit – by him or others. The Station Hotel was our territory, but the cinder path by the goods yard . . . Well, it seemed to me that ought to be ours as well, for not much happened on that path that didn't have something to do with the movement of goods on the railway.

I had been ordered to keep away from the station in daylight hours, and I wondered whether that included the Lost Luggage Office. At any rate, I meant to collect my missing bag once again, if it hadn't been nicked. I also wanted for some reason to set eyes on the mysterious Lund again. I looked up towards the bike stand, and my portmanteau was there, not three feet from the back wheel of the Humber. A quarter of a minute slowly dragged itself out as I stood there in the rain staring at it. It couldn't have been there at 5.55 when I'd arrived. I'd have run straight into it. Then again I'd been in a tearing hurry, so might have missed it. I looked inside: the magazines were all there, the top one a little damp. I picked up the bag, and heard a smooth Yorkshire voice saying, 'The first article is described as a brown canvas bag, about three foot in length, corded, with "Nursing Sister Harper" printed on it in white letters. It contains a bed, one black mackintosh sheet, a pair of rubber boots, one rubber pillow, one ordinary pillow, one wash basin and one collapsible basin.'

It was the assistant Stationmaster, protected from the wind and the rain by his long black coat, and his silk topper. He was holding some papers, and reading from them for the benefit of Parkinson, the morngy lost-luggage superintendent, who wore his overcoat and bowler, and carried an umbrella, which he was fighting to keep still in the wind. He was looking sidelong as the assistant Stationmaster addressed him.

'I will have the porter make a special search, sir,' he said.

'See that you do,' said the assistant Stationmaster. 'It's the third letter I've had about this bag. Now,' he continued, shuffling the papers in his hand, 'listen to this.'

'Might we stand under the portico?' said Parkinson.

'It will only take a minute,' said the assistant Stationmaster, who began reading from a second sheet. 'The undermentioned luggage is missing. Large-sized wooden suitcase, brass studded, two side clips, centre lock, bearing label addressed "Williams, 60 Forest Walk, Scarborough." It may also carry labels for Chatham and Newhaven. Contents . . .

Japanese gown, nightgown, tweed golf coat, black blouse
and slip, felt hat, black straw hat, woollen hat, girl's dress,
four pair stockings, grey silk scarf, black crepe scarf, comb,
sponge, silver-backed brush, skunk fur for neck, opossum
ditto, white circular jade pendant, tiger claw and chain . . .'

The rain redoubled, and Parkinson gave a sigh.

'Am I boring you, Mr Parkinson?' asked the assistant Stationmaster.

'Not at all, sir,' said Parkinson.

'Two pair trousers,' the assistant Stationmaster continued,
'three petticoats, boy's shirts and vest, two nightdresses,
child's war game, belt, leggings, Burberry, tennis shoes,
walking boots, and toilet articles to wit toothbrush, face flan-
nel, nail clippers, tweezers, soap times three, tube of Euthy-
mol, hand cream . . . Have you seen this luggage?'

'No,' said Parkinson.

'Will you have the porter make a special search?'

'I will.'

Parkinson trudged on towards the Lost Luggage Office,
and I watched him go, wondering: did he return my magazines to me? It was possible, since I'd come upon him standing so near to them. Set against that, though, was the
thought that returning my magazines would have involved
work, something Parkinson was evidently not over-keen on.
And he had not acknowledged me or even looked in my
direction while being lectured by the assistant Stationmaster.

I cycled off legs akimbo, with the portmanteau balanced
on the crossbar of the Humber, for I could see my way clear
to using it at the Garden Gate. If anyone had returned them
to me, I thought, pedalling away in the direction of town, it
had surely been Lund – making, perhaps, his early round of
lost-property collections – rather than his governor, Parkinson.

I knocked about York all morning, fretting about the Camerons, Lund, the sharps at the station, and my prospects at the Garden Gate. At midday, I bought an *Evening Press* in Museum Street, and there were precious few details added to the story, only that the bodies might have been lying on the cinder track for a day or more before discovery. Otherwise it was all windy stuff: the case appeared to contain features of strong dramatic interest . . . a certain vicar meant to make mention of it in a sermon to be given in the Minster on the following Sunday. It was also pointed out that this was the first year in living memory in which two murders had occurred in the city. The previous year, there'd been none at all.

I turned around and saw the West towers of the Minster, the great bull horns, black against the grey sky. The shilling novels on the station bookstall had three-colour wrappers, but there were only two colours in central York at that moment. I folded my paper into the pocket of my new suit. A metal panel was nailed to the scrap of city wall that overlooked Museum Street: it said 'Uzit: The Ointment for All Occasions'. Beneath it stood a rough-looking bloke, smoking a cigar in the rain, watching me. I turned tail and rode the Humber along past the rattling carts of Coney Street, turning at the end into High Ousegate, where I propped the bike beneath a board that stuck out from a tobacconists reading 'CIGARS', the letters going round almost in a circle. I was not interested in baccy but the sign signified the start of an alleyway at the bottom of which was the office of a coal merchant, and a tiny rag shop that was half underground. The sign above the window read 'Clark' in very small letters – whispered it. You walked through the door, and immediately down some steps, as if a floor was too pricey a luxury. Inside was a small old man who'd shaved only in parts. 'I'm after a suit,' I said, since the old fellow had said nothing but just looked at me.

The place was dark and sour-smelling; the suits behind the man were like a pile of flat dead bodies.

'Suit for every day?' asked the old fellow, without removing the cigarette. Smoke came up with each word, so that he communicated by puffs of it, just as the Red Indians are said to do.

'Yes. The one I've got on is my Sunday suit,' I added, to make a straight story of it. 'Might I have a look?'

He turned away from me with his hands in his pockets, which was the signal that I should fall to on the clothes heap.

After a couple of minutes, I found a suit that was a sight worse than any I'd ever seen before. I put on the coat, and the old man turned back towards me, smoking out the words:

'Best class work, that is. You're well away with that. Couldn't ask for a better.'

I held the trousers up against my legs. The cost was sixpence, and as I paid the fellow, I leant into his smoke, and across some tins he kept full of dusty trinkets. One of these held a tangle of old spectacles. I picked out one pair, put them on.

'How much are these, mate?' I asked, standing before a fragment of looking glass that hung from the wall, but hardly able to see a thing.

The word 'tuppence' came in two puffs of smoke.

I handed over the coin, took off the eye-glasses, and pushed out the lenses. I put the specs back on, and my reflection came clear. It was a regular marvel: there was no difference between the look of glasses with lenses and glasses without. The old fellow, looking on, had at last removed his cigarette.

57

'More to your liking now, are they?'

'Aye,' I said.

'You're nuts,' he said, very firmly and definitely. Then the cigarette went back in.

I walked out of the shop with the glass-less glasses and the suit bundled into my portmanteau on top of the magazines. I walked towards the gentlemen's lavatory in Coney Street, down the steps to where the wash-and-brush-up man waited. I knew him to be a sensible fellow in a white coat (every one of the dozen or so hairs on his head very carefully Brilliantined), and he did not blink an eye at the sight of me in my spectacles. It was a test, and he – or I – had passed it.

I put a ha'penny in the door slot, and locked myself in one of the WCs, where I put the old suit on, laying my good one on top of the magazines in the bag. Then I pulled the chain for good measure. As I stood there amid the roaring York waters, I tried to tell myself: my blood is up; this is all quite a lark, and on better wages than I earned on the footplate. But I kept wondering: ought I not to have been given a police whistle or some other method of giving the alarm? I was too much at large in the world; I wanted the rules and protection of the railwayman's life.

I stepped out of the WC, and the wide looking glass was before me. The sight checked me for a second. I was Allan . . . Allan something, late of Halifax. Factory turns and work in the fields – that had been my lot; and a spell in the workhouse at Bradford. I saw myself as Allan, approaching York on foot from Leeds, alone in the wide fields, with a griming of snow on the soil. Plainly I was in want of a tattoo but otherwise I fancied I looked the part.

I now trudged miserably on, killing time around the narrow ancient streets, where the rain raced along the wide stone gutters, and the houses were kept up by force of habit alone. The York citizens, with their derby hats and celluloid collars, had the care of the city for a little while, but before long there'd be a new lot, with different hats and collars. I remembered a scrap of history about York from the school-room at Baytown: 'Here history is almost the history of Britain.' What were the deaths of two brothers when set against that?

I walked on, thinking about the wife at home typewriting behind the long garden with the washing line too high, like a telegraph wire. How could my work be kept secret from her? It seemed unimaginable, with her brains.

The stiff, damp suit wanted to walk in a different way to my way – or to lie down and die, just as its late owner had certainly done. At getting on for 3 p.m., I crossed over Lendal Bridge, went past the new North Eastern office – that great riverside stack of railway clerks – and through the arch in the Bar Walls towards the station. Walking through the portico, past all the shouting carters and cabmen, I thought: I should not be showing my face here. I was too close to the Police Office, base of my operations, but I had to stow my good suit.

This I did in the Left Luggage Office, a far brighter and cheerier spot than the *Lost* Luggage Office, full of whistling blokes and light. I made sure the warrant card and the Der-bies were in the pocket of the suit I handed over; I held on to the *Railway Magazines* though. As I turned away from the office, clutching the ticket I'd been given in return for the suit, I saw the Lad, rushing along with his telegraph form. 'How do . . . Cheerio,' he said, laughing as he shot past. I walked quickly off the platform. It was then that I saw, over on Platform Six, which was generally the one for Leeds, an engine belonging to my former employers, the Lancashire and Yorkshire Railway, the black paint with red piping. It was a 0-6-0 Class, one of the Wigan Bashers, good for any kind of work, from pick-up goods to main line. The Wigan Basher had four coaches on, and it was heartbreaking to see it pulling away, not tied down to rain, cocoa smell and dreary York ways.

I took my dinner at the bargeman's café on the King's Staith, walked about a bit more; took a pint at the Ouse Bridge Tavern, then stepped out into lamplight and dark rain shine.

It was nigh on four o'clock when I struck out for Layerthorpe.

Chapter Eight

Carmelite Street I knew to be somewhere in the shadow of Leetham's Flour Mill, which was nigh-on five times higher than the terraces roundabout. Evening was coming down fast as I walked towards the mill, which had three silos, like cricket stumps, connected at the top by the conveyor, which was like the bails. On its other side, the mill looked onto, and dropped things into, the River Foss, which ran along as best it could between the little terrace houses of Layerthorpe. No trippers came this way; the *Illustrated Guides* had nothing to say about Layerthorpe, except maybe to warn strangers off.

Carrying my bagful of *Railway Magazines*, I entered a dead-end street. At the bottom of it was a wall covered in an advertisement for boot polish. It held a picture of a bootblack calling 'Shine, sir?' then, in bigger letters 'SHINE, SIR!' Wouldn't take no for an answer, that one.

I turned right down an alleyway between two houses, just in time to see a kid boot a dead rat along the road. Above his head, a wooden sign stuck between the two walls read: 'The Tiger'. That was another pub to be found somewhere in this maze, but it was a couple of minutes more before I came on the one I wanted.

There was no garden and there was no gate, and there was hardly any *pub* come to that. It was just one thin house in the terrace. Above the door and to the right, a tiny tin sign said

'ALES', like a stamp on a letter. The words 'Garden Gate' were spelt out in small white letters on the black door. I stood there picturing every kind of York cadger and area sneak putting back beer inside. I pushed at the door, and walked in.

His cap was off, and his hair was round and white like a jellyfish, but it was the big oaf, the Blocker, all right – standing just inside the door with his coat open in a tiny blue room filling with smoke from a badly laid fire, which set my eyes stinging straightaway. The Blocker seemed to be looking directly at my glass-less spectacles. Then, to my relief, he turned away. Approaching the bar, I glanced down and noticed my wedding ring. Allan Appleby was not a married man. I pulled it off as I stepped up to buy a drink. Serving on was an old fellow who stared at me all the while as he raised up a pewter of beer from somewhere below the bar. Leaning on the bar to my left was another elderly party, like the barman seen in a looking glass. And there was another present, sitting by the fire on a rocking chair: the Brains, the dip who haunted the Scotch expresses.

A bottle of stout was on the floor by the side of his chair, and he was raising and lowering two long keys on a rusty ring that hung from the end of the longest finger of his right hand. He sat in his coat, but his hat was off, and he had scant black curly hair and sleepy eyes. He looked like a musician, I thought, and I wondered why he could not have put his long fingers to better use by learning to play the mandolin, or some such thing.

He was watching me as I walked towards the bar, and the Blocker spoke up as I walked past, but I didn't catch the words. I ordered a pint of Old, drank it off fast with shaking hands; ordered another. I stood side on to the bar, my portmanteau at my feet. The Blocker was leaning on the door, blocking it, giving me the eye. The Brains was still playing with the long keys.

Taking a deep breath, I pitched in:

'I'd be obliged for another glass of Old,' I said to the barman, 'and two more for these lads.'

I pointed at the Blocker, and the Brains. They were looking back at me, holding fire, waiting further developments. Then, as the landlord started to pull the beer pump, I added: 'Can you not do owt about your fire?'

'Want more coal on it, do you?' he said.

'Less, if anything,' I replied, 'and a little air put to it, perhaps.'

This drew the Blocker, who said: 'Who are you giving orders to?'

'Nobody,' I said.

Silence again. The Brains had put down the keys, folded his arms. He was watching me.

It was the old barman who spoke next:

'Are you a sanitary inspector by any chance?' he said.

I shook my head.

'Because you better fucking not be,' called out the Blocker.

The drinks were now being set on the bar. I put one on the fireside table in front of the Brains; handed one to the Blocker.

On receiving the ales, neither man said anything; but they continued to stare.

At last, the Brains spoke up: 'I'm obliged to you for the pint,' he said, 'but what's it in aid of?'

'Just being hospitable,' I said.

'But the Gate's our boozer,' said the Blocker, 'so by rights, it's up to us to be hospitable to you.'

As he spoke, I heard a sound from the direction of the door. It was the Blocker, sliding home the bolt.

A longish silence, broken once again by the Blocker:

'. . . Speaking of hospitals,' he said, 'you're going just the right way to ending up in one.'

'I've come to see you specially, like,' I said.

The Brains said: 'How did you know we were here?'

'Might as well give out that I followed you last night,' I lied.

'But we never came here last night,' said the Brains, sounding curious more than anything, 'not directly at any rate.'

'That's right,' I said.

'I know it is,' said the Brains.

'You went somewhere else beforehand,' I said.

'Where, for Christ's sake?'

'Over yonder,' I said, moving my hand so as to maybe indicate everywhere else in the city.

'But where *exactly*?' asked the Brains, almost smiling.

'You went to a pub,' I said.

Well, it seemed a fair hazard.

'*What* bloody pub?' said the Blocker, impatient.

'Don't recollect the name,' I said. 'I'd spotted the pair of you at the station, see? A chap had on a very heavy coat. And you lightened it for him. It was a very good bit of work.'

The blackness rolled from the fire; the old boy at the bar said another thing I couldn't catch.

'Well,' said the Brains after a while, 'what's your interest in the matter?'

'I was thinking you might be able to use another pair of hands.'

Long silence. The Brains stood up.

'I've never seen you round the rattler before,' he said.

'I'm new in town, like.'

'From where?'

'Hebden Bridge.'

'And where's that, when it's at home?'

This was the Blocker speaking.

'Next door to Halifax,' I said.

'How did tha get bread there?' asked the Blocker.

'Had a go-on in a factory, like.'

'A factory making what?' asked the Brains.

'Screws,' I said.

I looked at the Brains: a foxy-looking sort: skimpy hair, sleepy eyes; a lot of eyelid visible at all times. Pickpocket . . . Well, it was a skill above the ordinary thief.

'I had a bit of a run-in with the charge hand . . . got stood down over it, so then I worked in the fields for a time . . . Over Bradford way. That was last back end – harvest time.'

'And when the harvest was in?' the Brains asked.

'Workhouse,' I said. 'It was a pretty soft doss.'

'Got a name?' said the Brains, with the creeping smile about his lips as before.

'Allan,' I said.

'Allan bloody what?' said the Blocker.

'Allan Appleby,' I said.

'Bollocks,' said the Blocker.

I gave a glance down at the portmanteau, saying, 'I had this away earlier on.'

I kicked the bag over towards the Brains, who stood up, plucked out one of the magazines, leaving a page dangling on which we both read the words 'British Locomotive Practice and Performance.'

From over by the door, the Blocker said: 'What's this rubbish?'

'*Railway Magazines*,' I said.

'Short of arse wipe are you?' he said, striding over, taking that particular number from the Brains and pitching it on to the fire, where it just lay in the smoke for a while. Presently, though, it began to burn, signifying as it did so the end of all my railway hopes for ever. I did not want to be in this smoke hole, I did not want to be in the Pantomime Police, and the anger came up in me all at once.

'You're a fucking rotter,' I said to the Blocker.

I heard the Brains say something surprised-sounding as the Blocker closed on me. His fist went back, and I fancy that I said out loud, 'Here we go, then', just before spinning back under the blow, feeling the bar floor come up towards me like something carried on a wave.

I put my finger towards my eye, and it touched my eye too early. Some things had happened. The fire was smoking even more strongly, and the place was becoming like a damned kipper house. I put my hands to my eyes again. Of course . . . the fake spectacles were not there. It was all up with my disguise. I was propped against the bar, and the Brains had swapped places with the Blocker.

'You in the York workhouse?' he said, in a kindly sort of tone, with folded arms.

'No,' I said, and I saw the specs on the floor beside me, good as new. The want of glass in them might not have been noticed after all. I picked them up, and put them back on my nose.

I was all right really, refreshed somehow by the thought that the worst had passed for the moment. My eye was swollen. I could force it open, but it wanted to be closed so I left it be. As the water from the stinging smoke rose within it, I wiped it away with my coat sleeve.

'I'm in a lull just at present,' I said, 'but I'll turn me hand to outdoor portering . . . handyman . . . spot of cow walloping now and again on market days. You can get half a crown a day at that lark.'

66

'Who maintains you in between times?' asked the Brains.

I looked at the fire, where the magazine number was one big cinder under the flowing smoke.

'Me old man has a bob or two put by. It's him I lodge with . . . over Holgate way.'

'You'll take a pint?' said the Brains, and he stepped back and nodded at the Blocker, who stood up and walked around the bar, to draw the pints himself. Of the landlord there was now no sign. The fossil at the bar had pushed off, too. The Brains jabbed at the fire, reached into the chimney and moved the flue, and an orange glow was revealed in the grate.

He pulled two more chairs from the far side of the room over to the hearthside, and we all sat down as the Blocker came back with the beer.

'What's your game then, mate?' said the Blocker, after necking most of his ale.

'Well, I've seen you operating up the station,' I said, 'and I liked the look of it. You know, steal from folks before they get on a train then don't get on yoursen . . . And I was wondering whether I could lend a hand.'

'Put 'em up,' said the Blocker suddenly, and I made two fists thinking: is he going to lam me again?

Then the Brains was shaking his head.

'Fingers held out straight, like,' he said, and I did as he said. The Brains looked at my fingers, looked away.

'You've the right-shaped hands for a hoister,' he said, staring into the fire. He turned to me once again, saying: 'Ever done the work?'

Before I could tell another tale, the Blocker was reaching out towards my glasses.

'Let's have a skeg through those gogglers, mate,' he said, and I swayed back away from him.

'Leave off,' I said. 'I don't like other folk . . . looking through 'em.'

The Brains laughed.

'Well, we're all cranky *some* way,' he said.

He stood up; the Blocker stood too.

'Finish up,' said the Brains, looking down at my beer.

'What's the programme, lads?' I said.

'Little stroll,' said the Brains, '. . . maybe look out for a soft mark while we're at it. Look slippy now.'

I downed the beer, picked up my bag, and followed them out into the street. I was very glad to be out into the cold and rainy air . . . and my bad eye was now giving less trouble. It had simply gone to sleep. Directly we turned the first corner, the Blocker said, 'Bears.'

As Chief Inspector Weatherill had told me, there were two of them – two coppers, thin men in capes, walking fast with their dark lanterns in their hands. They passed us by without a glance. I was next to the Brains. The Blocker had fallen in behind – he was the owl, keeping eyes skinned to protect the Brains. As we walked, the Brains put his long hand out to me. 'Miles Hopkins,' he said. 'Glad to meet you, Allan.' He had a good grip, and shook my hand hard as I hazarded his age (he was perhaps thirty-five, a good ten years older than me at any rate).

We came to a rare gas lamp. It illuminated a curved wall covered with posters – a great, glowing bay of advertisement, with nobody about to read the words: '*Aladdin* at the New Theatre Royal', 'The *Yorkshire Gazette* – for the Farmer, the Sportsman, the Fireside', 'Turn Right For Capstan's Cigarettes.'

But we turned left, striking a row of pubs – a good hundred-yard run of pubs or jug and bottle shops before the cobbled road rose, becoming a little bridge over the River Foss. Some light leaked from the pubs, which were mostly ordinary terraced houses that had a different life at night. The front windows were low, and Miles stooped to look through some of them as the wind and rain picked up. He looked with an expert eye into those parlour bars. The first few were silent, but desperate shouts came at intervals from the fourth or fifth one, as if orders were being passed among the crew of a ship. Some of the houses had names: the Full Moon, the Ebor Vaults, the Greyhound. Others didn't run to names.

I thought my nerves would either get set or get shattered, but they did neither, and all I could do was wait, trying to disguise fast breathing in the meantime. On the little bridge, Miles Hopkins and the Blocker stopped for a conference. I looked down at the river. The Foss was not more than five foot wide, compressed by factories, and darker than the night. I thought of my bike, waiting in High Ousegate to carry me back to Thorpe-on-Ouse and the wife. It was a breakaway I could not easily imagine making.

The conference was over. Miles Hopkins touched my arm, and we crossed the bridge to see a stubby little street of crumbling bricks blocked at the far end by a high wall, as if somebody had tried to cross it out, a mistake having been made. In the street stood one house, one shop – 'Todd for Meat' – and three pubs, all bigger than the earlier ones. Going by their names, these pubs did not seem to know they were in Layerthorpe: the Cricketer, the Fortune of War, the Castle Howard.

With Miles Hopkins leading the way, we made directly for the Castle Howard. It was one wide, low room, half full, and with a wooden framework in the middle that made it look like a barn loft. Just inside the door, a man stood drinking slowly, with his glass held horizontally at his face as he turned back and forth, like Admiral bloody Nelson with his telescope. He broke off from this performance as we entered, grabbing the Blocker's sleeve and pulling him away into a corner. I heard one word from the two of them before Hopkins pushed me gently towards the bar: the word was 'Cameron', and I was running again through the engine shed at Sowerby Bridge, riding a locomotive with no brakes.

On a trestle behind the bar sat a row of big barrels, like cannon. Three men crossed back and forth, working the taps. A dozen men stood at the bar, and one sat on a high chair. Hopkins was pointing towards this fellow, but my mind was on the Camerons.

'Who's whatsisname talking to?' I asked Hopkins.

He looked quickly backwards.

'Never mind him,' he said, and he gave a grin, adding: 'He's allus boozed.'

Whether he meant the man with the glass or the Blocker I couldn't have said. Hopkins was nodding now towards the one man sitting at the bar, and I too looked at the fellow with my remaining usable eye. The fellow was all wrong for this pub: youngish, fresh-looking, cap neatly doubled over by his pint glass – not a working man but a clerkly sort, I guessed. He was the soft mark, at any rate.

'That cove there,' Miles Hopkins was saying, 'has a box of choice cigars in his left-hand coat pocket. Let's 'ave 'em, shall we?'

'You want me to lift 'em?' I said, wondering, If you commit crime to prevent crime is that a crime? I did not believe the answer to that lay in my *Police Manual*.

'It's not really my game, you know,' I said to Miles Hopkins. 'I'm bound to make a bloomer, and then we'll have a scrap on our hands.'

'Got the collywobbles, have you?'

It was the Blocker; he was right behind me.

I was thinking of the Camerons, but I was supposed to be concerned with a different matter. I spoke up again:

'Something more in my way,' I said, 'might be lifting articles from the goods yards. I know a deal about what goes on there. Done a spot of portering you see, and . . .'

I looked at Miles, who looked at the Blocker, who said, 'Stop monkeying about, you daft bugger.'

I had no choice. I would never get the goods on this pair otherwise. I walked up to the bar, and formed a tale in my mind. If I bungled the theft of the cigars I would say that the owner had whipped them off me earlier on. I moved next to the man, next to his *pocket*. I was within range of the smell of his hair oil, and I could feel his breath on my raised left hand. But the fellow was a regular dolly daydream, staring straight ahead towards the barrels at the back of the bar. Looking in the same direction myself, I sank the fingers of my left hand into his pocket, and straightaway my heart beat slower. There seemed a whole world in there – many articles rolling between my fingers in the slowness of the new world I had entered. There was certainly more than just a packet of cigars in there. There was a solid article besides: bone – and I immediately knew it for the handle of a clasp knife, and a good, weighty one at that. I caught it up, and as I swivelled away from the fellow I couldn't help grinning at Miles Hopkins, who was grinning back at me.

'It's a wonder that bloke can *live* with no nerves at all down one side of his body,' he said, as I walked up to him, with the trophy in my hand.

'You what, mate?' I said, and I realised that I was bathed in sweat.

'When that bloke gets off his perch, you'll probably see that he's immobile all down that half of him.'

He looked at the knife.

'Think I've got the makings?' I said, in a kind of breathless whisper I had not meant to use.

'You've a little ground to travel,' he replied. 'Come on.'

We stepped outside with the Blocker in tow. He took up position on one side of the little bridge, with his back to the lamp that sprouted from its low wall. The cold air made my sweat turn colder. I stood with Miles Hopkins on the other. It seemed that Hopkins's opinion of my abilities had slipped a notch, because he said to the Blocker:

'Our friend will never be a hoister as long as he's got a hole in his arse.'

'Might be good for some other business, though?' said the Blocker.

No reaction at all from Miles Hopkins.

We all three had our hands in our coat pockets. I waited; something was on its way.

'I know all the railway territories around York,' I said.

The rain fell; still nothing was said, so I went further: 'Reckon I can put my hands on a goods yard pass, n'all.'

At this, a look went between the two.

'I heard you speaking of the Camerons,' I said to the Blocker. 'I've seen those two about . . . One of 'em's nuts.'

The Blocker said:

'That bastard's in the morgue.'

'Which one?'

'The York morgue, you fucking idiot.'

'Which *brother*?' I said. 'They both caught it from what I heard.'

'They both caught it,' repeated Miles Hopkins.

Suddenly, he looked up at me:

'There's a job on,' he said.

I nodded back at him.

'I'm on for any mortal thing,' I said.

'There's a fellow you've to meet first,' said Hopkins. 'Big Coach, Nessgate. You know it?'

'I do that,' I said.

'Quarter to six day after tomorrow suit?'

'OK,' I said in a trembling tone, and the two of them walked off back the way we'd all come.

Standing there on the bridge, I realised that what had just passed matched firing an express for excitement. The difference was that with this business, you were glad when it was over.

I looked back at the door of the Castle Howard, and the man whose knife I'd lifted walked out. He came up the bridge towards me, and it was his fifth step (which went more to the side than forwards) that told me he was canned.

'Evening,' I said, as he walked past. 'You ain't lost a knife, have you?'

He turned and looked at me, and kind of sagged. His hand went up to his eye, and he said something that wasn't quite a word.

I put my hand up to my own eye. I must look pretty bad.

The tipply bloke walked on as best he could, and so I kept the knife. Or Allan Appleby did, at any rate.

Chapter Nine

That night, I biked back to Thorpe-on-Ouse the long way round: along past the big country houses of Tadcaster Road, and down along Sim Balk Lane, running parallel to the Leeds line. 'Never go home straight,' Weatherhill had said, 'always by a roundabout route', but there were only two routes really, short of riding a horse over the fields. The wife was asleep when I got back, but I stopped up, drinking coffee and writing out my report on the whole evening (making a copy using some of the wife's carbons), and taking care to mention that the name Cameron had come up. I also requested a goods yard pass made out to some made-up name, my intention being to pass it off as something stolen or somehow unfairly come upon by Allan Appleby.

Next morning, the wife was up and at her typewriting first thing, and I stepped out of the house to post the report the moment the village post office opened. My eye was practically healed. In any case, the wife had not remarked on it; and nor had she yet mentioned the stolen knife, which I had placed on the mantelshelf because, for some reason that I preferred not to think about too closely, I wanted it to hand.

It was a white, misty morning as I stood in Thorpe's main street. Amid the distant river sound, the usual things were going on. Kettlewell, the carter, was leaving it from the other end – the Palace end – making for Thorpe-on-Ouse Road,

going into town by the sensible way, with two paying cus-
tomers up on his wagonette. A trap stood outside the chemists:
Birchall's, late Pearce and Sons. That was a sad do. Old Pearce
had died the year before – heart gave out – and his son had
gone soon after, most unexpected. Everybody had liked the
Pearces, and nobody liked Birchall. There was only one of him,
which made him seem mean somehow, and he didn't give the
kiddies fruitdrops with the medicines as the Pearces had done.

We'd had all this from Lillian Backhouse, a skinny woman
with shiny black hair that was never worn up, and who went
about the village with an airy, high-stepping walk, and
looked to me like a female pirate. She'd had seven children,
and not one born under the doctor. Yet she was not worn out.
In fact, she believed in 'freedom's cause' – votes for women
– and had become great pals with the wife as a consequence.
They were both liable to fling at you questions, or more often
statements, regarding the status of women and so the best
thing, I found, was not to be in the same room.

Lillian's husband, Peter, was the verger at St Andrew's, a
quiet chap, who in practice lived in the graveyard and the
pub, with the balance of his time at present spent in the second because he knew that in the end the balance would be
spent in the first.

Major Turnbull came sweeping out of the post office as I
approached. He lived in one of the big houses by the river.
He would have been sending a telegram, I guessed. He was
a nice man who'd been in the Zulu Wars. He was in business
now, and all his dealings lay far beyond the village. He wasn't
a swell, but more of a practical, hard man – not unfriendly
though. He gave me a quick nod as he, too, turned away in
the direction of the Palace.

Outside the post office stood a trap. A lady in a white cape
sat inside with a white dog on her knee. They made a ghostly

pair in the white morning mist. I noticed her gloves. They were trimmed with fur. The wife had been after a new pair of gloves.

I gave the report to Mrs Lazenby, the postmistress, who worked behind the counter under a great clock and a photograph of a man and woman sitting at either end of a long table. There was too much light in the picture, so there was a burst of whiteness in between the pair. As Mrs Lazenby took the envelope she read the address, which vexed me. She was the postmistress, and could not send envelopes without reading the addresses. And she knew me for a railway policeman in any case. As she put on the stamps, I read it as well: 'Chief Inspector Weatherill, Police Office, York Station'. It would get there in the afternoon, but I said: 'Can you mark it down as urgent?'

Mrs Lazenby looked up at me, and I thought she was going to ask, 'Where's your specs then?' It was quite a nice calculation to work out where I ought to be wearing them, and where I ought not. Instead, she gave me a big smile and said: 'Not long now, is it?'

It came to me after a few seconds that she was talking about the baby.

'Well,' I said, 'it's a month, you know.'

'Could happen at any time then.'

Thank you very much, I thought. The place smelt of food. There were stacks of letters and parcels on the sofa, around the fireplace. The post office was also Mrs Lazenby's living room, and it was hard to make out where one ended and the other began.

'My first was six weeks before time,' she said.

I had lost my job on the footplate, joined a criminal band, and was about to become a father 'at any time'. It was all too bloody drastic.

And yet Thorpe-on-Ouse was quiet as I stepped back into

the main street. The trap with the white lady in it was gone. I stood still, fancying I could hear the river running away out of sight towards the locks at Naburn. I walked on, and could hear the wife at her typewriting from half way along the garden.

'What are you doing still here?' she said when I pushed open the door.

The words of the Chief came to me, and I said: 'I can't be clocked to my new work with a patent time clock, you know.'

'Well *I* can,' said the wife. 'I've an armful of correspondence on behalf of Cooper and Son.'

There were sweet jars next to her machine: Opopanax and Parma Violets.

'Who are Cooper and Son when they're at home?'

'Saddlemakers.'

'Never heard of 'em . . .' I said, sitting down on the sofa and picking up my *Police Manual*. 'Keep a shop, do they?'

'Railway Street,' said the wife, continuing to type.

'Where on Railway Street?'

The wife stopped typewriting for a moment, and gave me an interesting look; then pitched a bundle of flyers over towards me.

M. Cooper and Sons were at 4 and 6 Railway Street. Besides saddles they made pair and single-horse harnesses, horse clothing, hunting and riding bridles. 'It says here they're Patronised by Royalty,' I observed.

'Yes,' said the wife. 'I'll *bet* they are.'

I opened the *Police Manual*. It must have been a mystery to the wife – me sitting there reading, in the middle of what ought to have been a working day. I'd so far managed to keep back all details of my secret work, and there'd been no mention of the Cameron murder between us. The book fell

open at 'Stolen Goods'. 'See "Receiving"', I read, 'and "Resti-
tution."' It struck me that, the night before, I'd stolen a knife.
The wife was sitting in a room with a thief.

I looked across at her, and it was just as if she knew, for
although she was still typewriting a tear was now rolling
down her cheek, like a small intruder running away across a
field.

'Now hold on a minute,' I said, getting up fast, and walking across to her. There was her *work* typewriting on one side
of the machine, and her personal church-ladies' and suffragist typewriting on the other. One side represented the
world as it was; the other side how she wanted it to be.

I kissed her and said: 'What's up, kidder?'

'It's *all* up,' she said. 'When the baby comes . . . That's me
finished.'

Another shocking thought came: in all the past eight
months something had been missing, namely happy
remarks about the baby from the wife. I hadn't noticed.

'It is not over,' I said. 'I make fair wages in the police; we
are to have our new house, and we will have a skivvy.'

'We can't run to a skivvy, and you know it.'

'We bloody can.'

She looked at me, saying nothing, and the decision was
made. We would have a skivvy or help of some kind.

'You should go upstairs and have a lie down.'

'What earthly good will that do?'

'I don't know,' I said.

I looked at the wife.

'I could come with you,' I said.

'And what will you do?'

'You'll see. You'll have plenty of time free to carry on with
your work for the women's movement,' I said as we climbed
the stairs. 'I was thinking that in about a year's time you

78

might have a demonstration in the station. Very likely I'll be a detective-sergeant by then, and I'll be the one to order all your arrests . . . We'll be quite a team.'

The wife fell down on the bed saying nothing, and I fell down next to her.

'How do you feel just now?' I said.

'Overcrowded,' she said, and she nearly laughed.

Love-making with a woman who's in the family way was a speciality that Mr Backhouse the verger might well have mastered over the years, but I was still finding my way, this being the first child.

'It's a bit of an obstacle course, this is,' I said to the wife.

'Bit of an obstacle *race* more like, the way you go at it,' she said.

Downstairs again shortly afterwards, the wife went back to her typewriting. I built up the fire, and settled down on the sofa with my *Police Manual*, at which point the wife ordered me out.

I walked over to the Fortune of War for a pint, and I saw, three doors down from the pub, the doorway of Scott Johnson, Boot and Shoe Maker. Scott was in the doorway on one side, his son, William, was on the other. They wore the leather aprons they worked in. In between stood a fellow wearing a brown suit and a bowler, and sucking on a long clay pipe. They were all three watching me, and Scott Johnson was nodding in my direction while saying something to the smoking fellow, as if he'd just pointed me out.

They watched me cross the dusty road, and my feet and their heads were the only things moving in Thorpe-on-Ouse. And there was no noise but for the unseen river and the twisting sound of one bird singing.

In the pub, I said to Bill Dixon, who kept the Fortune.

'Any idea about the new hand at Johnson's?'

'What new hand?' he said.

'There was a fellow in the doorway with 'em just now.'

'He'd be having a pair of boots made.'

'Why would he be staring out into the street? It just looked rum, that's all.'

'If he was in the doorway, he'd be staring out or staring in,' said Bill Dixon. 'He'd have to be doing one or t'other, do you take my meaning?'

He went off upstairs and I was quite alone in the pub, trying to picture the *Police Gazette* face of the man who'd be waiting for me the following day in the Big Coach.

After dinner – corned beef, fried potatoes and a pot of tea – I had a bit of a kip on the sofa, and when I woke up it was four o'clock and the wife was standing over me with a telegraph form. The Chief had got my report; he wanted me in the next morning at six once again.

PART THREE

The Big Coach

Chapter Ten

Chief Inspector Saul Weatherill was sitting back in his chair, scratching his scraps of hair and yawning, and the more he scratched the more he yawned.

'But was any offence committed other than by *yourself*?' he said, at last.

I thought for a moment. The gaslight shone blue and white – the colours of coldness – and steam rolled from our mouths. The chief sat in his overcoat, as before, and (also as before) looked as though he wouldn't be stopping.

'Well this, sir,' I said, indicating my eye, although there was hardly anything left to see. 'The one I've called the Blocker belted me, as I said.'

Weatherill had turned up late, and it was now 6.35 a.m.; the fish train was in, having arrived early, and we could hear the crashing all along Platform Three.

'So what's going off tonight?' he said, over the racket.

'As I said in the report, sir, I can only make a hazard as to that.'

'Where exactly did you say that in the report?' he said.

'At the end, sir.'

He nodded thoughtfully, looking at the two pages of the report, which lay folded on his desk. Next to these was a small envelope. He slid it over to me, and there was a goods yard pass, made out in the name of Gordon Higgins.

I'd set out in my report my reasons for requiring it, but still the chief said, 'Why do you want it, again?'

I thought: wake up, can't you?

'I want it because I've told 'em I've got it. It's just my way of getting a leg in.'

I looked down again at the goods yard pass.

'Why Gordon Higgins?' I asked.

'Why not?' said the Chief. 'You wanted a made-up name, and they don't come much more made up than that . . . Reckon it could be another railway job?' he asked, leaning forward, suddenly keen.

'I reckon it is, sir.'

'If it's not, of course, we father it on to Tower Street.'

A great roaring from Platform Three checked us for a moment, then silence – the fish train had gone, leaving only the sound of the Chief breathing through his 'tache.

Presently, he stood up.

'You'll go along to meet this new fellow, and see what's what.'

'Any idea who it might turn out to be, sir?'

'Have I any idea?' he said, quite amazed to be asked. '*Me?*'

He fished a stack of newspapers out of his desk.

'A few of the local lot have picked out Shillito,' he said, pitching across to me a heap of newspapers tied up in brown paper. They were all *Police Gazettes*. 'Commit the faces to memory, and you might find you recognise one tonight. Chuck 'em away when you've done. We have more than enough copies of each edition. Remember,' he added, walking towards the door, 'keep your mouth shut as far as possible and your eyes and your ears open.'

I could have done with some advice of a more specific nature.

'If my lot do nothing more than make a plan this evening,

then that's conspiracy, isn't it?'

'It is,' he said, nodding, 'and it will be open to us to indict them for that.'

'And will we?'

'Reckon we'll get 'em for the *act*, eh?' he said. 'That generally goes better in court.'

It was the answer I deserved. I had been trying to bring the matter to an early end, and had been doing so out of funk, but the chief didn't seem to have noticed. He didn't seem to have noticed *anything*, really. Only now he was giving me a good, hard look up and down. 'It really is a shocking suit,' he said, from by the door.

I put the glass-less spectacles on.

'And they set it off to a tee,' he added. 'They make you look like a fellow whose woodcut was circulated to us just before Christmas: Herman van . . . summat or other. He'd come over by steamer from Rotterdam.'

'Oh yes, sir?' I said.

'Fellow was a sodomite,' said the Chief, scratching his wisps of hair. 'Still is probably, because we never caught him . . . I'd bring you into the hotel for bacon and eggs, lad, only it wouldn't do for us to be seen in company.'

'Not to worry sir,' I said, 'there's plenty of dining rooms along the river'll see me right.'

He was about to make his breakaway, so I said:

'I wanted to ask you about the Camerons, sir – the pair that were done in by the goods yard.'

He looked at me without any trace of expression.

'That's Tower Street,' he said at length.

'Do you *want* it to be Tower Street, sir?'

He looked at me steadily for a while, and for a moment I thought his temper would give way. But he just gave a sigh, walked around to the mantelpiece and lit a cigar. Leaning on

the mantelshelf he began smoking, still looking at me directly and saying: 'Do you realise how much work we have on
here?'

'No,' I said.

'Make believe for a minute that our job is just the policing
of this railway station. Now, there are fourteen platforms
and it is the biggest railway station in the country. It is also
the busiest. Besides the engines of the North Eastern, it
receives those of six other companies, and if our duties as an
office were just confined to crimes committed within the station we would be over our ears in work . . .'

Ash was falling from the cigar on to the Chief's open coat,
on to the suit beneath. He paid it no mind. The suit wasn't up
to much, but he wore gentleman's boots. He turned at the
mantelpiece – a giant of a man really, and case hardened.

'. . . The next thing to imagine,' the Chief continued, 'is that
we are responsible solely for the railway matters carried on
within York as a city. York is the administrative centre of the
Company, it's also the geographical centre; the Company is
the biggest employer of its men by far, and the city has its
racecourse, its market, and is a holiday ground in its own
right. Shall I name you one thing in York that's not to do with
the railways?'

'Go on then,' I said.

'*Go on then*?' he said. '"Go on then, *sir*", you mean.'

'Go on then, sir.'

'Well I can't,' he said quietly, 'which just proves my point.'

'What about York Minster, sir?' I said, but he ignored me,
saying: 'York alone would stretch us to the very limit and
beyond, but it's not just the station, and it's not just York. You
see, lad, in theory we cover about a third of the Company
territory but in practice, should any affair begin on our part
or finish up in it, then that's very likely to be ours as well.

The fact is, we look to the whole of the North Eastern railway for our work, and this is the biggest railway in the country in geographical extent and it's the biggest carrier of goods and people . . .'

He pitched his cigar into the cold grate, and began moving his arms.

'. . . Berwick to the north, Hull to the fucking east, Carlisle to the west, Sheffield to the south. Five thousand route miles of track, seventeen docks; sixty-eight million passengers carried in the last year alone . . .'

'There's one more thing I think we should be looking into,' I said.

'Oh, for crying out loud,' said the Chief.

'Richard Mariner. He was night porter at the Station Hotel here, and he committed suicide.'

'How do you know about that?' he said sharply.

'It was on the front page of the *Yorkshire Evening Press*, sir. He was a railway employee – so was one of the Cameron brothers and I'm wondering whether what happened to them was to do with the matter that I'm investigating.'

'But we don't *know* what you're investigating,' said the Chief. 'That's why you're bloody investigating it.'

'The Camerons were shot near the goods yard . . .'

'Outside it,' he said, 'and don't you forget.'

'Two bits of business in the file that you gave me were carried on in the goods yard. Richard Mariner worked at the hotel, where another of the jobs was done.'

The Chief said nothing.

'Can I go to the hotel, and ask questions about Mariner?'

'I'll do it,' he said, very quickly and surprisingly as he adjusted his coat. He was striding towards the outer door of the Police Office now. 'Come on,' he said, 'time you were out of here – bring those papers.'

On Platform Four, I was saying good morning to the Chief under the finger-pointing sign reading 'To the Hotel' as a short train pulled away alongside us. There was a shout, and a bloke came running from the ticket gate, hailing the train. Somebody in a carriage opened a door for the bloke, and the bloke was up on the footboard and in.

The Chief turned to me:

'Offence, is that,' he said sharply.

'I know, sir,' I said. 'It contravenes a railway by-law but I can't quite remember the number.'

'By-law ten, section (a),' said the Chief.

Well, he knew *that*, and he'd come up with the goods yard pass as requested. Maybe he wasn't completely barmy, after all, I thought as I walked off with the *Police Gazettes* wrapped in brown paper under my arm.

Chapter Eleven

It turned out the sunniest day for weeks.

To my right, as I made my way from the station into the city centre, battalions of clerks flowed into the new North Eastern Company head office, the company badges glinting gold on its balconies. It was said the North Eastern was six months in arrears with its accounts, which no doubt explained the great rush. I walked across Lendal Bridge, freezing cold in my bad suit in the golden light. Nobody stopped for this moment of sun. On the south side of the river, Rowntree's factory was making its cocoa smell, which somehow made you want to pay a call of nature. The river barges fitted underneath the bridge but the smoke they put out didn't, and clouds came up from either side as two farmers' carts rolled over the top. These were followed by a hearse, and I watched the horse – a fast trotter – bringing its glass box with a coffin inside, the sight a warning to all.

Scurrying down the stone steps on the south side, I thought of the dead Camerons, and how they'd had all the energy needed to commit a felony just days before. I took a little turn through the Museum Gardens, past the peacocks, the ladies in white with baby carriages. I bought a sausage in bread and a billy full of coffee from the barrow parked near the Abbey ruin and sat down at a bench with the bundle of *Police Gazettes* given me by the Chief.

There were half a dozen of them. I turned the pages secretively, for they gave my profession away. Mostly, they were just lists of people wanted or missing. Usually there were photographs or woodcuts, and remarks as to appearance: 'scar at eyebrow', 'scar at bridge of nose', 'fourth left finger crooked'. And the tattoos of course: crossed hands, ship, flower. Certain of the portraits had been ringed in pencil as Weatherill had said, the local lot: a man wanted in Malton for stealing from his lodgings; a man wanted in York for stealing gold rings, pendants and medals from a jeweller's. He looked a respectable sort. It was stated that he had a Union Jack tattooed on his chest, and I wondered whether that was meant to go in his favour or against.

I read on at the bench for a while, then, after returning my billy to the barrow, pitched five of the six *Police Gazettes* into a dustbin outside the Yorkshire Museum. The sixth – which I hadn't got round to – I put in my inside coat pocket, holding it in reserve for later in the day. A vicar watched me at the dustbin, and I tipped my cap at him. I then walked out through the back gates of the Gardens into Marygate, where I entered St Olave's church for a bit of a kip on the back pew.

I was woken by the tower bell ringing eleven, and went out again into the bustling streets, trying to walk off cramp and dampness, and thinking of Allan Appleby, my other self, lying in his dark lodge over at Holgate, listening to the crashing of the trains over the great tangle of Holgate Junction. He might be getting up about now, thinking about taking a drink, putting on his glasses . . . I lifted those very same from my pocket, settling them on my nose in Duncombe Street, opposite the West Door of the Minster, spying, as I did so, a prime candidate for the *Police Gazette*, although not in the 'Wanted' columns, but the 'Missing': it was Edwin Lund, sitting on the steps of the war memorial on the patch of green that faced the Minster. I removed the glasses, and watched the fellow for a while.

The memorial was to those soldiers of the Yorkshire Hussars killed in the war with the Boers. It was like a church steeple standing on its own, and there were three steps around its base. Edwin Lund was sitting on the middle one, looking down at his boots, and looking blue – glummer even than the last time. As I approached, he lifted his head, and watched two carts going along Duncombe Street. His little valise was alongside him. He turned his head, saw me, and left off chewing for a second. I sat down near to him on the cold stone, and he rubbed his sleeve across his nose, which I took to be his 'Good morning.'

'Dinner break?' I said.

'Aye,' he said.

'You look done in,' I said, really meaning something else.

'Been on since six,' he said.

'What time will you book off?'

'Six again,' he said. 'Well, half past.'

There was a copy of the *Press* in his pocket – early edition.

'Long day, is that,' I said.

He nodded for a while, presently adding:

'I've put in for overtime.'

'Why?'

'Mother wants a linoleum.'

'Do you mind the work?' I asked him.

'Whatsoever thy hand findeth to do, do it with thy might,' he said slowly, looking down at his boots.

Well, he'd told me he was chapel, and that lot were all Bible bangers. Besides the Minster, there were three churches in sight, and they had the look of giant tombs even in the brightness of the day, but still the carts and horse trams flowed on.

'How do you pass the time in the Lost Luggage Office,' I said '. . . at slack times, I mean?'

'Searching the Gospels.'

'Searching for what?'

'The light.'

A few pigeons came up, but Edwin Lund was screwing up the brown paper. The bread was gone.

'Do you read owt else, Edwin?'

'Oh aye,' he said, stuffing the paper into his valise. 'I read a good deal.'

'What though?'

'Lost books,' he said, and he might have laughed, only I couldn't make out his face, the monument being half in between us. If he was at twelve on a clock face, then I was at four. Ought I to have been speaking to him in the middle of the town, in full view of anyone passing? And if so, ought I to have been doing so as Allan Appleby or as Detective Stringer? I should've had it all calculated out, but I hadn't.

'By rights I shouldn't be speaking to you in a public place,' I said, 'since I'm a detective operating in secret, and you've supplied me with information. Do you want me to push off?'

I stood up, brushing down my trews.

'Sit down but round t'other side,' he said. 'We might be two strangers then.'

I sat down again, and this time if he was at twelve, I was at six, and while he faced out to the road, I faced the Masonic Hall and the backs of the buildings in Stonegate. Presently, Lund spoke up again:

'Operating in secret, you say? What's secret about it?'

'Well,' I said. 'That's one of the secrets.'

'Get over to the Garden Gate, did you?' he asked.

'I did,' I said, not sure how much information to give out.

'It's railway treasure they're after,' he said.

'Reckon it is,' I said.

'More than just pocketbooks.'

'I'm keeping cases on a couple of those blokes.'

'The Brains and the Blocker?' he said.

I made some sound that might have meant anything or nothing.

Peering to the left, I could see a line of trippers filing into the Minster. Tours were given at certain times.

'Why do you sit here, Edwin?' I said, after a while.

'Keep these fellows company,' he said, and I could make out that he was tipping his head backwards, indicating the monument.

I turned about, reading something of the list of names, also the inscription at the top: 'Remember those loyal and gallant soldiers and sailors of this county of York who fell fighting for their country's honour in South Africa.'

'Our kid was after enlisting,' said Lund.

'What happened?'

'Rejected.'

'On what grounds?'

'Undefined.'

'Failed the medical, did he?'

'Not sent up for it . . . Want of physical development. They told him not to go to the bother of removing his coat.'

'And what's become of him?'

'Passed on, three year since.'

'Died?' I said. 'Sorry to hear it.'

'Passed *on*,' said Lund, again.

Silence for a while.

'He was right with God at the end, I believe,' said Lund.

I asked Lund: 'Never thought of enlisting yourself?'

No reply.

I asked again and after a space, Lund answered:

'Wouldn't have an earthly.'

'Why ever not?' I asked – just to see what he'd say.

'Dull intellect.'

'Come off it.'

'And I'm subject to bronchitis, like our kid.'

'You haven't coughed for a while.'

'Don't say that, you'll set me off . . . See that bloke?'

He was pointing at a carter.

'Who's he?'

'Mr Laycock. Famous gentleman, he is – Rowntree's carter.'

'I've seen that gent,' I said. 'He takes cocoa to the station
. . . only now he's heading into town.'

'He'll do his run to the station come six o'clock,' said
Lund. 'That's cocoa for . . . Could be County Hospital. See
that horse?' he said, pointing to another carter, who was
making his way across the west front of the Minster with a
load of steel poles that rattled so loudly that I couldn't make
out what Lund said about him, or his horse. Then the bells of
the Minster struck up, adding to the racket.

'Ringing practice,' said Lund, in a louder voice, '. . . generally starts about now of a weekday.'

'You're a human directory to everything in York,' I said.

The voice came round from the other side of the monument after a while. 'Good-sized town is this. Big enough to
provide interest, small enough to get about on Shanks's
pony. I do know the pubs, I'll say that.'

He rose to his feet.

'Reckon I know the York public houses better than anybody else doesn't take a drink.'

It was a peculiar boast, I thought.

'*How* did you get to know them?' I asked, twisting about
towards him somewhat. 'Band of Hope?'

(For that lot often toured the York pubs.)

'Just with the chapel, like: city mission. We'd go round handing out cards giving times for tea treats. Handsome teas, they were . . . And no preaching the first time but just two hymns at the end.'

'They'd be a bit of a rough house, I expect?'

Lund was shaking his head.

'Treat folk as *gentle*folk, and they behave according.'

'Daresay,' I said, though doubting it.

'One o'clock,' announced Lund. 'I'd best be off.'

At that very instant the bell-ringing practice broke off to let the hour bell strike one. Lund walked around the monument a little way, his valise over his shoulder.

'What's up with your eye?' he said, turning back.

'Nothing to speak of,' I said.

He'd noticed such bruising as remained, and the wife hadn't.

He passed me his copy of the *Evening Press*, saying, 'Want a look?' I nodded at him; he went his way, and I turned to the second page of the paper. The article proper began: 'The shooting to death of John and Duncan Cameron, brothers, continues to agitate the minds of the York police.' Not the York *railway* police, I thought. It didn't seem to have been agitating Chief Inspector Weatherill's mind in the least. I read the article from top to bottom, and it was plain as daylight that there were no clues, and precious few conjectures from any quarter. I looked back towards the great cathedral where the same trippers – or perhaps another lot – were threading their way out. You'd have parties like that criss-crossing the city in all seasons; they'd check you for quite minutes on end, and there was nothing you could do to break through. I wondered how many more killings it would take before they stopped coming.

I put on my special glasses and rose to my feet.

95

Quarter to six. I'd eaten a late dinner on the river, and the light was falling fast as I entered the Big Coach on Nessgate. The place was packed out, and there was a dancing class happening, not too daintily, on the second floor. When you walk into a pub you want a moment alone to get your bearings and settle, but Miles Hopkins hailed me immediately from a table in the corner. He sat with another fellow, whose back was to me but I could tell it wasn't the Blocker. Of that big bastard there was no sign. As I approached, I saw that a copy of the *Evening Press* was on the table, folded so that the latest report of the Camerons' death was uppermost, but the gent with his back to me was intent upon a different publication – a sporting paper. As Miles Hopkins looked up at me, I could read over the new bloke's shoulder: 'Gatwick Meeting; Capital Afternoon's Sport; Gossip from the Course.'

I touched my spectacles, to make sure they were in place. Miles tapped the other man's arm, and he stood up and turned about. Miles Hopkins stood too, saying, 'Sam, like you to meet Mr Allan Appleby.' It was all very mannerly and all very different from Layerthorpe. The new man stood, turned with hand held out, and I certainly did not recognise him from the pages of the *Police Gazette*. He was medium height and broad, although not as big as the Blocker, and more compressed. If the Blocker was an elephant then this one was a bull, and a distinguished-looking bull at that, with belted Norfolk coat, grey, bristly hair, a sharp grey beard, and regular face that was all-in-all the shape of a shield. He looked a little like the King himself, and would have looked still more like him had he been wearing the Homburg hat placed at his elbow. He was smoking a cigar. He had a strong grip, wore two rings to each hand, and it turned out he had the name to match:

'Valentine Sampson,' he said, in a deep voice, and with an accent that was . . . out of the way.

The teeming pub seemed to come to a halt as he gazed at me. He had peculiar eyes, between blue and brown, with the result . . . violet. The light seemed to be revolving inside them, winding you in towards him.

'Allan Appleby,' I said.

Had he taken the name? It was hard to say, since the moment I uttered it, he was signalling to a barman for three more pints of Smith's.

We all sat down.

'Will you excuse me for five minutes, Allan?' Valentine Sampson said, as the drinks were delivered, and the coin paid over.

I glanced over at Miles Hopkins, who gave a humorous sort of shrug, and began with his customary finger fiddling, moving a sovereign between the long fingers of both hands, and gazing about the pub – taking in all the gaping pockets, as I supposed.

'Sam has an appointment with a layer in half an hour,' he explained presently, 'and he's only just getting to grips with tomorrow's cards.'

At which Valentine Sampson looked up from his reading, and said:

'Don't fret, Allan, I'm a quick study.'

He spoke in a smooth, low rush – almost gentlemanly. I sipped beer, trying to slacken my nerves as Sampson turned again to the pages of his paper. I was glad that Sampson was due elsewhere before long – it might mean a short evening's work for me. At intervals, the fellow would make a mark with a pen, and slide the paper across to Miles Hopkins with a question or remark. 'What's your fancy?' he asked at one moment; at another, after some ferocious underlining of a horse's name, he observed: 'Be all right if I could get on after time.' He laughed at this, and Hopkins, smiled, still rolling the coin from finger to finger. Neither paid any attention to the murder report staring up from the *Evening Press*.

After ten minutes, the business of the betting programme was finished, and Valentine Sampson folded the paper into his pocket, turning towards me: 'You play the horses, Allan?'

'Not regular, like,' I said.

'Been at it since I was a nipper,' he said. 'But I'm kept back by want of knowledge – in sporting as in other matters.'

I didn't like this. Was he referring to his lack of knowledge of myself? He'd necked his beer very fast, and was raising his hand for another three. His requests seemed to cut through the crowds immediately, for the barman was at our table within a second of being summoned.

'These are on me,' I said, but the offer was ignored just as though not heard. Valentine Sampson paid up once more, before turning to me:

'Sorry for cutting to it directly, Allan,' he said, 'but Miles has told me you might have been able to put your hands on a goods yard pass.'

'I have it here,' I said, reaching into my pockets, and laying it out on the table. Sampson read out loud the name on the pass: 'Gordon Higgins', testing it out. Underneath, the words:

'Permit the bearer to walk over and along the Company's Railway at the Goods and Mineral Yard, York.'

'That's up to snuff,' said Valentine Sampson, after a moment. 'I'll not ask where it came from. Now . . . you've no employment just at present?'

'Nowt to speak of,' I said.

I picked up the pass, and returned it to my pocket, as Sampson said: 'Miles tells me you're from Halifax way.'

'Aye,' I said.

'And that you had employment in a screw factory?'

'It didn't just make screws,' I said.

'What else did it make?' asked Miles Hopkins, grinning.

'Nuts,' I said. 'Nuts and . . . you know, bolts.'

'Metal factors,' said Sampson, nodding.

I looked over at Hopkins. He was moving the coin, looking about the pub.

'Miles let on you'd had some magazines away,' said Sampson.

'*Railway Magazines*,' I said, 'complete set of 'em . . .'

'Complete set of 'em?' said Sampson. 'Somebody's pride and joy they would have been. Well worth having away, Allan.'

'It was a complete set until the big sod pitched one into the fire.'

Sampson shook his head, saying:

'Well, that blighter's not exactly a big reader, Allan.'

'A *small* reader,' said Miles, 'that's what Mike is. Can he read at all, Sam?'

'Oh aye,' said Valentine Sampson; then, turning to me once again:

'You been inside, Allan?'

'No,' I said, for I was not about to try inventing prison experiences.

The pair of them hadn't left off eyeballing, so I said:

'Don't *mean* to be, either.'

Sampson nodded.

'Liberty is sweet, Allan,' he said.

I'd been looking out for a change of front, but the two had continued quite friendly through this quiz. Now Sampson sat back and folded his arms, nodding towards Hopkins as he said: 'We've done a bit, Allan . . . Armley Gaol. Two years I was in that fucking barracks, and one thing kept me from going doolally, and that was meeting this gentleman here.'

He indicated Miles, who was looking all about, a half-smile on his lips from the compliments he was half-hearing.

'We were on the same landing early on, but then I got into a bit of bother, Allan, and I was put away on me tod for a spell. We managed to keep in touch though, and with the help of a few good lads we put together a line of communication as you might say.'

'The underground railway,' said Hopkins, before going back to his study of the pub.

I leant a little forward, and it suddenly came to me: the sixth *Police Gazette* remained in my inside pocket.

'We'd pass messages back and forth, trying to settle on a cute scheme, Allan,' Sampson was continuing. 'We fell to talking counties and towns and Miles being a York lad, born and bred, I said to him one day: "Well, what *about* that place? What's York?" And what did you tell me, Miles?'

'Old buildings, trippers, chocolate, railways, and pubs,' Miles Hopkins replied, the distant half-smile still on his lips.

'I told him it sounded very interesting,' Sampson continued, 'all except for the old buildings, the trippers, the chocolate and the railways. But then Miles here said: "As far as York goes, the big show is the railway."'

He leant towards me, smoke streaming from his nose and mouth like a dragon.

'Miles here,' he went on, 'said there's real possibilities there; that there's hundreds of blokes on the North Eastern Railway Company who are straight sorts, up and down, white as you like, and can't be touched for owt.'

At that word he put his cigar out with a crash, or tried to do so, but the thing burnt on, and he had to positively murder it, twisting and turning and dragging it back and forth.

'. . . And there are hundreds more, Allan,' he continued, still screwing down the cigar end, 'who are *not*.'

He sat back, arms folded, looking all around the pub. Then his eyes were back on me, and he was smiling.

'To make a long story short, Allan, the first fix went in about a year ago today.'

'Bribery,' I said.

Sampson looked away sharply, looked back, and held me with his eyes again for a while, the smile quite gone.

'Speaks plain, does Allan,' said Miles Hopkins as the smile returned to Valentine Sampson's face.

'You speak as you find, Allan,' he said, 'and that goes pretty well with me, I can tell you. Miles says you put the knock on Mike.'

'I won't be made to eat dog,' I said, 'not by any bugger.'

'And the bad sod crowned you, didn't he?' said Sampson.

I put my hand up towards my eye.

'I'll give him change for that,' said Sampson, 'don't you worry, Allan. I'll give him a talking to. See, I don't go in for knocking people about, and anybody that does . . . I'll put their *fucking* lights out.'

I was scared of the man, and that was all there was to it.

He rose to his feet, collecting up his soft hat, his gloves and his *Evening Press*, saying:

'We have business in hand in Allan, a very great doing – see you right for life if it comes off. Are you with us?'

'Reckon I'll knock along,' I said, nodding, and wondering what terrible event would have happened if I'd said anything but.

Chapter Thirteen

Could I hold my own on this dangerous ground? I hung about at any rate; and I knew I must get rid of the *Police Gazette*.

First off, Valentine Sampson had to go and see his layer, and this cove was evidently stationed on or beyond the street called Pavement, because that was the street he ducked into, having had a quick chat with Miles Hopkins.

'Where's the layer?' I asked Miles Hopkins as we stood at the west end of Pavement, outside Wood and Co., cutlers and surgical instrument makers.

'Oh,' he said, '. . . *Layer*thorpe. Can you credit it?'

He grinned at me, and I wasn't sure whether I could credit it or not.

I chanced another question.

'What'll happen when he comes back?'

No answer. There was a sharp coldness to the lamplit evening. It quickened the steps of the later shoppers and working people heading for home. A steam lorry came down towards us from Pavement, its own fog riding above it. Being modern, it looked all wrong in York.

I asked my question about Sampson's return once again, feeling daft for doing so, and Hopkins said, 'Sam'll be half an hour or so – he generally takes a pint with the bookie. We'll all hook up together . . .' He looked at his watch before continuing: '. . . Half an hour touch at the Blue Boar in Fossgate. I'm just nipping off for a tick, myself.'

'Where to, mate?' I asked, casual like.

'Railway station,' said Miles Hopkins.

'Off to catch a train, are you?' I said, frowning.

Miles Hopkins thought for a while.

'That's it,' he said, presently, 'I'm off to catch a train.'

'But you'll be back in half an hour?'

'Now that I think on,' he said, 'it's not really me that'll be catching it, but others.'

He gave a grin and walked off, and as he did so, the light dawned.

It was getting on for half past six. I pictured the Scotch express, the line of lights shaking over Holgate Junction getting on for a mile away, the toffs gathering at the north end of Platform Fourteen where the first-class carriages came to rest. I pictured Miles Hopkins, landing on Platform Fourteen, like a bird, with his long hands in place of wings. I wondered whether Mike, the Blocker, would be on hand once again.

What to do? What would Chief Inspector Weatherill have recommended? I looked along Pavement. Where were all the bloody coppers – railway coppers or otherwise? Where was Shillito the detective sergeant, and all the rest of the fellows I'd thought I was on the edge of getting to know? And where was Weatherill himself? If that fellow was so hard pressed, why did he spend so much time eating breakfast?

I turned to look at the strange articles for sale in Wood's: an artificial leg stood in the window, watched from a higher shelf by an artificial eye sitting in a velvet-lined box, like a jewel. There were trusses, hosiery, all kinds of secret, shameful things; and a rack of knives. I put my hand into my coat pocket. I meant to drop the *Police Gazette* at the foot of the window.

I began to lift it from my coat when a hand was placed on my shoulder. A beer smell came with it, and Valentine Sampson said: 'You could have some bugger's eye out . . .'

'Eh?' I said, turning slowly about to face him.

'. . . Then make amends for it, you know,' he continued, '. . . with the *glass* eye in a nice silk presentation box.'

The remark was too strange to answer, so I said, 'Seen your layer then, mate?'

He grinned.

'That bugger's always the same,' he said. 'Always sharps me on the prices.'

He seemed glad to have got the business out of the way, just as if it was a job of work. He no longer carried the racing paper, or his copy of the *Evening Press*.

'Miles has gone off to the station,' I said, as we set off for the Blue Boar.

Sampson took out a pocket watch, and looked at it, shaking his head.

'From what I understand, his trip ought to put him in funds later on,' I said.

'In funds or in chokey,' he said, striding on. 'Do you know, Allan, they've got bears on the fucking railway station nowadays?'

'Aye,' I said, fairly croaking out the word, 'I did know that.'

'It's just bloody well not *on*,' he said, striding on.

What was the great doing that was in prospect, and when would the doing be done? When would Weatherill think it the right time to jump in, and put the kybosh on? And what if the great doing was on the cards for this very evening? I couldn't afford to worry about that. I just had to go along, keeping my ears open and my mouth shut. I thought of the Blue Boar in Fossgate. The trouble with that street, to my mind, was that it led back in the direction of Layerthorpe, and the Garden Gate, and talk of murder.

We turned into Fossgate, where I suddenly saw my whole life standing six feet before me: the wife in her good maternity dress with the warm blue wrap on top, and the unknown baby seeming to ride out before her. Had she been doing her marketing? No. She did that on Wednesdays. Rather, she'd been to collect her week's typewriting, for there was a paper parcel under her arm. She was looking into the illuminated window of the shop that stood beside the Blue Boar: Dove and Crenshaw, Bespoke Tailors for Ladies and Gentlemen. She was looking at the millinery corner – no, the gloves, the fur-lined ones. I couldn't help but notice this even as I swayed out into the middle of the road, almost into the path of a bicyclist, who shouted out just as I gained the kerb at a point ten feet or so beyond the wife. I saw her turn towards me as I set foot into the Blue Boar, where Sampson was already giving his report from the parlour bar.

'No sign of Miles,' he said.

I just stared back at Sampson, struck dumb. I knew all the blood had run from my face at the sight of the wife . . . But had *she* seen *me*? The worst of it was the glasses. How to account for the peepers? Another pint was coming towards me from Valentine Sampson. He didn't play low with the drinks, and that was a fact. My mind was full of new horrors: the Camerons lying dead on the cinder track and the wife sitting quite alone in the dark parlour at home. I had never kept anything from her before, and now it was as though the locking pin had been pulled out from our marriage. One thing I could take comfort from: the wife would not follow me into the parlour bar of the Blue Boar. Even Lydia would not do that.

Miles Hopkins did step into that small crowded parlour bar though, and just a moment later.

'Sorry, mates,' he said with a grin, 'my train was late.'

He swirled Sampson and myself into a tight circle of three and, saying nothing more, produced from his coat a fine pocketbook stuffed with folded banknotes. The three of us stood there breathing beer fumes onto this money, and there was not only the smell of beer, but the smell of sweat and of greed. One word was uttered as we broke, and it was Sampson who spoke it.

'Good-o,' he said.

I looked across the bar top, where gas jets burned for cigar smokers and saw, at the foot of the back wall, that the low double doors giving on to the cellar were open. I could see into the pit of the cellar, but not to the bottom of it, and I had a picture in my mind of this tiny pub perched on top of a great hole. It was a smarter place than the Garden Gate though. A cut above. More drinks were bought, with whiskys to go with the ales, and Valentine Sampson led us over to a table. Here, the pair produced their own stolen or somehow purloined goods yard passes. They matched mine in all particulars except for the name.

'It's well minded is that place,' said Sampson, meaning the goods yard. We all nodded for a while. Then Sampson said: 'It was hardly likely we could fix all the guards on the gate.'

'. . . So we fixed the bloke who prints the passes,' said Miles, who had become not so watchful, but quite larky after his triumph at the station.

'Fixed him? How much?' I said.

'Two guineas, I think . . . That right, Miles?'

'Two *quid* is what he was promised,' said Miles. 'What he got was a different matter.'

'What *did* he get?' I asked.

'He got what was coming to him,' said Sampson, putting his glass up for more beer. The fellow drank like a pond. 'See,

Allan,' he continued, 'once you've fixed a bloke . . .'

'Once you've tickled him out of the narrow path of rectitude . . .' put in Miles Hopkins, who was tossing and catching a coaster.

'Once you've done that, then you *have* him,' said Sampson.

'You have him because you can rat on him,' I said, regretting it directly because once again Valentine Sampson put his eyes on me with no accompanying smile.

'Not so much rat on him, mate,' Miles Hopkins said quietly, 'as let on you might do.'

'You see, Allan,' said Sampson, 'if you rat on the Company blokes, who are you ratting on 'em *to*? Some toff, that's who. Because when it comes to it . . . who benefits? Top brass. You know who the top man on the railway is, don't you? Fellow name of Lord Grey.'

'It *was* him,' I said, 'but now he's chucked it in.'

Hopkins was looking at me; Sampson was frowning.

'Why has he chucked it in, Allan?' he asked.

'Gone off to be Chancellor of the Exchequer in the government.'

'Bloody typical is that,' said Sampson, sitting back.

Silence for a space, then Hopkins said:

'Most blokes of your stripe wouldn't be expected to know that, Allan.'

'Aye,' I said, colouring up, '. . . daresay.'

'Most blokes of your stripe wouldn't be expected to know anything at all, Allan,' said Sampson, 'and don't take that amiss, brother.'

'I'm a great one for reading,' I said. 'If I take a pint, I'll usually read a paper at the same time. Drinking beer somehow doesn't quite seem enough in itself if you know what I mean.'

Sampson was frowning at me again.

Hopkins, leaning forwards and grinning at me, said: 'So the more you drink, the more you read?'

'Well . . . up to a point,' I said.

'Point is, Allan,' said Sampson, 'you put the fix on a bloke, you buy his silence at the very same time, and very little further action needs to be taken as regards that.'

'Except in the odd case,' said Hopkins, with a distant look.

We talked on, and I was half pleased, half worried that I seemed to be getting along well with Sampson in particular who, come nine o'clock, rose to his feet saying, 'Hadn't we better be off, mates?'

I half expected the wife to be still standing outside the door of the Blue Boar. She wasn't of course, and I didn't like to think of the moment at which she must have turned away to go home.

In Fossgate, Miles Hopkins hung slightly behind – watchful again – and I fell in with Sampson, who walked just as fast as before despite all the beer he'd taken, and looked just as spruce and kingly in his salt and pepper suit. The only thing that let him down was the sharp and sour smell coming off him, and an over-eager look to his walk. He was like a fine steamer that was shipping sea secretly, out of sight, far below the water line. He led us along Pavement, through Parliament Street, through Davygate, our boots clinking on the cobbles. It was cold, and the streets were mainly empty, except for the buried noise coming from pubs along the way. I could feel the *Police Gazette* in my coat pocket, burning away there, as it seemed to me. As we pushed on, the Minster bells struck nine, sounding soft and yet loud, filling the whole city, and when they'd finished, a new sound took their place: an echoing rattling and clanking. We were in Leeman Road; the passenger station was to our left, and the goods station stood directly before us with light blazing at all their windows.

Chapter Fourteen

The goods offices were at the front, and the goods station stretched out behind under a glass roof. From here, half a dozen lines reached out, soon multiplying to dozens and curving away to merge with the lines from the passenger station. An aeronaut flying over the whole mass of tracks might have understood it in a moment; anybody else would have taken years.

The booking office stood guard before the main building on its own island, under a great four-sided clock. Wagons approached the station from either side of it, and we came in behind a load of timber under a tarpaulin with our passes in our hands. Inside the main door was a wide, cold, white-tiled room. There was a long table and some blokes in long coats milling about it. Any one of them might be a goods yard guard; any one or none. Their main purpose seemed to be keeping warm. Valentine Sampson walked past them at a lick, holding out his pass, and Miles and myself fell in behind, our passes also held out in a grudging, take-it-or-leave-it sort of way.

In ten seconds we were through the offices and into the station, at the buffer end of the platforms. Valentine Sampson stood before us, breathing it all in, nodding to himself and giving Miles and me not a glance. He was a different man on a job: sober-sided all of a sudden and the more frightening for it. I realised that he was scouting about for somebody or something, and I looked out into the station with him.

The place just seemed too small for all the clutter within. Lines of tall vans stood in each of the stalls, and the platforms, backed in by engines out of sight. The platforms were clarted with spilt paint and flour, half-cabbages, and the remnants of long-gone cargoes; all about the place stood goods lately taken down from the vans, goods about to go up, or goods just simply forgotten about: casks of grease, sacks of slag chippings, a children's merry-go-round in pieces, a big crate with the word 'Furniture' branded on the side, another stamped 'Clocks', half a dozen ladders stacked together and held by wire, a dozen new bicycles held upright by nothing but themselves. There was a weighing machine to each of the platforms, sometimes more than one, and a few of them crocked. On the platform before us were two high desks, one abandoned together with all the papers piled on top of it; at the second sat a clerk under a swinging gas bracket. With steam coming from his mouth, he was talking to a workman, saying: 'You've no bloody forwarding orders . . .'

Just then one rake of vans jerked into life, and began to be withdrawn from the station; they moved slowly, like a dozen convicts manacled together, and as they went, Valentine Sampson took a step forward. A fellow in a bowler and a paper collar – a clerk of some description –was coming along the platform as the train departed; he was a small man with a small moustache. He and Sampson closed, Sampson saying, 'All set?'

The man nodded, turned about, and we set off along the platform after him. Above each of the platforms were metal signs hanging from chains, and I spied 'Peterborough', 'Birmingham Curzon Street', 'Glasgow General Terminus', 'Liverpool Great Howard Street'. These were other goods stations, and this was the shadow railway, the ones that your average Joe Soap, taking his railways to work or holidays knew nothing of. But I knew it from my days on the North Eastern and my time on the Lanky, and as we walked forwards, it was as though I was walking back into my own past.

We walked through the goods station, and out into the tracks beyond, where the business of loading and unloading continued without benefit of a roof. On the longest, straightest road were more wagons covered right over with tarpaulins, like beds with the top covers pulled right up – beds with a body lying in them. A fellow walked alongside it, a hand lamp swinging in his hand. As he approached, I whispered to Miles Hopkins: 'Is he one of our lot?' Miles shook his head, and the man with a lantern seemed a hero as he passed by with nothing more than a nod. He had not been 'fixed' in the parlance of Sampson and Hopkins; he would not have to go down in my report. He was a railwayman of the right sort. He had the greyhound looks of a driver, and I had a bet with myself that he was in the running department.

I looked again at the ink-spiller walking ahead of us, alongside Sampson. He was nattering away in an underbreath to our leader, but getting precious little back in return. I could not hear their speech because of the jangle and clang of the sidings, and the great boom of the passenger station away to our left. We had walked through into an area where it was not so much the goods that were being moved as entire wagons and trains – these were the marshalling yards. A line of hopper wagons kept pace with us to our left, winched forward by a capstan, hydraulic powered, attended by blokes in long coats, one of them working the treadle with his foot. Beyond it, a horse walked a line towing a single wagon full of broken wood and metal – a wagon full of *nothing*. There was a great crash to the other side, and a rake of vans, shoved by a pilot engine, moved on their own as though blown by the wind. The shunter trotting beside like a cowherd with his long braking stick in his hand was half in control of those vans, and half not . . . for any marshalling yard was a wild and dangerous spot.

Gaslight came and went as we marched on; braziers and blokes came and went. These gangs of fellows would look up to us, and we would walk on, and I'd think; good for you, mates, you're off the hook.

Ahead of us, there was a conference under a gas lamp between the ink-spiller and Sampson. As a result of this exchange we now struck out to our right, crossing tracks by barrow boards, proceeding away from the direction of the passenger station. We came to a tall row of vans, each with the same slogan on the side: 'This Van Contains 500,000 Tins of Rowntree's King Chocolate'. It was a private siding for Rowntree's factory, and the thought crossed my mind: we're never going to have sweetmeats away, are we?

Hard by the line of chocolate vans was a shunter's cabin made of old sleepers but half gone west. The clerk and Sampson walked up to it, and the clerk ducked inside, emerging presently with a long iron bar – a crowbar, I saw, as he came closer – and a hand lantern.

'These'll see you right,' he was saying.

We now moved on, same direction as before. There were just two shorter sidings beyond the chocolate road, before the limit of the railway territory was marked by a high brick wall. One of the sidings was a van kip – half a dozen reserve brake vans on a slope; the other was a rake of vans on which the names of different companies were painted:

'I have a copy of the manifest here,' the clerk was saying to

113

Sampson. 'It's the fourth from the right, you want.'

I made out the names of the three vans directly before us: 'Finsbury Distillery Company', 'Morrison and Co., Sail Makers & Co., Rotherhithe', 'Nairn Bros, Spirit Merchants, Strand'. To either side, the train stretched away into darkness.

Sampson was nodding: 'All for London, right?'

'No, no,' said the clerk, 'all *from* London. This is a "down" road, you see. "Down" is away from London, while your "up" lines . . . they take you *to* it.'

Sampson fixed a glare on the little man. There was a pause; the wind made a winding sound, as if working up to something. Sampson spat:

'Where they all off to?' he said, nodding again towards the vans.

'All different places. See, they're about to be cut. The Morrison and Co. – that's for South Shields. The Spirit van – that's . . .'

'Leave off for Christ's sake,' said Sampson, seizing the crowbar and lamp from the clerk. 'How long are they going to *remain*?'

'I have it set down just here,' said the clerk, turning the pages of the manifest; but he couldn't make it out in the darkness, and Sampson was already striding off over the cinder road towards a fourth van. As he closed on it, the white-painted name seemed to flare up: 'Acetylene Illuminating Company, Queen's Road, South Lambeth, London, S.W.'

Well, I'd seen those words before: in the Occurrence file handed me by Weatherill.

Sampson set down the lantern by the track and, gaining a foothold on the bogey, began scaling the van like a mountaineer on a rock face.

'New thing for me, this is,' said the clerk, looking on.

No answer from Miles Hopkins, who was watching his

partner with a worried look. Sampson was trying to jemmy open the door on the van, which was locked with a padlock, and sealed with wire and a ball of wax.

'Come away, you bastard!' roared Sampson, who was spread out against the van.

'. . . Been writing abstracts all morning,' continued the clerk.

No reply again from Hopkins.

'I spent the best part of the afternoon consigning potatoes . . .'

Hopkins looked around, and down, at the little fellow.

'Best thing to do with 'em,' he said.

As Sampson grafted away with the crowbar, I heard the beat of an engine away to our right, towards the front of the rake of vans. This'll put a crimp in, I thought . . . If they're going to pull the vans away . . . Sampson continued to labour with the jemmy, and curse at the lock, while the talkative little clerk tried his luck with me:

'We had a new lad on this week,' he said. 'Silly bugger was charging for the weight of the sacks as well as the spuds.'

He looked up at me.

'You don't do that.'

'I know,' I said, and watched Miles Hopkins as I did so, but his eyes were stuck on Sampson. I wanted to say to the goods clerk: I'm on your side, pal, but then I thought: I'm not on his side. My job is to see him put away. I thought of asking his name – for the report – but he wouldn't have given it, and I would hardly have been able to bear hearing it if he had.

I looked again at the van. Acetylene was used to give light, but it could also be used in place of coal gas for burning through metal and *was* so used in any up-to-date engine shed. I looked down at the clerk: 'How long you been with the company?' I asked him.

'Nigh on forty year, and no bloody pay increase in ten. Four nippers I have, it just won't do . . . A fellow must keep his soul in his body. How long you been working for Mr Duncannon?'

He was nodding towards Sampson; this was evidently the name he knew him by.

'About an hour,' I said.

Sampson had climbed down from the van, the door still fast. But no: as he raised his lamp, I could see that the lock was busted, that the thin wire of the seal was floating in the wind as Sampson drew back the great sliding door like a mesmerist revealing something miraculous. I could make out only blackness inside, though.

'Bingo!' said the clerk. 'Nobbut six penn'orth o' steel, those padlocks!'

As Sampson strode back towards us, there came a jangle from the right hand end of the rake. He wheeled about at the noise, and the vans jumped . . . then they settled again.

'They'll not move till midnight, I swear,' said the clerk.

Sampson had the crowbar raised as he closed on the clerk.

'I'll bloody coffin you,' he was saying.

'I en't lying,' said the clerk. I'd taken his constant nattering as a sign of nerves, but he was turning out to have a lot of neck.

'How much money have you had off us?' said Sampson, still with the crowbar raised.

'Five quid,' said the clerk, 'and the rest promised, but it ought to've been ten quid down, that was the agreement as you know very well. We shook on that – thee and me.'

The clerkly language was going to pot now.

'. . . And that chap was looking on . . .'

He pointed to Miles Hopkins.

'Ten quid down, and ten to follow, you said, if I could

show you to the acetylene van. Well there it bloody is!'

'It's not going to be there for long though, is it?' Hopkins said quietly.

Squinting through the bogies of the vans before us, I saw a pair of boots on the far side. They paused, turned, walked. That would be the goods guard or shunter, signalling to the engine driver.

'I've never worked out why you don't order the stuff direct from the bloody company in London,' said the clerk.

Sampson shook his head as he swung the iron.

At the same moment Hopkins called 'Sam!' which might've been enough warning for the clerk, who any rate stepped back from a blow that would have done for him, had it struck him.

'Five quid,' continued the clerk, looking only a bit surprised at having missed death by an eighth of an inch, 'and I know I've not a cat's chance in hell of seeing the rest.'

Sampson was looking at nobody and nothing. The rake of vans seemed to fidget once more. What was going off on the footplate of that shunting engine, I could only guess.

'I'll settle this,' I said, and Valentine Sampson looked at me:

'You'll fucking *what*?' he said, with dead eyes.

'I'll settle it,' I said again, rather shakily.

He nodded and, speaking softly for the first time since we'd entered the goods yard, said: 'I know you will, little Allan. I know it.'

I walked up to the train, which was still shifting, restless. It was going to be shifted at any moment . . . and I didn't step between those wagons for the clerk's sake. It was for my own, for I'd look such a clot if he was brained on my watch. The high side of the acetylene van was on one side, the spirit merchant's van on the other, and as I bent down to the coupling, I thought: I am in the valley of the shadow of death. Going under a train without the knowledge of the driver was not so much against regulations as plain suicide. I pulled up my sleeves. The wagons were loose-coupled, thank Christ – anything else would have been irregular for freight – and there was no vacuum pipe to wrestle with. I lifted the great, greased hook, and just then the train rolled, throwing me down on the sleepers, but there was suddenly freedom and space to one side of me. I stood up to see the back of the spirit van being pulled into darkness. I stood up at the side of the track, and thought I could make out the guard's van in the opposite direction; I was still standing. The engine had taken roughly three quarters of what it wanted. On the footplate, they should have been able to tell by the beat, and the guard would stir himself before long, but we had a couple of minutes while perplexity set in.

Valentine Sampson was walking towards me, the iron bar still in his hand. He flung it down and embraced me, fairly squeezing the life out of me for . . . Well I counted the time in my head: one, two, three, four, five clear seconds.

'Tell you what,' he said to Miles Hopkins when he'd finally left off, 'we've struck lucky with this one.'

Then he was up in the van, monkey-like again, and Miles Hopkins with him. All the rest happened at a lick: the two in the van grafted away and after a few seconds I saw what looked like a cannon sticking through the door of the van – the thing weighed about as much too, as I found out being the one expected to steady the brute as it was lowered down. It was a white, steel, gas cylinder, evidently full, with a big brass nut on the top, and warnings of fire, explosion and other scrawlings in chalk on the side. Sampson and Hopkins leapt down after it, and the three of us were just about able to manage it as we made our escape towards the wall of the goods yard. This time the clerk led the way, gabbling away as before:

'Ten tons of spuds I've to get away before sparrer-fart, and more besides. I'm going to have the bloody A1 Biscuit Company down on me like a ton of I don't know what, bloody biscuits, I suppose, and all the kid's bloomers to set right. Sacks he charged for, which he shouldn't have; porterage which he *should've*, he bloody did *not* . . .'

We'd come to rest by the goods yard wall – at what turned out to be a gate in the wall, which happened to be open – and the clerk was pointing the way, as though seeing us out of his parlour. There was a sign next to the gate: 'North Eastern Railway: Public Warning. Persons are warned not to Trespass on this Railway or on any of the Lines, Stations, Works or Premises connected therewith. Any person so Trespassing is liable to a Penalty of Fifty Shillings. Signed, C. N. Wilkin, Secretary.'

The three of us heaved up the cylinder again, and carted it through the gate into a black, windy, dog-barking wilderness, where Mike, the Blocker, stood waiting with a pony and cart.

Chapter Fifteen

After we'd been rolling for half a minute, I realised that we were on the cinder track, where the Camerons had been done in. The excitement of events had bolstered me up, but now I wanted to go straight to the Chief with my evidence. I had no time for my own thoughts though, for Mike was looking back at me from his driving seat.

'Reckon I should apologise for lamming you in the face, mate,' he said.

'Right,' I said. 'Well, I'm sorry for calling you a fucking rotter.'

'Fairly brings a tear to the eye, it really does,' said Miles Hopkins, grinning. He was on the perch next to me, while Sampson was crouching over the cylinder. It was as if he wanted to prettify the thing, for he was brushing off the chalked warning that began: 'DANGER! On no account to be used except by . . .'

I should not have let things get this far.

Instead, I asked, 'What's this thing in aid of, then, mates?' pointing at the white cylinder.

'We'd have been in lumber back then, but for you, Allan,' said Sampson, not answering the question.

He was now rolling the cylinder into a tarpaulin that had lain on the cart. He did it as carefully as though putting a baby in a blanket.

'You were just champion, Allan,' he went on, 'the way you fettled that train . . .'

Miles Hopkins, the weird smile once again about his lips, began a speech I wasn't keen he should finish:

'How come you knew what was what on the . . . ?'

'Nowt to it,' I said, interrupting.

'You're coming on like anything, Allan,' said Sampson as the pony and cart approached the goods station, the centre of events, once more. The drays were still flowing in, either side of the clock house that stood in front of the entrance.

We struck Leeman Road before turning into Station Road, right in front of the railway offices. There was a small dark court between the offices and the building facing, which had been the old station hotel, and was now used for storage. The main doors of each building faced one another, with their gas lamps dangling above, but the lamp over the entrance to the store was never lit. Beyond the two buildings ran a cobbled lane called Tanner Row, which was one long terrace of tall black houses. Set in the middle of that terrace, and overseeing the stand-off between the old hotel and the offices was a pub: the Grapes. Its front window was in three sections, and each one carried a word. The three words glowed out darkly towards us: 'Wines' 'And' 'Spirits'.

Sampson, with one foot steadying the gas cylinder, was looking thoughtful.

'What's the next business?' I asked.

Sampson's and Hopkins's eyes locked.

Sampson said, 'A week Sunday?' speaking more to Miles Hopkins than to me.

He got the nod from Hopkins, and said again 'A week Sunday', this time addressing me.

'Quite a long space between now and then,' I said, and it

was queer: I felt somehow let down. I would be back to waiting and worrying for a week.

Sampson nodded, seemingly to himself.

I risked another question.

'Will that be the day of the big show?' I said, '. . . the great doing?'

'We've a few more movables to collect first,' said Hopkins, and I thought it a little odd that *he* should have answered the question.

Mike had turned us over the river by Lendal Bridge, and along Blake Street, where half a dozen gas standards awaited us, and no people.

'Where are we to meet then?' I asked.

I noticed another glance fired between our leader and his lieutenant. At the end of it, Miles Hopkins shrugged, and Sampson looked down at his boots, and his beloved gas cylinder. I knew what he was about: he was revolving in his mind the low pubs of York.

'The Grapes,' he said, looking up.

'The one we've just passed?' I said, for there were half a dozen houses called the Grapes in York. The one in Tanner Row was a smart place, frequented by a superior grade of clerk. It was as though, having netted the cylinder, the gang could afford to put on swank.

I decided to go fishing again.

'So it's one more little job, with a big one to follow?'

Sampson nodded. 'Big one's a little way off, though.'

'What he's saying,' said Hopkins, nodding towards me, 'is that he's not had his wages.'

He was wrong over that, but I was glad he'd spoken up. The only reason I'd not mentioned the matter of payment was that I was a policeman playing a double game – simple as that.

Sampson put his hand in his pocket book, and after some

thought gave me a pound, saying: 'You kept the line beautifully today, kidder.'

My first thought was: that's the wife's new fur-lined gloves paid for. A lot of other thoughts came as I pocketed the note – of some vicars I'd known, of Dad and the family name, written above the butcher's shop in Baytown . . . But in the working world of York, extra money was something miraculous.

There was silence as the pony plodded on, and it seemed to mark the end of the night's business, or my part in it. 'I'll get down here,' I said. 'My lodge is t'other way.'

Sampson stood up in the cart to see me off – very courtly, he was.

'Keep it dark about tonight's work, won't you, little Allan?' he said, as I climbed down.

'You bet,' I said.

'And you're all set for Sunday week?'

I nodded again, watching the cart roll on. As Mike steered into Lendal, Miles Hopkins turned his head, and looked back at me, not breaking off his stare until buildings came between us.

As I biked back home past the dark villas of Thorpe-on-Ouse Road, I kept trying to think when I might've shown my hand. Favourite was the moment when the cylinder was being extracted from the van. That's when I could've raised my arm to declare: 'It's all up for you lot. I am a detective with the railway force, and I am arresting you on a charge of theft.' I might also have mentioned trespass, assault, a spot of blackmail (in the case of the clerk, no doubt), and then the bill topper: the Cameron brothers, side by side in the York mortuary.

Valentine Sampson was nuts and the other, Miles, was clever.

Which was worse?

And where was Edwin Lund in all this? He was clever *and* nuts.

I stowed the Humber by the cottage wall and, removing the fake glasses, opened the door to see the wife, who was at her typewriting of course, by a dead fire.

'Well then?' she said, not stopping typewriting.

She *had* seen me in Fossgate. It was ten-thirty by the mantel clock . . . And there was a bottle of beer waiting by it, which was a good sign – a sign that I might kiss her, which I did. I had half expected to find the wife in tears. As it was, she just looked tired.

'Just at present,' I said, standing by the rocking chair, 'I'm put to spying for the police.'

It sounded like a confession.

'Does that require you to wear funny glasses?' she said.

'What's funny about them?' I said, removing them from the pocket in which I'd just stowed them. 'They're a pair of perfectly ordinary glasses, except that they don't have any glasses in them.'

'And a terrible suit,' she said, standing up from the typewriting table and walking over to the sofa. She sat down here, sprawling rather, with legs wide underneath her skirts. Her condition probably made this a necessity, but it was all for it in any case. She was brownish, skinny but for the football under her dress, and altogether indestructible-looking, somehow.

'That can't be helped,' I said, taking a pull on the bottle of Smith's. 'You have a husband who's pretending to be a vagabond.'

I sat down next to her. 'I suppose I must admit,' she said, 'that with many women it's the other way about.'

She fiddled with the locket at her chest, then looked up at me, and said:

'Let's have it, Jim.'

I gave her the tale, the whole of my double game, leaving out only my suspicion that Sampson had done for the Camerons, and concluding:

'By rights I'm not supposed to have told you any of this.'

The wife was looking at me in a mysterious sort of way – half amused, I thought.

'You are to keep it dark,' I said, thinking of Sampson standing in the cart.

Still no reply – just the dark eyes looking at me in the dark room.

'You wanted me in the police,' I said, 'and this is what police work comes down to.'

'I wanted you out of an occupation that was not suited to your intellect,' said the wife, after a space.

It was the first time she'd come out with anything of that sort. I'd thought all along she'd set her face against railway work because it was mucky.

I said: 'Firing's no picnic, you know: one shovelful of coal in the wrong spot, down goes the pressure and you're knackered; and driving's just as tricky.'

I finished off the bottle of Smith's, and turned towards the wife.

'What is the effect of notching up the gear upon the steam cycle within the cylinder?' I asked her. 'Any notions on that point? No? Try this then: what are the eight name positions of the crank?'

'You're the crank, Jim Stringer,' she said.

'Tell you what,' I said. 'You're off the hook if you can name me one.'

'You're not happy in the police, then?'

'You know very well I'm not.'

I walked through to the kitchen to collect another bottle

of Smith's from the pantry.

'Off the footplate,' I said, returning to the parlour, 'you see the world as it really is . . .'

'And how is it?'

'Everybody spends too long in one place. I have a need for speed.'

I sat down on the rocking chair, and the wife came over and sat on my knee, saying, 'Well, you have the Humber.'

We sat there in silence for a while.

Some voices came from the direction of the Fortune, but just when I thought they were about to grow loud, they faded away.

'There are three people in one rocking chair,' said the wife, after a while.

'I wouldn't half mind putting the fixments on that lot,' I said, thinking of the cart rolling away down Lendal, the cutting cylinder rolling back and forth inside it, like a clock ticking.

'I'm doing some letters for Hunter and Smallpage just at the moment,' said the wife (who was evidently still thinking of the rocking chair, for she was speaking of the shop where we'd bought it) '. . . they call themselves "a firm of forty years' *standing*",' she continued, '. . . and yet almost all their business is selling chairs . . .'

I looked at the wife; she could be a queer sort, at times.

'You've your report to write tomorrow, I suppose,' she said, standing up, for I'd mentioned that part of the job, too.

'Aye,' I said, 'in fact I think I'll make a start now, while it's all fresh in my mind.'

I moved the typewriter and the sweet jars across to one side of the strong table, laid out on it the papers given me by Weatherill and, having placed carbons beneath, began to write. With the wife looking on, I set out at the top of the first page the headings insisted on by Weatherill, thinking, now ought I to begin with meeting Lund at the War Memorial? I decided to leave him out of it, as before, and so started with the moment I walked into the Big Coach.

After five minutes of watching me write, the wife said: 'You're not to eat the Opopanax, but you can have one of the Parma Violets.'

I took one of the sweets, looking at her, thinking hard. I was now up to the point at which Sampson went off to meet his layer, and Hopkins was preparing to leave for the railway station.

After another five minutes or so, the wife rose swiftly to her feet, went into the kitchen, and came back with some bread, soup and hotcake, which I ate as I continued to write, and the wife continued to watch.

Suddenly, she stood up, declaring: 'I cannot stand the slow travel of your pen!'

'You said I was an intellect!' I shot back.

'I'll type your reports,' said the wife, and she was already at it: chivvying me out of the chair, and winding a new one of the report sheets into her machine.

'It's late,' I said.

'What do you put at the top?' she asked.

'"Special Report",' I said, 'then "Subject: Persons Wanted".'

'That's a waste of words,' said the wife, but she was typewriting all the same, asking, 'And how do you begin the actual reports?'

'How do you mean?'

'What form of words do you start with?'

'You've to start: "I beg to report".'

'That's ridiculous,' said the wife. 'We'll start with "I respectfully submit . . . " Now, you speak it out, I'll take it down.'

And so the wife learnt in more detail about Hopkins and Sampson, and all that had happened in the goods yard. And it was much quicker this way, for she typed fourteen to the dozen – at least as fast as I could speak. Occasionally she would eat an Opopanax, occasionally she would ask a question. She wanted to know what was in the cylinder, and I explained as best I could.

'They're safe-breakers,' she said, quite delighted. 'It's like a penny shocker.'

When we reached the point at which we'd all spilled out of the goods yard, I thought I'd better let Weatherill know that this occurred at the very spot where the Camerons had been shot, and so the wife learnt all about this matter too, at which she stopped typewriting, saying: 'You're in danger here, you know.'

'Once things get too hot, I'll just do a push,' I replied. 'Besides, I don't think they'd run to shooting a policeman.'

'But they don't know you're a policeman.'

'That's true,' I said. 'I was forgetting.'

'You're quite certain of that, aren't you?'

'Of what?'

'That they don't know.'

'Do leave off,' I said, 'of course I am.'

She carried on taking my dictation until I came to the moment when Mike, the Blocker, had apologised for lamming me, and I'd apologised for calling him a 'fucking rotter'. The wife was shaking her head, as I came out with this, saying, 'That goes down as "He uttered foul language".'

'You must write it out,' I said. 'Just put "f" and a line.'

'Why were you given this work to do?' said the wife. 'You're brand-new on the job. You've no experience.'

'That's exactly why,' I said. 'The Chief was taking advantage of the fact that I'm not known.'

'Taking advantage full stop, if you ask me,' said the wife.

PART FOUR

The Great Doing

Chapter Sixteen

'What are you reading?' asked the wife.

'*Police Gazette*,' I said. 'Deserters and Absentees from His Majesty's Service.'

We were in the living room, waiting for the knock that would signify the arrival of my father for his Sunday visit. I turned the page and it came.

Just as I stood up to open the door, I noticed, on the very top of the scrap papers in the fire basket, the words 'LADIES' COLUMN by "Lucy"'. It was one of the ones sent by dad to the wife in the hopes of turning her into the more common run of housewife, but it was too late to do anything about it now. I had the door open and Dad was stepping in, removing his brown bowler.

'Harry,' said the wife, and she rose from the sofa and they kissed.

'Now you mustn't stand up, dear,' said Dad.

Leaving aside his being forty years older, he looked like an indoor version of me: pinker and more rounded, better maintained.

'Well, you know, I *like* standing up, Harry,' said the wife. 'It is one of my favourite activities.'

'But in your condition, Lydia,' said Dad.

He was standing at the fireplace now, in his Sunday-best suit, boots gleaming. 'You do look well on it, though, I must say. Absolutely blooming, isn't she, James?'

He was looking about the room – searching for the sewing machine. I'd forgotten to put it out.

'Journey all right, Dad?' I said.

'Yes, all right, lad,' he said. 'A bit blowy coming along the cliffs.'

The wife was watching him very carefully as he folded his gloves and placed them inside his bowler hat. He knew she was doing this, and he coloured up a little. A good deal of his gentlemanliness was new, a luxury afforded by a comfortable retirement, and he was liable to be embarrassed over it. He said:

'The waiting room at Ravenscar blew clean away, last month, you know.'

'But how could it?' said the wife, evidently fascinated.

'Well, it was made of wood, for one thing,' said Dad.

'They built it out of wood with the gales they get up there?' said the wife. 'Has nobody in that company read *The Three Little Pigs*?'

Dad didn't know what to make of this, and went a little redder.

'I don't know I'm sure, dear. You must take it up with your husband . . . Oh, before I forget,' he said, and he took out from his inside pocket a pen which he handed over to me.

'Now you're working at a desk,' he said, and he handed me a pen.

I recognised it. This was Dad's Swan fountain pen, his best one. Receipts to the gentry were always written with it – and I'd often tried to puzzle out the secret of its smoky green and black decoration.

'I can't take this, Dad.'

'Look after it,' he said, 'and it'll be a lifelong friend. I always meant to give you it when you started work, but first you were portering, then on the engines. There was no call for a pen.'

'I'm not always at a desk,' I said, looking at the wife. 'A fair amount of the work is outdoors.'

'But it's not as if you're patrolling a beat . . . Is it?' he added, rather anxiously.

'I'm a detective, Dad, in the plainclothes section. I've told you this before.'

'Detective?' he said. 'That sounds a rather superior grade.'

'It is the very lowest grade on the plainclothes side,' I said.

'The lowest grade in a superior division,' said Dad, who was now removing another article from his pockets. It was small and squarish, and wrapped in brown paper. He handed it to the wife, saying: 'This is for you, Lydia, love.'

'Thank you, Harry,' she said. 'Whatever is it?'

'Cheese,' he said, 'best cheddar.'

'I'll go and put it in the pantry straight away,' said the wife.

'No, no, let me, dear. I need to go to the little room as well. That's . . .'

'Out in the garden,' I said.

Dad took the cheese back from the wife, and handed over a slip of paper to her as he did so.

'Brought you another of these, love,' he said.

He turned and walked through to the kitchen, and I looked at the wife. It was another 'LADIES' COLUMN by "Lucy"' snipped from the *Whitby Gazette*. She read out loud: 'There are many dishes which are much improved in richness and flavour by the addition of a sprinkling of grated cheese.'

'Well that's the mystery of the present solved,' she said, putting the cutting into the fire basket, from where I retrieved it and placed it on the table next to the typewriter.

The wife was now putting on her cape and gloves, while I took my cap off the hook on the front door. We had a plan for the day, and it was now being put into effect.

'We thought we'd go off to church,' said the wife, when Dad came back from the privy.

'Oh good,' said Dad.

And we all stood there looking at each other.

———————◇————————

The day was darkish, drizzly. A grey cloud sat squarely over Thorpe-on-Ouse like an island in the sky. On the long path cut diagonally through the churchyard, we fell in with a thin stream of churchgoers, as the sound of a distant train filled the sky: a Leeds train or London train. It rattled away, leaving the cold, old sound of church bells. The wife had spied Lillian Backhouse, and, having made her excuses to Dad, had dashed on ahead. Lillian Backhouse, I knew, did not believe in God but went to church only because her husband was the verger. As far as I knew, most of the suffragists were like Lillian: non-believers. But Lydia did believe, and I went to church – sometimes – because she went, whereas Dad went to church because he thought it was the gentlemanly thing to do.

St Andrew's Church smelt of damp kneelers and old flags and banners. These hung down dead from the roof. They were set in rows above the pews, and reminded me somehow of the moving cranes in a locomotive erecting shop. The wife had re-joined us at our regular pew, which was at the back. Major Turnbull's pew, of course, was at the front, and when he walked in, making along the aisle towards it, I pointed him out to Dad, who was not in the least interested, which knocked me rather.

'No fresh meat to be seen in your kitchen, James,' he whispered, so that the wife would not hear. 'Do you not have a joint on Sundays?'

'Not every Sunday,' I said.

'In your larder,' he said, 'the emphasis is rather on the can. A young lady in Lydia's condition,' he continued, lowering his voice yet further, 'needs a regular supply of good, fresh meat.'

'Well,' I said, 'she's living on raspberry-leaf tea and humbugs just now.'

'The baby will be small,' he said.

'They generally are, aren't they?'

He ignored that, but turned into a different channel:

'Where does Lydia wash the clothes, James?' he asked.

'In the bathtub,' I said.

It was the wrong answer.

After the service, I reflected that Dad was bringing out the suffragist even in me. He'd never done a hand's turn about the house. As a widower he'd always had help: a half-time maid when I was a boy, and now Mrs Barrett, his housekeeper.

Afterwards, the three of us stood in the churchyard, and the wife said: 'Lillian's going to look in later.'

Then the wife said, 'The river's just nearby, you know, Harry.'

'We thought we might have a swing out there,' I said, for this was the second part of the plan.

Dad said: 'Are you sure you're able, my love?'

'Quite sure,' said the wife, shortly.

'How are things in Baytown, Dad?' I asked as we set off past the front of the Archbishop's Palace.

'I'm kept pretty busy with the meetings of the Conservative Club. It was our annual meeting on Monday. Very good attendance, considering . . .'

'Considering that you lost,' I put in, which I'd done because I'd feared the wife might, and it would come much worse from her. Dad already knew me for a Labour man, his own son a lost cause.

'I consider it a blessing in disguise that the Liberals got in, James. It'll give us the chance to put our house in order.'

He turned to the wife.

'You're still campaigning, are you, dear?'

We're in for bother now, I thought, as the wife nodded, saying:

'Church League for Women's Suffrage and Women's Social and Political Union.'

'Well, that sounds enough to be going on with,' said Dad, as the wife strode on ahead, opening up a little ground between herself and Dad and me. We were walking past the old, ruined church on the riverbank now, and the few gravestones that stood at crazy angles around it.

'You know,' said Dad, to the back of the wife's hat, 'women have got along perfectly well up to now without the vote. Why should they want it now all of a sudden?'

'This is a new century,' said the wife, striding on, as though about to walk into the river, 'and women want new things.'

'They want the vote,' said Dad.

'And other things besides,' said the wife.

'Such as what?' said dad.

'Sexual liberation,' said the wife, without looking back, and Dad turned to me with his mouth open and a look of panic on his face.

We are unbalanced, I thought, as we came to a wet, slippery sty, and Dad helped the wife over, neither of them saying anything; there ought to have been another female in the picture, but there again perhaps there would be in a little under a month's time. We were right by the river now. It was wide and cold, carrying more brightness in its golden colour than the sky, and hard to look at, somehow.

To our left were the private riverside grounds of the Archbishop's Palace, to the right the muddy path that lead towards Naburn Locks. We walked on in silence for a while, then Dad said to me: 'Hodgson has a new shed down on the front.'

'What for?'

'Boils crabs in it.'

The wife looked back at us, pulling a face.

'He doesn't do it for fun, you know,' I called ahead to her. 'He's a fisherman.'

The Hodgsons were one of the three or four big fishing families in Baytown. Dad didn't hold with them. They were vulgar sorts, he thought, stinking at all times of fish or foul cigars. Also, anybody eating fish was not eating meat, and Dad had been a butcher most of his life. Thinking on, it was a wonder he stayed put in that spot for so long. If he could have, he would have taken a rope and dragged the whole of Baytown up the cliff and away from the sea.

We began to hear the noise of the weir, and presently we stood before it, the water racing over the smooth stone slopes. It was not possible to speak in that stream of din. The swing bridge that carried the London trains over the river lay beyond. It looked like a steel tower that had over-toppled.

We turned about, and were back home for two o'clock. It was dinner time but there was no dinner, only tea, which the wife had half-prepared, so I put off the subject of food, made up the fire and lit the gas (for it was already dark outside). Dad looked at the pocket knife on the mantelshelf, saying:

'This is a handsome one, James, where did you get it?'

I don't recall answering, but poured him out a bottle of beer, and sat him on the chair near the fire, where he went to sleep in short order. I suggested that the wife have a lie-down, but she went off to the kitchen to finish the tea, and I picked up the *Police Gazette* once more. At first, I didn't read, but thought of Baytown, stacked up on its cliff – not so much streets as steps. If you let fall a marble anywhere in the town, it would be on the beach within a minute. I thought of the fishing families, and how they carved model ships and sailed them in the rock pools, which proved they liked the sea in some way. It wasn't just something they were stuck with. Anybody could join in too, even the butcher's son, so I liked the fishermen . . . But the railway ran around the headland, high and free, and timetables had held more fascination for me than tide-tables.

I looked down at the *Police Gazette*, and, without thinking, turned over the page reading 'Deserters and Absentees from His Majesty's Service' to that reading 'Portraits of Persons Wanted'.

I read the by-now familiar words: 'Apprehensions Sought.' 'Metropolitan Police District,' I read, lighting on the top one on the page. 'Joseph Howard Vincent, whose arrest is sought for the murder of two police detectives at Victoria on August 23rd, 1902.' There was a bad picture. The fellow was blurred, and further away than the usual *Police Gazette* lot, as if he'd already started making his escape at the moment the picture was taken. He looked to be on a gangway of a ship. The sky was very large behind him, and half of it might have been sea, when I looked closer. 'Complexion fresh,' I read, 'rather high cheekbones, carries head rather forward, beard, dark grey mixture jacket suit, silk hat. Eyes small and shifty. Blue. Erect bearing; has a habit of biting his nails. Until the date of the murder he lived on the prostitution of a murdered woman. Two days after the murder he is said to have been at Great Grimsby. Sentenced at Durham Assizes, 21st April 1890, to seven years' penal servitude for burglary at a pawnbroker's and shooting at police. Will probably be found in hotels. Warrant issued. Information to be forwarded to the Metropolitan Police Office, New Scotland Yard, S.W.'

It was Valentine Sampson.

Dad moved suddenly in his chair. I looked slowly across at him, thinking: it should have been me giving a jolt like that.

'I wasn't asleep was I, James?'

I said nothing; my mind was elsewhere, but he really wanted to know. The wife was setting out the tea things.

'I wasn't *asleep*, was I, son?'

There was a loud pounding on the door. The wife stepped across, opened it, and in walked Lillian Backhouse. The wife was introducing her to Dad. I was distantly aware of things starting badly, when Lillian handed a package to the wife, saying: 'Here's the scented oil. Now you are to rub it on *here*.'

She was pointing with two hands down towards her cunny. Dad was looking across at me, his face red from the fire, looking like a man trapped in his seat.

Was it Valentine Sampson? That was just the kind of name you might make up if you were swell-headed . . . He did have a fresh complexion, but did he carry his head forwards? I couldn't have said.

Dad was now talking to Lillian; or the other way about. He was saying, 'You have children yourself, Mrs Backhouse?'

'I was continually pregnant for eleven years,' she replied.

'Eyes small and shifty.' Valentine Sampson's eyes were not small. They were *large* and shifty.

Dad was looking puzzled. He was turning to Lillian Backhouse.

'But you must have had a child at the end of all that time?'

The wife was laughing, trying to steer the sound of it in the direction of politeness, but not quite succeeding. Lillian Backhouse was standing in the centre of the room, hair down like a girl, her legs set further apart than is generally considered ladylike. She was swaying her middle back and forth, moving her thin dress, and saying her piece:

'Eleven children, eight survivors; two miscarriages, and not once under the doctor, and never once with chloroform either.'

Valentine Sampson's eyes were large sometimes, at any rate. Small at others? Maybe.

'. . . And that was when I felt my membranes go,' Lillian Backhouse was saying.

The wife was remarking upon something.

'My first?' Lillian Backhouse was saying, evidently in reply. 'With my first I had a straight labour but I flooded afterwards.'

'Flooded what?' I thought. Dad was on the edge of his chair, wanting to go but unable. Tea had to be eaten first, apart from anything else. Meanwhile, his object was to shift the talk away from Lillian Backhouse's insides.

'What did you find was the best diet for building up your strength, Mrs Backhouse?'

'Oatmeal and bacon,' said Lillian Backhouse.

'Ah now, bacon,' said Dad in a firmer voice – at last he had something to hold on to.

They were not blue – Valentine Sampson's eyes – so much as blue-ish. But the *Police Gazette* didn't run to 'blue-ish'.

'The second and third,' Lillian Backhouse was saying, '. . . things ran along smoothly.'

Valentine Sampson at Victoria Station . . . I could just picture him there, sweeping towards the trains of the London, Brighton and South Coast Railway. I saw him in Brighton, looking nobly out to sea while dreaming up villainy. The man haunted railways; railways and hotels, it now seemed. Very well then: railway hotels too. He would have a gun about him at all times, of that I was now sure, and the

Camerons, I was equally certain, had taken lead because Sampson had brought his gun to York.

The wife was still bringing out the tea things. Lillian Backhouse was watching her, saying, 'A mother should have nothing to do with heavy labour for three months before or after.'

'It's only a few potted meat sandwiches,' I heard myself saying.

I could send a message to the Chief straightaway, and he could telegraph the Metropolitan Police, South Western Division. We had run their man to ground after all. Why, this might be the end of the matter!

Dad was up and out of his chair at last, as Lillian Backhouse was saying, 'With the baby always writhing and turning like a . . .'

And now Dad was in front of me, with his gloves, cane and bowler collected up.

'His lungs were not inflated by the midwife,' Lillian Backhouse was saying, as Dad said:

'The three o'clock train'll suit, James, if you don't mind.'

And so, with a kiss, and apologies, for the wife, and a bow of a very peculiar sort to Lillian Backhouse, he was out the door with me following along behind.

'Who's her husband?' Dad was saying as we crossed the front garden.

'A man of a rather delicate constitution,' I said.

'I'm not bloody surprised,' said Dad.

Kettlewell, the carrier, did a three o'clock run into York on Sundays, and we waited for him at the Palace end of the main street, just outside the ill-fêted, never-occupied cottage with the wild garden. Dad was saying something about a Middlesborough ship, lost off Filey the week before, and I made a few comments here and there, but I was wondering

141

all the time at the near identity of Valentine Sampson and Joseph Howard Vincent of the *Police Gazette*.

As I stepped back in through the door of 16A, the ladies were obviously talking about me, because they *stopped* talking at just that moment.

'Well, shame on me for saying the father ought to be present,' Lillian Backhouse muttered after a short pause.

She looked directly at me, saying: 'We'd all have fewer bairns if fathers attended births, I'll tell you that for nothing, Jim Stringer.'

'I shall be here, Lillian,' I said, sitting on the sofa, '. . . only downstairs.'

'Lydia will be downstairs, for the hot water,' said Lillian Backhouse. 'That kitchen,' she added, pointing, 'is going to be a hot water *factory*.'

'Then I will be *up*stairs,' I said, but with Valentine Sampson to settle, another thought was beginning to cross my mind: would I be here at all?

Chapter Seventeen

Sunday to Sunday.

I had a week of waiting and clearing the broken-down pig sties out of the front and back garden. Meanwhile, the wife sat at her typewriter getting bigger by the day. She was in better spirits now though, Lillian Backhouse's bloodthirsty talk having seemed to galvanise her in some strange way. On the Monday, I cut the picture of Joseph Howard Vincent from the sixth *Police Gazette*, and sent it to the Chief. I had no word back until the Friday, when a telegram told me to report to the Police Office on Sunday morning at seven, later than usual on account, I supposed, of Sunday being a quieter day in the station therefore a safer one for me.

I left 16A on the Humber at six-thirty, wearing the bad suit, and with the glass-less specs in my top pocket. I had the Chief to see, and I was due at the Grapes in the evening, so I would make a day of it in town.

The smoke smell was thin in York station at seven o'clock, for there were long intervals between the trains. The book-stall was open, with the stout party still in place. It was weird, given his full figure, that those books he sold that were not about murder concerned the suppression of fat. There were about fifty souls in the station proper, every one of them on Platform Ten: an excursion party, heading for Scarborough most likely, for a bit of a blow. I wondered if it could possibly matter that some of them were looking on as I walked into the Police Office. I was not yet wearing the glasses, not yet Allan Appleby.

The Chief was waiting at his desk with the *Police Gazette* photograph of Valentine Sampson or Joseph Howard Vincent before him.

I saluted, and the Chief winced.

'There's no need to do that, you know.' he said. He sat back looking at me; he had a different suit on – a little better than his regular one, and wore a diamond stick-pin in his neckerchief. It seemed that he became half-gentleman come Sunday. But he was still too big and wild-looking, cut out for desperate deeds, not Sunday visiting. He moved forwards, saying:

'It's much like when you go into a Church of England service . . . You don't need to cross yourself.'

'Oh,' I said. 'But you do need to take your hat off.'

'What the heck's that got to do with it?' said the Chief, who seemed quite put out. He shook his head for a space before picking up the page I'd sent him.

'Now this scoundrel's been cropping up in the *Gazette* for donkey's years, always the same photograph, always the shooting of the two detectives mentioned. I think they put him in at slack times, fill up space.'

He held up the page featuring the photograph for us both to see.

'I've spoken on the telephone to the right fellow at the Met,' he continued. 'And they know him only as Joseph Howard Vincent, not . . . whatever you said.'

'Valentine Sampson, sir,' I said, adding rather sharply: 'It's a hard name to forget.'

The Chief gave me a warning look.

'How did they come by the picture?' I asked.

'It was taken by his fiancée.'

'Where?'

'Not known,' said the Chief. 'Some holiday ground. He's at the start of a pleasure cruise by the looks of it. The fiancée sent it to the police with a note: this is the fellow you want for that shooting at Victoria. She kept her name back but offered to make a statement, and so a time and a place was set, but she never turned up.'

'Why would she make an offer then withdraw it?'

'There can be no great mystery there,' said the Chief, kicking his chair back, and putting his arms behind his head, like a man preparing to go to sleep in a play. 'She knew he'd done it, perhaps witnessed the crime; he then chucked her over, which sets her thinking: blimey, he really is a rotter, this one.'

The Chief shook his head.

'Stupid bloody cow,' he said.

'Why were the detectives after him in the first place?'

'Attempted robbery of a bank.'

'Is it known how he was attempting to rob it?' (Of course, I was thinking of the cylinder). 'Was there any machinery involved?'

'Yes,' said the Chief, 'a revolver.'

'Well, I think it's my man, and I'm going to meet him this evening at the Grapes on Tanner Row.'

'Convenient, is that,' said the chief. 'Why, it's just around the corner.'

'Convenient for an ambush,' I said.

The Chief said nothing.

'Am I not to have any support from fellow officers?' I said, and I couldn't help but give a quick glance behind, through the open door towards the general office beyond, which was, as always, quite empty.

'If I get in much further with this lot,' I continued, 'I'm going to have burnt my ships with the law.'

'How do you mean?' said the Chief, and I surprised myself by what I said next.

'I was given the shove by the Lancashire and Yorkshire,' I said, 'but what happened wasn't my fault. I was always up to the mark with the work. Given a job to do, I'll do it well, whether it be firing an engine or robbing a bank.'

The Chief was grinning at me. He seemed to like this talk.

'You want me to save you from yourself,' he said.

He took out a cigar and lit it.

'You hungry?' he said.

I knew straightaway that he meant to take me over to the hotel.

'I'd best change my suit,' I said, shocked.

'That's right,' said the Chief. 'Can't go in your knockabout clothes.'

'It's my disguise,' I said.

The Chief nodded, mind elsewhere once more.

I dashed off to Left Luggage (which had just opened for business), took out my best suit, changed into it in the gents, and replaced it with the bad suit, all at the cost of a tanner.

'Natty,' said the Chief, when I returned to the office, and five minutes later we were aiming for the dining room of the York Station Hotel or rather, one of the three dining rooms. The one we were after lay on the second floor, and, as we approached along a corridor wide as a road, I heard a droning noise to the right: there was a housemaid, alone in a ballroom and pushing an electrical cleaner. The Chief grinned at me as we passed her, and the sound of the machine was gradually replaced by a mighty rising tingle-tangle. We turned a corner, and doors opened on to something resembling a great wedding feast or banquet: Sunday breakfast at the Station Hotel.

A man in livery approached us, and led us towards a bonny serving girl. She said, 'Do you wish to view the breakfast?' You'd have thought it was a work of art, and in fact it was – all laid out on three sideboards before the high windows over-looking the hotel pleasure gardens. I noticed for the first time that Sunday, 11 February had become a fine winter's morning, and this feast required nothing less. At the sideboards, well-to-do folk were eyeing bacon, scrambled eggs, sausages, devilled kidneys, haddock, hams and cold meats and roasts, all on silver plates and warmed by spirit lamps. We took our seats, informed a waitress of our selections; she brought the preliminaries of coffee, toast, pots of marmalade, honey, unknown imported jams. She smiled often as she worked and it was a very good smile indeed; you didn't tire of it.

'This keeps you going until dinnertime, you know,' said the Chief, and his face could not contain his twisted, half-embarrassed smile. He was thinking of the morning he'd left me in the cold Police Office with nothing but a cold kettle. But I was wondering whether we ought to be in the hotel at all. It was the Chief himself who'd made all those rules about our not being seen together, after all.

'You're not a dog, lad,' said the Chief, as he poured coffee, 'a creature trained to absolutely obedience at all times. You must operate in two minds. What most folk – most police-men especially – don't understand about police work is that it's *brain* work of the most confoundedly difficult sort.'

As he said this, the swell sitting opposite a woman at the next table turned to face us, and it was like a field gun swing-ing on its pivot. He was a bastard – I could see that right away.

'You must go along with your bad lads,' said the Chief, 'but stop short before the point of no return.'

'And what then?'

147

The Chief spooned a lump of marmalade on to his toast. It fell off. He spooned it on again.

'Remember,' he said, 'that you will not have brought the business to that point. It would have arrived there anyway, and when it does come, if there's no help to hand, you must do your best to face down . . .'

'Face down what?' I asked after a while, but the Chief was eating his toast and marmalade.

'Evil,' he said, when he'd finished.

'But I have no means of giving the alarm.'

Our neighbour, the toff, was prodding at bacon with a fork. He seemed very down on the whole show. This was not a very good breakfast as far as he was concerned. He looked up at the woman sitting before him:

'Want fruit?' he said, in a dead voice. I did not hear her reply.

The Chief picked up another bit of toast. It was fascinating to watch him eat, and also quite off-putting. I suddenly remembered what the *Police Gazette* had said about Howard or Sampson: 'Will probably be found in hotels'.

'Look,' said the Chief, 'we must net these lads, and we must net them *finely*. And that means an ambush, yes, but at the right time. At the moment what've we got? Theft of a cylinder of some sort?'

Was the aristocratic misery alongside us listening? He was looking at the woman. It was hard to say.

'It'll be used to cut metal, sir,' I said quietly, 'as I've already mentioned.'

'Theft of a cylinder,' repeated the Chief, 'pick-pocketing within the station; an assault. Other minor matters possibly. It's very thin pickings, and yet you suspect this scoundrel – the number one man – of all sorts.'

'I'm sure he killed the Camerons,' I said, in an under-breath. 'They were in his way somehow.'

'Add to that,' said the Chief, who continued loud, in spite of my whispers, 'the fact that you say the next meeting is not the actual doings, but more in the way of . . . plotting?'

I nodded, although I wasn't quite sure of that. As I tried to recall exactly what had been said on the cart coming away from the goods yard, a question came: why would Sampson want Allan Appleby involved in the planning of the great doing?

'We'll meet tomorrow in the Police Office at six in the morning,' the Chief was saying. 'No, meet at five. I've to be in Newcastle at half-past seven. We'll talk over whatever happens tonight and see if we have a better understanding of their final object.'

I asked the Chief: 'Any news on Richard Mariner?'

'Mariner?' said the Chief, a strange look on his face.

'The night porter here who did away with himself.'

'I asked about him. Spoke to the general manager. Nothing in it. The fellow always was a miserable sort – he'd had the morbs for years . . .'

The girl came up again, with the bacon and eggs and related matters. She served very daintily, but clumped off when she'd set it all out, which made her even more charming somehow. The Chief watched her as she walked away.

'One curious thing about Mariner though . . .' the Chief continued. 'He'd worked in the housekeeper's office, later with the banqueting staff . . . knew all about glass, linen and silver.'

'That fits the bill,' I said, and I thought of the riches of the Company. The glasses on our table, the cruet, the cutlery, the cloth – all carried the North Eastern insignia. I was sure that Sampson had got at Mariner somehow.

'I've hours to kill until I go along to the Grapes,' I said. 'Might I go back to the Police Office for another look at the particulars in the occurrences file?'

'There've been no occurrences since you last looked,' said the Chief. 'None in that line, I mean.'

He appeared to be thinking; he pulled out his pocket watch, saying, 'It's eight o'clock turned.'

He then took out of another pocket a silver key, which he handed to me.

'I want you out of there at eight-thirty sharp,' he said, passing me the key.

'Should I lock up when I'm finished?'

'Leave the door open and put the key in my desk,' he said, 'Shillito will be in at nine.'

He was calling for more coffee as I walked away.

Chapter Eighteen

The breakfast had fairly dazed me, and I walked back into the station wondering who I ought to be: myself or Allan Appleby. I worked it out by degrees as I strolled along Platform Four, and I saw the Lad, the telegraph boy, watching me from the footbridge, as if he was trying to puzzle it out at the same time. I stopped before the Left Luggage Office, where I collected my bad suit. I changed into it in the gentlemen's, and took my good one back, receiving the ticket in lieu, which I placed in my trouser pocket.

In the Police Office, I picked the 'Occurrences – Large Theft' file out of the cabinet near the door. I read again the first one: 'Attempted (possible actual) burglary at office of goods superintendent, York Yard South . . . Mr Cambridge (Goods Super) will endeavour to ascertain losses.' The writer of that was a great one for brackets. *When* would Mr Cambridge make that endeavour? Or was the setting down of the intention the end of the matter? I wondered which of the absent sportsmen had written this: Shillito? Langborne? Wright? If I hung on, I'd be able to ask Shillito directly, but no, that was not permitted; I must be kept from him, and all the other railway coppers of York.

I turned over the leaf, and read again of the assault on the wagons – also in the South Yard. I knew all about that, and had a fair idea who'd replaced the broken seals – Valentine

Sampson's tame little goods clerk. They'd tried the Acety-lene company van on the same night but given up because they couldn't put their hands on the right cylinder, as I sup-posed. Well, they had it now. I turned over again, and read of the robbery at the Station Hotel on 16 December, only this time the list of missing items went on to another sheet, and seemed to run on too long. I was reading of 'silver cigarette cases (two), silver snuff boxes (two), gold Alberts (three), good jewelled bracelets (two), cash (estimated £200)', and more besides until the penny dropped. This latest sheet did not belong to the account of the hotel robbery. I went back-wards through the pages, and saw that there was another stray mixed in with the papers to do with the burglary at the office of the Goods Super. The two went together and the second one I'd found was meant to be read as the first of the two. I looked to the top of this page: the date was 21 Decem-ber 1905, the occurrence detailed as follows: 'Theft from Lost Luggage Office'.

I stared at the words while an engine pulled out of the sta-tion, somewhere on the down side. The rising bark from its cylinders ought by rights to have ended in some mighty explosion, but instead the engine simply left the station. Silence returned, and I had the great perplexity of this new occurrence before me. There were no more details – only the list of items stolen. Had no statements been taken for this or any of the thefts?

If this matter was part of the series then it was an inside job, and there were only two blokes on the inside of the Lost Luggage Office: Parkinson and Lund. I bundled up the file again, and returned it to its cabinet. Why had I not seen those papers before? Had I simply missed them? It was not out of the question. I'd first looked at them on my first day in the job, and I'd been in a tearing hurry. It was very important to find out how Lund was connected to Valentine Sampson and his band – and that before I met Sampson at the Grapes. I could do with knowing about Parkinson too but I had no address for him whereas I had a street name at least for Lund: Ward Street, Layerthorpe.

◦

The sun was doing its work, even in Layerthorpe. The shadow of a cloud moved faster than me along Fossgate and, running on ahead, it rolled easily up and over the silos of Leetham's Mill. The same breeze made cigar and cigarette stumps tumble along the cobbles at my feet. Although I wore the Appleby suit, I did not sport the fake spectacles. Some of the pubs had their windows open; they were getting an airing, and the voices that floated out of them were still at this time of the day normal voices, kept low. In between the pubs were the tiny alleyways and side-streets where the constables walked in twos. Ward Street was one of them, or connected to one.

I turned into one of the entries, and saw two men standing in the doorway of a little broken-down hotel called Hemming's. One was peeling an orange, and throwing the peel at the other as he did so. It might have been a lark, but neither one was laughing. I turned again, and was facing the curved wall with the posters on it – the one I'd seen after quitting the Garden Gate on my first meeting with Miles Hopkins and Mike. The gas lamp was there but, not being lit, looked different. The advertisements for the pantomime remained, and if they'd survived this far, I reckoned, they'd probably see out the year.

On this occasion I obeyed the order: 'Turn right for Capstan's Cigarettes', and I was now into a new part of Layerthorpe, walking along a terrace where there was not enough window, so that the people in the houses had not been accommodated so much as bricked up. From somewhere, one voice was screaming out 'Dad!' over and over, and a dog barked after every cry. Eventually the voice gave up, but the barking continued, the loneliness of the sound driving the dog itself crackers. I didn't know the number of Lund's place and, as I walked, I realised that the matter was complicated by the fact that the dull, brown doors came irregularly. Some in the terrace were shuttered so that two houses were turned into one, and there were intervals of wall in between the houses, as though the builder's meagre supplies of glass had run out completely while his abundance of bricks had continued or increased. But the real surprise came at the end of the terrace where the last two houses had collapsed, or been demolished, with the rubble remaining, so that the terrace was like a cigar which had been smoked up to a certain point. On the facing terrace, the opposite numbers of the fallen houses remained and one carried a sign, not proudly but against its will as it seemed to me: 'Ward Street.'

But which was Lund's place? I turned around, and there was a man approaching one of the doors. I walked towards the man.

'How do?' I said, and he smiled.

He'd looked all right until he did that, but the inside of his mouth was a calamity: too-many-teeth and no-teeth all at once.

'How do?' I said again, for the sight of the mouth had knocked me. 'I'm looking for a fellow called Lund.'

The man pushed at the door, and walked in, motioning me to follow, which I did with no time to prepare for the second shock: the reek of the room. The man did not explain himself, but just sat down on a broken-down sofa next to a broken-

154

down woman. Half a single curtain at the window, no fire; poker in the middle of the bare wooden floor, tab rug hard up against the wall. It was as though a wind had lately blown through. The pair in the room were canned, and I was somehow sure they were drinking at that moment, too but I could see no bottles. The man leant forwards, slowly revealing a worn spot on the top of his cap, like a bald patch.

Silence until the woman spoke up:

'You must take us for what we are,' she said.

Was this Lund's mother? The person in want of a linoleum?

'I'm after a word with Lund,' I said, 'Edwin Lund.'

It was as if the man had forgotten what I was about but, now remembering, he rose to his feet, and caught up the poker that lay in the middle of the floor.

'Cold is cruel, en't it?' said the woman as he did so.

The man continued forwards, holding out the poker, making towards the fireplace, where something smoked in the blackness of the grate. He pushed the poker up the chimney, and rattled it against the flue. As he leant over to perform the action, a ripped part of his coat slipped, taking with it a portion of ripped shirt, so that I could see clear through to his white, washboard ribs, and what might have been the beginnings of a scar. Soot came down into the grate as the poker rattled, and then, behind me, something else that was coloured black settled quietly into the room: Lund. He wore a black suit, old and not pressed. His kerchief was something special, but not elegant; he held two black books in his hand. He nodded slowly at me; he didn't seem put-out, as I'd hoped, and he suddenly looked to me like a crafty, secretive fellow. He might have been about to say something – it was impossible to guess what – when the man holding the poker righted himself with a loud groan. The woman on the sofa was looking towards him; she then nodded at me, saying, 'Weakened insides, Mister.'

'I went under an operation,' said the man, sitting back down on the sofa.

'He has a want of strength on the insides,' said the woman, as if that added anything to the general understanding. All the Lunds had this in common: riddled with illness, and very vague about it. The man was smiling at me again, as though he knew I was looking without success for the spirit bottle that lay somewhere to hand. Lund, at the foot of the stairs, was holding his hand in an unfamiliar way: moving it across his mouth, as though feeling the flesh after a narrow shave. He wanted to be out of the house, I could tell. He offered no greeting, but said, while moving across the room:

'I'm off to chapel – want to walk along with me?'

I nodded to the pair on the sofa and stepped out of the door after Lund, closing it behind me. It was a relief to be back in the open air, although the street looked worse, now that I'd seen the inside of one of the houses.

'No one comes to visit our house,' said Lund, walking along in the direction from which I'd come. 'You must have had all on to find the place.'

'You told me the street once, if you remember,' I said, 'and then I saw your dad.'

He shook his head as he walked on.

'That's not your dad?'

'That's Mr Pickering. He's Mother's friend.'

'Do they work?'

'Not over much.'

'Then yours is the only wage coming in?'

'We have a little from the Chapel Poor Fund besides . . .'

We were back in Fossgate now, and there was a little life both inside and outside the pubs. A kid on the opposite side of the road who was wearing boots that were far too big for him (or just had outsize feet) was waving his cap at me. I tipped my own back at him, and he did a little dance with an evil expression on his face, as if saying: 'I've just bagged another idiot.' Looking away from him, I saw a man barring our way while nodding his head, thoughtful-like, as if to say: 'Now what do we have here?' There were tattoos on the backs of his hands, the leftovers of long-lost high spirits. We skirted around him easily enough, but Lund said: 'You're a little out of the tourist track here, you know. You should keep your eyes open.'

The sound of church bells, calling from the centre of the city, was being ignored by everyone except Lund. They acted on him like a capstan, winding him in. He was walking with an elastic stride, and not coughing. He seemed surer of himself than before though he still looked like a scarecrow – a stick in a suit, and the blackness of his suit made his thin head look whiter. He was the undertaker and corpse all in one.

'I've read about the robbery at your place,' I said, 'at the Lost Luggage Office, I mean.'

Lund walked on, saying nothing.

'Do you know anything of that?' I asked.

'It might have been done by the lot you're after,' he said.

'Why did you not bring the matter up, though?'

'Because I know nowt about it.'

'You must have known I'd get round to it, though.'

'I thought you'd get to it in time,' he said, and I had the idea that he was baiting me.

'When you gave me the little tour of your office, you never showed me the safe,' I said.

'It's kept out of the way,' he said. 'I'm asked not to show it to strangers. By rights, anybody who's lost valuables must wait on the other side of the counter.'

'Whoever did it knew the combination of the safe,' I said. 'I reckon it's a put-up job like all the others, which is a bad look-out for you and your governor Parkinson.'

Lund said nothing.

'Were you not questioned over it?'

'There were some questions, aye.'

'And what did they amount to?'

'Nowt.'

'Who asked 'em?'

'Station Police Office bloke.'

'Name of Weatherill?'

'Shillito,' said Lund, turning about to face me.

We were at the top of Fossgate by now, just by the Blue Boar.

'I may have to run you in,' I said, 'you and Parkinson both.'

Lund moved his hand to his face in that new way of his.

'But to do that,' he said, 'you must first . . . come out of hiding, so to speak.'

One idea was strong on me: this was a threat. *Could* it be? Lund had pitched me into this secret work, and by his knowledge of what I was about, he had power not only over my investigations but also – at a stretch – over whether I lived or died. Across the road, a happy crowd was forming before the mighty pillars of the Centenary Chapel: ordinary-looking York folk revealed at that moment as Wesleyan Methodists. All across the crowd, hats were being lifted in greeting like flaps on the tops of organ pipes; and still more came, all on foot – there were no carriages, as you might expect to see outside a church of a Sunday morning. There might have been hundreds in the street, waiting not just for the Centenary Chapel, but the other chapels – and the one church – that stood in St Saviourgate besides.

'Go *every* Sunday, do you?'

'Every *day*,' said Lund. He was directly opposite me, but looking away. 'Past ten year . . . only missed once in all that time.'

He hurriedly looked away, just as a gust of wind struck us. Then, with his head still averted, he added:

'Went again next morning, mind you.'

'The prodigal son,' I said, glancing down at the book in his hand, and added, 'What's that?' pointing at it.

He looked down at the book. 'Prize for regular attendance.'

I read the title on the spine: *The Great If, and Its Greater Answer*.

'Looks rather dry,' I said.

'It asks for a little thinking,' said Lund, looking up, and meeting my eyes for an instant.

Behind him, the doors of the chapel were opening.

'Read it in the services, do you?' I said.

'Get away,' he said, and now there might just have been a small smile. After a short pause, he said: 'I could have had *A Historical Geography of the Holy Land* but decided against.'

'I en't bloody surprised,' I said.

His eyes flickered and closed again and for a longer time, which seemed to seal the whiteness of his face, making him look for an instant like a white pole, a ninepin. He was, perhaps, keeping a cough down.

When he opened his eyes again, he said:

'We must be born again, you know.'

I made no reply, but wondered whether it was the church bells ringing out all across the city that had brought this on.

Lund said, 'Well, I'm off in now,' and moved away, beginning to make his way through all that stack of folks, still coughing, and the cough seemed to take all his attention,

159

requiring him to remain outside, leaning against one of the mighty pillars, as everybody else filed in through the doors. Presently, he mastered his cough, but for all his chapel-going ardour of five minutes before, he just stayed leaning against the pillar and looking down at his boots. I watched until he entered the chapel, which he did just as the first hymn struck up, and with a half-glance in my direction.

'The Great If,' I thought, finally walking away from the top of Fossgate . . . that was just about right.

Chapter Nineteen

It was getting on for ten o'clock; I was in Coney Street. I touched the eye-glasses resting on my nose, and once again pictured Allan Appleby. He'd taken his dinner-time pint, maybe at the Fox Inn on Holgate. It being a Sunday, he might've been the only solitary drinker in there. He'd have drunk while looking down at his boots, adjusting his specs occasionally; he'd have gone back for a couple more after his tea. Then he'd have walked over Holgate Bridge, staring down at the tracks as they divided towards passenger station or goods station. On a Sunday there wouldn't be much action: the odd engine dawdling along with a rake of empties, its column of steam toppling forwards rather than flowing behind. And if an engine had gone underneath the bridge just at that moment, and Allan had caught a belt of smoke and steam, he wouldn't have flinched, but just walked on, being a man used to small setbacks of that nature.

He would turn left at the end of Blossom Street, entering Station Road, with the Institute and the Lost Luggage Office to his left, and he would walk up the incline that took him over the sidings leading into the Old Station. He would be a little anxious on approaching Tanner Row, but quite resigned to going along with whatever desperate scheme was being got up in there. He had nothing else in prospect, after all.

By the time I brought my thoughts of Allan Appleby to a close I was at the door of the Grapes, where I was confronted with three further doors. The decorated glass in the panel of the first read 'Snug', the second 'Sitting Room', the third 'Smoking Room'. Where would Valentine Sampson and Miles Hopkins be? They'd want to be *snug*, they'd want to be *sitting*, and Sampson at least would want to be *smoking*. I tried first the Snug, and there they were – it was quite a thrill to have guessed right first time, like winning a prize in the tombola.

I joined them at the table, to be greeted with nods. The three of us were the only ones in the Snug. Red leather benches ran around the white walls; brass table legs shone in the half-dark. The place was like a courtroom or a first-class railway compartment of the best sort. There were many empty glasses on the table before Sampson and Hopkins. Sampson still looked like a fashion plate in his kingly way, but was canned, or on the way at least. As for Hopkins, some of his hair seemed to have fallen out since last time – making me feel that I wanted to pull the remainder out, have done with it – but his eyes danced as before. He was a man always in the middle of some game I didn't quite understand. He was fiddling with a pocketbook – I could guess how he'd come by it – for he always had to be using his marvellous hands. But things were different this time somehow. I hadn't been offered a drink, for a start.

'Where's Mike?' I said.

Nothing was said, and I thought: they've done the bugger in.

'Mike has to watch how he goes,' said Miles Hopkins slowly. 'He's not fancy-free like the rest of us, you know.'

'How come?'

Sampson was staring straight ahead, not smiling.

'He's just come off ten years hard. He can't be pulled again.'

Didn't stop him assisting in the taking of pocketbooks from Platform Fourteen, I thought. Was he scared? I didn't like the thought of being on for something that he'd jibbed at.

Sampson's face was changing. A smile coming from far away.

'Well, Allan old lad,' he said when it had finally arrived, 'it's a go.'

Miles Hopkins was watching me very carefully.

'The great doing?' I said.

'The very thing.'

'You said there were more movables to collect first,' I said in a very peevish little voice, because the rough sort of plan I'd made with the Chief was now destroyed.

'So I did,' said Sampson, 'and they've *been* collected. You see, mate, we were waiting for a particular circumstance before we could set to.'

'Waiting for the circumstance to *stop*, that is,' said Hopkins, who then took a drink, one laughing eye watching me over the rim of his glass.

'What?' I said.

'The strike,' said Sampson. 'You'll have read of it in the *Press* or heard of it somehow.'

'You having such a good knowledge of railways,' put in Hopkins.

'I *have* heard of it,' I said.

'Unofficial-like, it was,' said Sampson. 'Some blokes in the Associated . . . Amalgamated Society of summat or other. The tough nuts, the diehards. Some bloke was reduced in position for no good reason, and they stuck by him. Good socialists, those fellows are, and I raise my fucking glass to 'em.'

He did not do that, however. Instead, he sat back in his chair, and said:

'But I'm still going to steal all the silly fuckers' money.'

Miles Hopkins was still watching me as Sampson rose to his feet and, striding across the room, collected his overcoat from the door back. We were done with the Grapes, I realised, although not done with drinking, because there was a bottle of whisky rolling in Sampson's pocket.

Hopkins was rising to his feet too, his coat already on.

I thought: I can stop this. Three words will stop it: Joseph Howard Vincent. Or perhaps only two: Edwin Lund. But I don't say them, and was instead swept along behind Hopkins and Sampson. We were striding through the door and now we were out into York, dark, rain and cold. It could not have been any other way.

'It's coming on to rain,' said Sampson, walking on in his jaunty way. I hurried to keep up, even though I'd rather have put a hundred miles between myself and him.

You could forgive Sampson remarking on the state of the weather – it had evidently been some time since he'd been out of a public house. Inside the Old Station, on the other side of Tanner Row, an engine was in steam, like a memory, moving goods into or out of one of the stores built on top of the long-dead passenger platforms. They were secret, shameful exchanges carried on in the Old Station. Just then, it struck me that Hopkins wasn't with us. I looked back, and he was fifty yards behind, talking to a stranger: youngish and well set-up. Only . . . I'd a suspicion I'd seen that stranger's face before. As I looked back, so did Samspon, and Hopkins broke away from the stranger, walking fast to catch us up.

'Who's he?' I said, looking back at the well set-up man, who was walking in the opposite direction, hard by the new Company offices.

'Him?' said Sampson. 'That's Five Pounds . . . He's five pounds' worth of man.'

I nodded; it wouldn't do to enquire further. The man would be a worker for the Company; a key-holder of some sort, repository of trust, and now receiver of the wages of sin.

Hopkins came up to us, and Sampson, nodding back down the hill to indicate the stranger, said, 'What's he want?'

'He's in a funk,' said Hopkins.

'Over what?'

'Nowt in particular.'

'All right, are we?'

Hopkins nodded, and we continued walking up Tanner Row, turning left along Bar Lane . . . and then we were in Micklegate, the 600-year-old Bar – the greatest of the gateways in the City Walls – standing before us like a castle front guarded by gas lamps. The town was quiet, but a man was standing underneath one of the arches, and we didn't stop for him, but rather we collected him, for he was following on behind as we walked on, turning right into Station Road. The City Walls, high on their steep embankment, were to our right. In the darkness, rain fell softly on to them at a slant like a thousand tiny missiles trying to broach the city defences. We crossed Station Road, which was quite empty, and then we were in Queen Street (which was likewise), walking down its slope towards the Institute and the Lost Luggage Office. Were they going to rob that place for the second time? Would Lund step out of the shadows, and join us as the other fellow had?

Now Sampson had stopped under the lantern that jutted out from the front of the Institute; Hopkins joined him there and they began talking. The stranger was at my shoulder now. I turned quite slowly, and looked at him, but he couldn't meet my eye. He wasn't one of the burglar brigade, I knew.

He was a railwayman, and a very anxious one at that – a railwayman who'd been fixed.

I watched Sampson and Hopkins. If they were thinking of going into the Institute for a drink then we were going to go in for a drink, and who did they think they were kidding by pretending to talk it over? But then came a second thought: it appeared to me, from a twenty-foot distance, that Sampson wanted to go in, while Hopkins did not.

Sampson at last turned around towards us:

'We're going to take a last drink, boys,' he announced.

So we stepped into the Institute, our silent newcomer removing his cap and smoothing his hair with the look of a man trying hard to master himself. I felt a little in the same way. I'd nerved myself to the business that lay ahead, and now this – further delay. It was already gone eleven.

We didn't go into the snooker hall, but – once Sampson had brought the glasses of Smith's on a tray – just stood in the tiled vestibule of the Institution, loitering beneath a bright gas ring. We were only a couple of feet inside the front door, which was propped open, so it wasn't as though we were even warm. But I had my eye on the other door, the one leading to the snooker hall and bar. The barmaid in there knew me for a detective. Sampson was exchanging a few words with the newcomer, but not much was being said by anyone else. Presently, Sampson took out his watch, looked at it, and he didn't leave off looking at it either. He seemed to be simply observing time passing.

Hopkins was shaking his head. He was in fits, I could tell.

'We should be waiting outside,' he said, and so at last here it was: a set-to between the two leaders.

'Why?' said Sampson, still looking at his watch. 'It's fucking pissing down.'

I watched the snooker hall door.

Sampson was saying: 'We've a night's work ahead of us, and I don't want to be sodden while I'm about it, do you?'

The hallway was a carbolic-smelling limbo. The clash of snooker balls came from the snooker hall – the long roll followed by the crash, like the shunting of engines.

'And the four of us are leaving boot prints everywhere,' Hopkins went on, 'that's evidence, you know.'

'Boot prints?' said Sampson. 'Where?'

'On the fucking *floor*,' said Hopkins. 'Where do you fucking think?' But he was laughing now and Sampson along with him. Just then, a man walked through the door, and slap into the back of Sampson's flying hand. He went down onto the white tiles.

'Always a friendly welcome with you blokes, en't it?' said the man, picking himself up.

Sampson was holding up both of his hands: 'Sorry, mates, lost my grip there just for a moment,' he said, addressing everyone save the man he'd belted, who was the cocky little clerk – the one who'd guided us about the goods yard eleven days before. He'd come back for second helpings. He was back on his feet now, saying, 'Don't you think you might include me in that apology?'

Sampson was looking at the man.

'I'm thinking on,' he said.

There was no great harm done to the man, but the young bloke was sent off into the bar, and came back with a bit of something in a short glass to help get his nerves set.

'I'll not apologise,' said Sampson, watching the clerk drink. 'You were getting on for ten minutes late, and we're operating to a tight schedule.'

I began to edge towards the front door. I was reckoning out the amount of time it would take me to scarper to the Police Office in the station. But no, that would be shut. I

167

thought of Tower Street, and the constable whose patrol took him past the Institute and the station. The handsome, well set-up copper . . . It came to me then, with a feeling of falling: he was the man who'd been in the Grapes earlier . . . Five Pounds, as Sampson had called him.

But that shock was immediately overtaken by a second one, for just at that moment, the door to the snooker hall opened, and the barmaid walked out looking determined. It was horrible to see her at large, out from behind her bar. I had made the thing happen by willing it not to, and all I could do was turn away from her as she approached and move towards the main door.

'Evening, gents,' she said, as she approached the door in my wake.

Only Sampson responded.

'Rain's coming in,' he said, and even as he did so, she pushed the door closed, saying, '. . . Lot of other strange articles besides.'

The door shut on her voice, and on the band of burglars. I was outside and they were in. Here was freedom at last – I could run away and give the alarm. But instead I just stood there and counted to five before the door crashed open and they all came out in Indian file, Sampson at the head, saying:

'Will you walk alongside me, little Allan?'

Why had I remained? Perhaps the answer was something to do with the biblical words quoted by friend Lund: 'Whatsoever thy hand findeth to do, do it with thy might.' Sampson placed his right arm very gently about my shoulder, but his friendliness was not a safe guide to anything. As we walked, his free arm was rummaging in one of his pockets. He picked out two tenners and handed them over to me, saying, 'More to come later . . . Now do you have any questions for me, little brother?'

'Yes,' I said. 'Where are we going, and what are we doing?'

We were certainly not going towards the Lost Luggage Office, but had turned left into the tracks and shadows of the Rhubarb Sidings, where half a dozen wagons stood solitary. They'd either been a train or were destined to become one but, it being Sunday evening, any shunting would most likely be put off till morning. So they just stood, like a lot of people in a room who didn't get on, and would not speak to each other.

'Tonight,' said Sampson, 'we're going to have away two thousand pounds.'

I immediately thought of the new villas along Thorpe-on-Ouse Road. You could buy the whole row for two grand. Sampson – the explanation completed as far as he was concerned – was now striking out across the tracks towards the buildings that lay behind the Lost Luggage Office. These were workshops where until lately a good many of the Company's engines had been built, but now the work had been moved, perhaps to Carlisle. I'd read of the change somewhere. The door of the first empty engine shop stood open. The inside was dark. I couldn't see a bit, but could guess at the size of the place by the extra coldness, and the ringing sound of a man's boots. It was the newcomer, the youngster, going on ahead. Hopkins was now standing alongside me, Sampson having moved forward with the new bloke.

'What's going off?' I asked Hopkins.

'. . . Scouting around for the bull's-eye they left lying about on the last visit,' he said.

For a minute nothing occurred except for bell-like sounds from the shed interior.

A light then flickered from twenty yards off, like something looking for balance. The bull's-eye lantern had been found. We moved towards it, as the little flame was replaced by a wide, soft red beam. It roved in a half circle around the shed showing a lake of oil on the stone floor, a row of barrels, a tangle of broken bogeys, and then a sight that stopped the breath on my lips: a long locomotive swinging in the middle of air, like a bear rearing on its hind legs. Nobody spoke, for it looked like a hanged man, too. It was Sampson had hold of the lamp; he played it over the dangling engine. It was only a boiler in fact, swinging at a forty-five-degree angle, suspended at the firebox end from the chains of an overhead crane.

The beam was at rest now, showing nothing but dust and cinders moving in the cold air – a red cloud. We caught up with Sampson, and he moved off again. Presently, he came to a stop, with the light steady again, picking out a tarpaulin. The young bloke pulled it away, to reveal not one but two cylinders half buried in a pile of coal with a sackful of stuff lying between them.

'There's the acetylene,' said the young bloke, 'and there's your oxygen.'

The second cylinder was a little bigger than the first – both were taller than a man. The first was the white one that we'd nicked from the goods yard. The second – the oxygen cylinder – was the colour of rust.

'Now, will it *act*?' said Sampson, and he fished in the sack for a tool with which he unloosened the top nut on the cylinder. The oxygen came out, with the sound of a man with his finger to his lips saying 'Shhh!' for a long time.

'. . . Tell you what'd be a bit of a lark,' Sampson said, over the noise of the leaking gas, '. . . send a bloke in here at night, give him a box of matches . . . put him to search out the cause of this noise. He'd find it all right . . . but it'd be the last thing he did.'

He turned towards the young bloke, saying, 'What do you reckon to that, Tim?'

Silence for a moment, before the young bloke answered: 'You'd need a fair amount of oxygen to cause a bang. It's the acetylene that's the dangerous stuff.'

Sampson thought about this for a minute, before asking:

'Can I smoke when I'm on the job?'

'That's *right* out,' said the young bloke.

Sampson and Tim were now heaving the oxygen cylinder on to their shoulders. Sampson then directed his lamp towards the second cylinder and the sack, before flicking the light towards Miles Hopkins.

'You and Allan take the tank, mate,' he said. 'And you . . .' he added, flicking the beam at the little clerk, '. . . you fetch the sack.'

He and the young bloke led off, with the red beam of light showing the way between the black objects inside the shed. The two of us had all on to carry the cylinder – I was beginning to see why I was needed. Behind us, the little clerk was saying: '. . . Only moved under special certificate, those things are.'

We all walked on, as the clerk continued: 'A carbon of every document touching the movement of inflammable gases is forwarded to a special office at the clearing house.'

He was at my heels now, saying:

'You seem a little out of your element here, pal.'

'Stow it,' I said. There was just the length of the cylinder between myself and Miles Hopkins, and I didn't want the clerk planting suspicions in his head.

'You're just the quiet sort, I suppose.'

'Aye,' said Hopkins from up ahead, 'and we could do with a few more like him.'

Chapter Twenty

We came out of the old loco erecting shop, and turned right, heading still further into the railway lands, and away from the city proper. We were in a place not meant for boots, but for wheels, and it was stumbling progress that we made towards wherever we were going. We'd left the Rhubarb Sidings behind now, and come to the railway and carriage sidings that lay alongside the dozen lines coming from the south into the station.

After a couple of minutes, we stopped for a breather, setting the cylinders down on the black track ballast before a row of sleeping carriages – Great Northern and North Eastern Joint Stock – and that's just what they were doing: sleeping. They screened us from the running lines leading to the station, so I could not see the train that went rocking past just at that moment with a tired, Sunday-night rhythm. Only it was probably Monday by now.

We trooped on, crossing the running lines. Why were there no watchmen about? The betting was that Sampson had fixed them, too. We crossed the 'up' tracks, and were about to step on to the 'down' lines when the young bloke pointed right. A train was at a stand within the station, down side. It would be heading out shortly. We set down the cylinders, and watched as it fumed under the great station roof. We could see the guard's green lamp moving on the platform alongside the locomotive, and what a fuss-box the bloody man was: to and fro, back and forth beside the boiler of the engine. The cylinder cocks were opened presently, however, and the engine began to move through its cloud of steam.

It rocked along in our direction, and every one of us turned to face away, yet the driver, a friendly sort, gave two screams on his whistle, and not only that (I couldn't help but turn about, so catching a glimpse of this), he also stuck his head out of his side window, and waved at us. He had to stand at a crouch as he did it, for all North Eastern Company engines had the cab windows placed too low. So the fellow had put himself out to be amiable, and got nowt in return. It would be nothing to him, though: he would have his mate to talk to, the tea bottle waiting on the ledge above the fire doors, the prospect of some good running on clear Sunday night lines. I admired the man – already gone from sight, Doncaster bound – and I hated him at the same time.

We picked up the cylinders once again, and I thought of Edwin Lund, searching the Gospels in the Lost Luggage Office, trying to seek out God's way. Was it God who'd set me down on the tracks and not up on the footplate? I had no answer to that, so I thought again of Lund: he was the winder; he turned the rope and I skipped. He had kept back the detail of the Lost Luggage Office burglary. Why?

Valentine Sampson and the young bloke were far ahead by now. Sampson was not over bright; he was not as clever as Lund or Miles Hopkins. But he was the striking arm, the man whose actions dictated the fate of his fellows. He walked steadily on, and I could see now that he was making for the south-side roundhouses: the first was the engine shed that stabled those North Eastern locomotives kept south of the station. It was in the cinder triangle between the lines leading into the station mouth, and those swerving away directly north towards the marshalling yards, goods yards and goods station.

Beside it lay the Midland roundhouse. The Midland was the main foreign company holding running rights into York, and such a company was entitled to its own shed, just as a government has its embassies overseas, but Sampson was paying that one no attention, for of course the blokes who booked on there had not been on strike. *Their* wages had not been brought to the shed week upon week to remain uncollected. We moved forwards, toward the pillars of a water tower, and Sampson motioned us to remain as he walked on with the young fellow yoked to him by the cylinder.

The two disappeared into the North Eastern roundhouse.

'Isn't there a watchman in there?' I said out loud, to nobody in particular.

It was the clerk who answered:

'Reason it out,' he said.

'Eh?' I said.

'Paid off, en't he?' he said. 'Like all of us.'

I nodded, looked away.

'How come you don't know that, mate?'

I made no answer. He was too curious by half, that bloke, and now he was looking at me sidelong. Had he seen me about the station? Might very well have. And if so would the glasses do their work? I heard a church bell floating across the darkness. It was the strike of one. The wife would be worried sick, or had she already become accustomed to my late hours? Sampson was now at the shed mouth, beckoning us on. Hopkins and I entered with our cylinder a minute later, the clerk coming along behind clutching the sackful of extra kit. And now he took over from the young bloke the task of escorting Sampson to the important spot.

As they went off to the eastern side of the shed, I looked

about me. It was the first time I'd been in an engine shed since the accident at Sowerby Bridge, and it was quite fitting, for I was returning to steal off the profession that had disowned me. The shed was a roundhouse, as I've said: tracks like the spokes of a wheel, the engines sitting upon them like a gathering of witches in the darkness, with the turntable in place of the boiling pot. Their high smokeboxes gave them a haughty look. There were sixteen stalls in all, only a dozen occupied. Sampson, or the young chap, had hung a dark lantern on the turntable crank handle. Another small allowance of light spilled in from the shed mouth, showing a shining pool of black water in the packed cinders. If the engines in this shed were to be used in the morning there'd be fire-raisers in here from four a.m. at the latest.

The clerk was in fidgets beside me, rattling the articles in the sack. Hopkins was smoking – the first time I'd seen him do so.

Sampson was coming back towards us. There was a revolver in his hand, and it was more of a relief than anything to finally clap eyes on the thing. The young man followed behind, looking sheepish-like. He was making towards the clerk, and I thought: he's going to do him, but no. Gesturing back to the young man, he said: 'Now you'll take no harm, but you must wait until the job's done.'

Sampson looked at the clerk, who was looking at the gun.

'How many poor buggers have had a taste of that, then?' the little bloke asked.

I looked across at Hopkins, who was shaking his head. The little ink spiller was past finding out.

'Four,' said Sampson, 'since you ask.'

I put two and two together: the detectives at Victoria . . . and the Camerons.

Then the clerk gave voice to my own thought:

'And I suppose two of those were the Cameron boys. I knew those lads – one worked at our place.'

Long silence. Sampson broke his gun, looked down at the cylinders, perhaps weighing up whether he could spare a bullet on the little clerk.

'I enjoyed that business,' he said, shutting the gun sharply and looking up. 'Clean sweep, you see. Once you've done one, what's the point of leaving the other hanging about in the world? I mean, it's fucking untidy. No earthly use to any living soul, the pair of 'em, and one's absolutely cracked into the bargain.'

All the men about ought to be given into the charge of the police without further ado. But it was past time for worrying about that. My job was to keep alive.

Hopkins crushed his cigarette stump under his boot. I heard a train go jangling past beyond the shed walls.

'Here, you,' Sampson was saying to the little clerk, 'show us your writing hand?'

'I'm right-handed,' the clerk said brightly. 'What of it?'

Sampson had picked up an old, dead lantern. He passed it over to the clerk, saying, 'Cop hold . . . right hand.'

He walked away ten paces, and asked the rest of us to step back from the clerk. He raised the gun, and I thought: this is worse than all; this is the point at which I must step in. But I did not, and the gun was fired and the lamp shattered. In the silence that followed Hopkins folded his arms, and I looked at Sampson. He was now side on to us, drinking whisky from the bottle.

The clerk was holding his hand under my nose, seemingly overjoyed that it was still attached to him. 'Five hundred invoices a day,' he said, making a writing motion, '. . . and demurrage bills are a great scarcity across my desk, I can tell you that.'

Sampson walked over to the clerk, and presented him with the whisky bottle; the clerk drank.

'Pass it round,' said Sampson.

As the bottle came my way, Sampson led us all off the part of the shed he'd visited a moment before. We were approaching a little brick room built on to the shed wall. The door to it was shut, and the two cylinders stood outside: the big man and the little man (as I thought of them), waiting to be put to work. The little clerk had the key, or *a* key, and he opened the door without being asked. We all then crowded inside. There was a gas lamp, which Sampson lit with a match, immediately turning it to the lowest setting. The room was somewhere between an office and a workshop. There was a desk, a metal cabinet, boxes of papers; boxes of engine bits. I made out some corks for oil pots, an old whistle, tins of screws. A smaller version of one of the shed's church windows was set into the back wall, and in the corner was the safe. It was about four foot high, with a metal crest on the front showing a lion and a snake in a tangle. Woven in between them was a ribbon on which appeared the words 'Croft and Son', and then something in Latin that probably meant: 'If you think you're going to break into this bugger, think on'. There was an ordinary lock, an American lock, I thought – a knob that you turned to find certain numbers. It was the opposite case to that of the Lost Luggage Office, in that they'd obviously not been able to find, or buy, the man who held the key or knew the numbers.

Sampson and the young fellow were now putting their boots to the top of the very dignified safe, and kicking it over. It fell on its back with a mighty crash, making matchwood of the desk chair on its way.

'Can we not bring it away?' said Hopkins, looking on. 'We're right underneath the fucking window.'

Sampson pointed at me, 'Fetch us a tarpaulin, won't you?' all friendliness quite gone, for now the business was under way in earnest.

I went out into the darkness of the shed, and Hopkins followed, although he then diverted away towards the shed mouth. Had he reckoned on me bolting? I walked between the locomotives. There was a Class R . . . also a Q Class, with its weird glass roof let into the cab top – that would give you a view of the clouds going in the opposite direction as you ran along. From the shed mouth, Hopkins was watching me as I looked at the engines. I fancied he knew that I was able to see them for what they were.

I saw a tarpaulin: folded over the boiler of a tank engine, like a horse blanket. I yanked it down, making a cloud of dust and muck; and a black lace was left dangling from my fingers: a cobweb. The sight of the thing checked me: I had given nothing but aid to this operation so far, and every new piece of assistance I gave made me less of a detective and more of a burglar. I wiped away the cobweb, and hauled the tarpaulin towards the little office. Hopkins closed with me as I did so, and I looked past him, beyond the shed mouth where – five hundred yards off – a figure was walking towards one of the cabins set between the tracks. Company man on a late turn. He might've had his hands in his pockets. At the same time I heard another train come rattling up, but it didn't go by the shed mouth.

Hopkins followed me into the crowded little room, where the cylinders – big man and little man – stood in place. Lengths of rubber tubing were now connected to the taps on their tops, and these came together in the brass blowpipe that rested in Sampson's hands. It was a double gun, able to mix the two gases.

'Put that against the window,' he ordered when he saw me

with the tarpaulin, so I moved around the desk. The thing was pretty stiff, and stood up of its own accord. I made a kind of cone of it, and it shut out the window pretty well.

'Good-o,' he said, so I'd got points for that, as well as everything else.

With stout leather gloves now on his hands, Sampson was removing his hat, putting on a pair of goggles. They were like the eye shades sometimes worn by the blind but they gave Sampson the look of one who could see everything, just as though they were a pair of giant black eyes. He had not troubled to protect his suit, which surprised me.

'Let's have the acetylene,' he said, looking at all of us at once. But it was the young man who answered the command. Taking his wrench or spanner he turned a nut on the smallest cylinder; there came a low whoosh, and Sampson lit a match, and put it to the end of the blowpipe. But the rushing gas simply blew it out. He tried again with a second match, obtaining the same result.

'Well I'd say you need a flint,' said the little clerk. 'You can't blow a spark out, you know,' he said, addressing me for some reason, 'instead of going out, it just blows away.'

Sampson turned his weird, goggle eyes towards the clerk.

He tried again with a third match. No go. I supposed that the room must be filling rapidly with the gas. It smelt like onions . . . fried onions.

Sampson tried a fourth match, and this one did the job, only the result was a let-down: a weak, ragged orange flame with a good deal of smoke into the bargain. I had expected the flame to be white, like the cylinder from which it came.

Sampson took a step to one side in surprise as the oxygen came, for the roaring increased ten fold, and the flame changed in an instant, both narrowing and lengthening into the shape of a sword. It was also now blue, and the young man at the cylinders was shouting over the roar: 'It's the light blue at the heart of it that does the cutting, mate.'

Sampson made no answer, but fell to his knees, and bent low over the safe, like a man praying. At the instant he touched the flame to the steel he was surrounded in a whirl of orange sparks. They flew about everywhere in the office, seeming to bounce and roll across the desk, quite able to survive an impact like game little acrobats.

It was hard not to think of this wonderful display as being the whole point of the exercise, and in fact Sampson did seem to be having some trouble with the cutting itself. He'd gouged a red groove across the face of the steel but as he moved the flame back and forth along it, the metal seemed to flow back into the trench, filling it in again, like time itself rolling forwards and backwards. The mark he'd made was no longer-lasting than a line drawn in sand. He looked up, once again staring at all of us and everything from behind the black lenses.

'Now he's thinking: maybe I ought to have spent ten minutes practising this,' said the little clerk, and the goggles turned once again in his direction.

The young man evidently called Tim was now at Sampson's shoulder. 'Don't touch the flame down so close,' he said, 'and go at it more at an angle.' He was so thoroughly in the know of the business that I wondered why he wasn't doing the job himself. But I supposed he would then have been a different order of helper, and liable to a longer sentence if caught.

The burning continued, and then there was an extra column of smoke, coming from beyond Sampson. The tarpaulin had caught light. The young man tapped Sampson on his shoulder, and yanked down the goggles, shouting straight at Hopkins, 'Water!'

At the window, the tarpaulin had slumped to one side, the flames beginning to creep across it from the corner place they'd started in.

The little clerk was shaking his head, saying: 'Beats all, that does.'

Hopkins looked across at me: 'You can give a hand,' he said, and we ranged out into the shed again.

'Where would you find water in a spot like this?' said Hopkins. I replied, 'How the bloody hell should I know?' but why had he asked me in the first place? Hopkins never called me Allan. Never believed it was my name, that's why.

Sampson was charging out of the office now, with the little clerk and the young bloke spilling out behind him. It was no longer possible to remain in there. 'Get a fucking shift on,' Sampson roared, 'the cylinders'll go up any second!'

'I can take a bucket to one of the water cranes outside,' I called to Sampson, but he wouldn't have that. There was nothing for it. If the cylinders blew we'd all be done for. I pointed down at the hydrant that lay at our feet. It was marked out for the engine cleaners by a square stone – there was even a canvas tube attached, though half buried in ash. I lifted the steel flap to get at the little wheel, which turned easily enough, and the tube stirred, leaping crazily three times as the water speed rose to its fastest. Sampson himself pointed the nozzle into the office, where the flames were quickly put out, and every light article sent flying by force of water in the process. The cylinders held their ground though: the big man and the little man, standing over the fallen safe.

Sampson and the young bloke fell to starting up the gas again, as we all crowded back into the little room – the floor of it was now a pond. The water continued to stream out of the hose in the shed beyond.

'Shouldn't have had a tarpaulin in here in the first place,' the little clerk was saying. 'It was bound to catch. Half of it's tar, after all. Why do you think it's called a *tar*paulin?'

I looked up to see that – as I had somehow suspected – he was addressing me again.

'What's that tap in the ground for?' he said, and I made no reply.

Sampson had the blowpipe lit once again, and was kneeling before the safe for a second go. If the flame was seen beyond the window, then it was just hard lines. Before he began, he called Hopkins across to him, and the two exchanged a few words while Sampson held the flame away. Then Hopkins motioned me and the clerk out of the room. 'Keep him pinned,' Hopkins said to me, and so the two of us sat down on a sleeper that had been placed across the tracks behind one of the engines – the weird-looking Q Class. I wondered whether they had any particular reason to fear that the little clerk would take off. If they did have a reason, then why had they brought him along in the first place? They could have had the keys off him with no bother. But the answer was easy enough to guess at: they wanted him involved – make him a guilty party. And if he was sitting here in the South Shed, then he couldn't be chattering to the night-duty coppers at Tower Street. Hopkins had returned to his former pitch at the shed mouth, so that the little clerk was now in a double prison: I was guarding him, and Hopkins was guarding me. If I made a run for it, he'd call for Sampson, who'd shoot me. Well, perhaps he'd miss, but Sampson and Hopkins would do a push in any case with one man gone and liable to split.

The cutting of the safe was continuing, with the door of the office kept open, so that I could see clear through to

Sampson as he worked away, like a magical figure in a cloud of bright sparks.

I thought I heard a church bell: three o'clock. But how could it be so late? I felt my eyes prickling. I ought not to be looking at the cutting flame. I remembered not to rub them by poking my finger directly through the frames of my glasses, but took the specs off first. It seemed as though my eyes were full of grit; and they felt better closed. I rested my head on my hand.

And then it was a different Sunday, late afternoon; darkness coming in to make sense of the gas lamps already lit across Sowerby Bridge, which rose on its bank above the engine yard. We'd run in light from Leeds – me and Terry Kendall. 'Grandfather Kendall', he was, to the blokes at the shed: the oldest driver on the goods link, or any link. The engine was 1008, the first of Mr Aspinall's radial tank engines, with bogies designed for making tight curves.

We were stood over a pit on an in-road, and it was one of those evenings with the coldness locked into the sky. No developments in the weather were imaginable.

I began lifting the fire out with the long clinker shovel, which was slightly bent a little way out of true, and when I'd done, I finished off the dregs in my tea bottle. Grandfather Kendall was fussing about somewhere near the front of the engine. I called out to him that the clinker shovel wanted replacing, and that I meant to go and see the toolman about getting another.

He said 'Right enough' to that, and I went off. When I returned with a fresh shovel, I expected to find 1008 in the shed – put there by her driver. But she remained over the pit on the in-road with Kendall now up on the footplate. There was a quantity of engines round about, most being prepared for stabling, and there were happy shouts coming up from the blokes at work, whether in the engines, on top of them, or under. It was coming up to the time when they'd stroll off to the pubs for the latch- lifter (first pint of the evening) and a smoke. To these shouts, I joined my own, for I called over to Kendall: 'Can I take her in myself?' Like most firemen I was keen for any scraps of driving I could get.

He climbed down and I climbed up, and I thought he looked a little dazed. We exchanged some words during this crossing over: 'Warmed the brake, have you, Terry?' I said. 'I have that,' he replied. There was nothing to that conversation; we were as casual as you like, but it touched an important matter. It was necessary to give a couple of tugs on the engine brake after the engine had been at a stand – this to put steam into its chambers, and prevent condensation occurring when it was next used in anger. If the chambers were not warmed, and condensation occurred, the brake would not do its job.

There was no fire in 1008, but there was steam in the boiler, and that would take her into the shed. It was magical: an engine rolling under the power of a memory. I gave a scream on the whistle, and a yank on the regulator, not thinking about the brake. I did not need to warm it, for Grandfather Kendall had told me he'd done that.

At the very moment 1008 went under the shed roof I knew something was amiss: not with the engine, but with the whole business of engines and engine sheds. This beast was meant to be at large outdoors, and now it was confined to a building, and, as we rolled on, past the workbenches on the south wall of the shed, I thought: this is like a lion in a living room; it is not right.

I pulled the brake as 1008 approached its berth. Nothing. I pulled again, only this time I did so as a dead man.

'Want to know what brought me to this?' the little clerk was saying.

'Eh?' I said.

'Miles away, en't you?' said the clerk.

The sparks were still flowing from the cutting flame in the little room before us.

'I said "Do you want to know what brought me to this?"' repeated the clerk.

'I shouldn't think there's any great mystery over that,' I said, replacing my glasses.

'I've been with this company since I quit school. I'm fifty-two now. This year I rose to thirty bob a week, and it en't enough – not when you've a wife and kids, and ten bob a week rent to pay. Even so, I'd always operated the rule book to the letter. No surreptitious removal by yours truly of little titbits from the goods yard.'

He turned and looked at me.

'Don't believe me, do you?'

I shrugged. My mind was still at Sowerby Bridge, my eyes were on the flying sparks.

'Six months back, I saw a fellow having his boots cleaned on Coney Street. Dazzled up lovely they were, by that little bootblack in livery outside the Black Swan. Do you know the fellow?'

I nodded; I knew the chap. He had deformed hands – no thumbs – but was a marvel with a shammy leather.

'Well, I was minded to have my own boots done,' the clerk continued, 'seeing the job he'd done for the other fellow, so I walked up and sat down on his chair, and after he'd done the first boot, I said, "By the way, pal, how much is it?" He said, "It's a tanner, guv", and I stood up there and then, gave him thruppence for the one boot he'd done, and walked off. The price was too high, and I en't saying it was unreasonable, but I couldn't run to it.'

The sparks had stopped now. Sampson and the young fellow were crouching over the safe. Sampson was looking chuffed.

'It's *pissing* through it,' I thought I heard him say.

'Well that was when the light dawned,' the clerk was saying.

185

'I looked down at that one clean boot all the rest of the day, and a fortnight later, I heard of a bloke who would be willing to supplement my wages.'

He nodded towards Sampson, who was back at his metal cutting.

'It was him, your governor, Duncannon. Of course he's not an easy bloke to get along with, but if I hadn't made his acquaintance I'd have run into debt six month since. Practically kept me out of the workhouse, he has.'

'And how will you feel when you come to serve your term?' I said.

'Beg pardon?' he said, in a startled voice. When I made no further remark, he rose to his feet, saying: 'Just going to see how things are getting on.'

He walked towards the office where, I noticed, the sparks had again stopped.

'Taking your flipping time, en't you?' the clerk asked Sampson, who was pushing his goggles up onto his forehead with one gloved hand.

'We're done now,' said Sampson. 'Here, you – catch.'

I believe that I tried to reverse that instruction, by shouting 'Don't catch' as the rough oblong of red-hot steel flew towards the little clerk. But he did catch it.

PART FIVE

The Crack Boat

Chapter Twenty-one

Whatever had happened to his hands, the clerk could run, and he could scream, and it was as if this scream was the particular cause of an event that had been inevitable all along: the clerk running out of the shed mouth, and Sampson calmly making *towards* the shed mouth while shooting the revolver at the clerk.

I ran at Sampson as one, two, three shots were fired. As the fourth bullet was loosed, I crashed into the side of Sampson roaring 'Police!'

Sampson went down with the gun in his hand, and before any expression could come over his features, I heard Miles Hopkins calling, 'He's fucking right n' all!'

From down on the ground, I saw a figure walking along the tracks towards us from the southerly end of the station. As I watched, the man's thin hair blew upright in the breeze that had come with the dawn, and then it fell again. What I had said had miraculously turned out to be the truth, for it was the Chief. He wore his long overcoat, and was carrying a walking stick, except that this stick never touched the ground. It was no stick but a rifle. Somebody had noticed the disturbance in the shed, and he had been sent for. A call boy would have gone out from the station. The clerk was between us and the Chief. He was a dark, low shape crawling along one of the tracks towards the station, and then he was just a dark low shape. The Chief was hard by him now, crouching down. After a moment, he stood up and walked on. Valentine Sampson was frozen into a firing position, gun pointed at the Chief. It seemed impossible that Sampson would ever move. He was like a signpost, and Miles Hopkins was next to him, talking fast, reasonable-like, saying: 'Put the gun down, we can take the readies and be out of here . . .'

Sampson seemed to think it over for a second.

'I'll fire once more; see us right,' he said, and immediately did so.

The Chief went down.

Sampson and Hopkins were straight into the office, pulling money out of the hole in the safe, and putting it into the sack that the clerk had been made to carry. I looked out again. The clerk was still down; the Chief was still down. Behind them, the station was making its own dawn: a few more gas lamps lit as work started; a few men moving about. Had they heard the shots? One engine was in – standing at one of the bay platforms on the 'down' side, and so looking the wrong way. I looked sidelong to Sampson and Hopkins, still stowing money in the bag. Of the young bloke, I could see no sign. I started to run for the shed mouth, and the Chief rose to his feet from down on the tracks; as he did so, his hair rose too, and he lifted his gun.

'Chief!' I bawled, but the shot came anyway, and it checked me at the shed mouth. Sampson was by my side now. If he'd heard the shout of Chief, and taken it amiss . . . well, there was no sign of that in his face. He was back in his gun-firing pose, only this time with the money sack over his shoulder. He tilted his head backwards a couple of times, as though aiming with his sharp beard. He looked like Robin Hood. He fired. I looked out again, and couldn't see the Chief.

'Chief,' I said to Sampson, so as to make him think I'd been calling for him in the first place, 'let's away.'

He clean ignored me. He was still in his firing pose, but he relinquished it a moment later, with a look of irritation. Hopkins was by his side once again. They were both going into a kind of crouch.

Sampson gave a roar, and they ran off to the right, out through the shed, skirting the tracks of the 'up' side. I ran a little way with them, keeping low, as they were, but as we came towards the carriage sidings where the joint stock sleeping cars were berthed, I thought: 'What am I about?' and stopped dead.

My body was perfectly still in the freezing darkness, and my mind in a whirl. If the Chief was alive, then . . .

Sampson was facing me, the joint stock carriage behind him. His gun was facing me, too.

'You come along with us, Allan,' he said.

'I'm just thinking on,' I said, for want of anything else to say.

I fell in behind them as they walked quickly over the tracks through the carriage sidings and towards the disused Queen Street loco erecting shop. No further shots came. The Chief had approached us alone. I thought of him striding south out of the station with his gun in his hand. There was more to him than breakfast, and that was fact . . . But he was crazy, as I'd suspected all along. He'd put me in this fix, and given me no way out.

We were into the Rhubarb Sidings once again. Two blokes stood by the wagons of the night before, but there was no engine in sight. They watched us as we passed. Had they heard the gunshots? If so, they might have taken them for fog detonators, because the darkness of the day was clearing too slowly, and it would be a misty morning. We pushed on up Queen Street, on to Station Road, and then turned right into Blossom Street, running now, away from railway lands.

Sampson, walking fast beside me, had the revolver still in his hand, although somewhat disguised by the money sack, which was half wrapped round his fist, like a bandage. We were on Tadcaster Road; trees and big houses to our right, Knavesmire and the racecourse to our left. A carriage or cart came past every couple of minutes, appearing from, or disappearing into, the rising mist. Lights were glowing in some of the grand houses, as the servants started them up, like fire lighters in an engine shed.

Sampson was crossing the road now, me and Miles Hopkins following. I wanted to think about many things, but the only thought that would come: I had failed in police work as I had in engine driving. I had failed (as I saw it) because of others, but was it right to be always throwing blame? Did the case not come down to this: that the world was more full of difficulty than I had ever imagined?

Sampson was climbing over the railings separating the road from the Knavesmire. I followed; Hopkins followed.

'Well then, little Allan,' Sampson was saying, as we strode through the wet grass, 'that's oxyacetylene cutting for you. Think it'll catch on?'

I made no reply; I was walking by his side, and that was as much as I would do to accommodate him. He seemed very keen that I *should* be by his side, and Hopkins too, who was lagging behind slightly in the mist. He kept checking on the two of us, with sidelong or rearward glances, and the message was clear: we are in a box over this, and we were to stay together. After all, anyone free of Sampson was free to talk.

'Well that was nice,' said Hopkins, 'two men fucking dead.'

'Trust you to bring that up,' said Sampson.

We'd stopped now, under a dripping tree, deep in the mist of the Knavesmire.

A cow walked out of the fog towards us.

'Fuck off out of it,' said Sampson to the cow.

It turned around and walked away.

'Who was that bloke firing on us?' said Sampson. 'That's what I want to know.'

He looked at me.

'Search me,' I said.

'You said it was a copper,' Hopkins said to me. He was dead-eyed now, all that mischievous sparkle put out.

'Aye,' I said, 'and you agreed.'

'Where did he get the bloody gun from?' said Sampson.

'Likely he was an old soldier,' I heard myself saying.

'The police ought not to be armed,' said Sampson. 'I don't bloody hold with it . . . And who alerted him?'

'Well let me make a hazard,' said Hopkins. 'Perhaps it was the sight of the sparks through the window, or the shot that rang out when you played your little game with the lantern; or the bloody great raging fire that broke out in the end.'

'I suppose you think you could have managed it better?' said Sampson.

He dropped the revolver into the sack, and slung it over his shoulder. In his countrified suit he looked quite at home, like a sort of gentleman poacher. He was shaking his head, saying: 'Some bugger split on us . . .'

'At least it wasn't the bloody Camerons,' Sampson continued, 'and that's for certain.'

Silence for a space.

'Well, we've got the money, and that's the main thing,' said Sampson, who was now pissing against a tree.

'I'm beastly hungry,' said Hopkins.

The carts and traps and wagons were going along Tadcaster Road towards town at a greater rate now, the rattle and

193

jingle of them was making itself heard even if they were still out of sight.

'Reckon we head back to the station,' said Sampson.

The cow reappeared from out of the mist, just as if it had been thinking over what Sampson had said, and decided it was owed an apology. Sampson looked at the cow and said: 'We must stay out of Yorkshire for a little while.'

I thought of the wife, waiting for me, and the sudden possibility of my travelling further away from her rather than towards. Sampson was now leading us back in the direction of the station as Miles Hopkins said: 'What makes you think it won't be ringed with bloody coppers?'

'It's the last place they'll expect us,' said Sampson.

I noticed that he kept his hand in the sack, where it rested (no doubt) upon the gun.

All along Tadcaster Road, workpeople were now filing into town, through the rising mist and falling rain. We walked faster than them, weaving in and out of the column.

We turned left into Railway Street, and there was a copper leaning against the inn that stood on the corner there. I turned my face towards him as we approached and, in my mind's eye, pictured my breakaway. I would cry out to him, 'These are the blokes you're after!' and he would take on Hopkins, while I . . .

No, because sacking does nothing to check the travel of a bullet.

I looked again at the copper. It was the well set-up copper from the Grapes; the one who'd been fixed, Mr Five Pounds. As he looked at Sampson there were about as many questions packed into his expression as I'd ever seen on one face, but nothing was said until, twenty yards further on, Sampson turned to Hopkins, remarking: 'That was money well spent.'

We marched through the station portico, amid the confusion of cabs and horses, and then we were into the smoke-smelling, reluctant grey-blue light of Monday morning in the world of work. We were still walking fast, the crowded booking halls on either side. We were not going to buy tickets, at any rate.

We walked through the ticket gate, and Sampson said to the fellow there, 'We're meeting someone in,' as if we looked like the sort of blokes who greeted people alighting from trains. We were on Platform Four now. I looked up at the footbridge, and saw the Lad, the telegraph messenger, but he was walking away to the 'down' side, thank Christ, because one cheery 'Good morning' from him could have caused more questions from the ever-watchful Hopkins than I could safely answer.

We turned left, and pushed along to the south end of Platform Four, where about a score of people, widely spaced, stood waiting miserably for a train.

At the very southern tip of the platform, where it sloped down on to the cinders, stood an abandoned baggage trolley. Hopkins climbed up on to it, and looked towards the southern sheds; two trains were rocking towards the station from that direction. It struck me for the first time that railwaymen were traitors in a way, for they took all the other workpeople to their factory and office prisons.

Sampson sat on the baggage trolley, facing the tracks before him rather than south. The sack rested by his side as he lit a cigar, saying, 'How many bodies do you see, then, mate?'

'None,' said Hopkins, who was still peering towards the engine shed, scene of our late adventure. He too now sat down on the cart.

Had the little clerk and the Chief been *carried* away, or had they *walked* away? I was gazing in a northerly direction along the platform – towards the door of the Police Office, and there was no sign of life *there* at any rate. It was coming up to six o'clock, too early in the day for Shillito and the other sportsmen to be in there. I saw instead a porter making towards us. I'd seen him about in the station, and he'd seen me, possibly wearing, and possibly not wearing, the glasses I was now lumbered with . . . But he gave no sign of knowing me. He stood before the three of us, saying 'What are you blokes after?'

We'd attracted his attention by sitting so far towards the end of Platform Four.

'Waiting for a fucking train, what d'you think?' said Hopkins.

'Any particular one?' asked the porter.

'Anything London way,' said Sampson, looking up at him, the sack once more in his hands.

The porter nodded, while I thought, I will *not* be carried away to London. I was no better than a leaf in the wind, blown in any direction.

The porter said: 'Six-eleven, this platform.'

He then turned and walked away, and Sampson said, 'I thought we might've had bother from him.'

'You don't know he en't run off to fetch a copper,' said Hopkins, but even as he spoke the bell rang, and the London train came around the curve at the station north end, driving through the rain with unstoppable force. I could not help but notice that it was one of the Class J singles, with one mighty driving wheel in either side. I waited on tenterhooks, thinking that something surely must come along to prevent me climbing aboard.

But nothing did.

196

Chapter Twenty-two

I boarded the train because of Sampson's gun. A second thought – a little more creditable – only came along later: that unless I stuck with this pair, they would very likely never be caught.

A new sky was coming: dark blue and rain-lashed over the wire works at Doncaster, twenty miles south of York. It was a non-corridor train, so we were all together in a first-class compartment. There was no one else in it. Doncaster was a run-through, and as we rolled out of the station, Sampson was sitting by the window with his revolver, pointing it at people in the terraced streets.

He caught my eye as I watched him, and he laughed, more embarrassed than ashamed, I reckoned.

'You could just go about on trains shooting people,' he said, '. . . if you were that way inclined.'

'Which you are,' said Hopkins, from his seat. I'd thought he was asleep up to that moment.

Sampson winked at me.

'Don't mind him,' he said. 'He's better with a drink in.'

As he returned the revolver to the sack, he was still eyeing me, so to distract him from any dangerous thoughts, I asked: 'What if a ticket inspector gets up?'

'Well, I've at least two thousand pounds and a gun in this sack, little Allan, so one way or another we should be all right.'

Hopkins gave a smile at that. He was a little more at ease now. As for me . . . I was half-dreaming of the great black cathedral at York, and the smallness of the carters and pedestrians who walked to and fro in its shadow. Many had gone before and many would come after. We were just the present-day lot. Anything we did or did not do . . . it came to naught.

I looked at the money sack on Sampson's knee, and I thought of the London line. A ticket inspection could only happen at Peterborough, for I reckoned that would be our only other stop . . .

At Peterborough the rain blew crazily around that city's own cathedral – which lay just beyond the station – as we all trooped over first to the gentlemen's and then to the bar on the platform. We drew a lot of glances as we stepped back up into our first-class compartment holding a bottle of beer apiece, and I had not the energy to look back at those who gawped. In addition to beer, Sampson carried a paper bag full of railway pies. He'd paid for this breakfast by pulling a tenner out of the sack, and I wondered about the denominations in there. There didn't seem to be a great bulk of money . . . but what engine man earned a tenner in a week? There would have to be a good many pound notes in the bundle. What was not in there was silver and copper, for the sack seemed easily carried and it did not jingle.

We made a slippery start away from Peterborough, the rhythm of the engine all wrong, but we were soon making seventy, eighty miles an hour through the rain, and I pictured those mighty driving wheels up ahead, racing on to London in spite of the mixed feelings or feelings of dread that anyone aboard might entertain.

We came into Platform One at King's Cross, and the moment we stepped down, Sampson put his arm about my shoulder. I wondered: is this a show of friendliness, or more of a manacle? We stepped out of the station, and the London day – crowds, rain, buildings three times the size of any in York – opened and closed quickly, for within a minute we were inside a hansom.

'Charing Cross,' Sampson called to the driver, and I thought: What are we about? A tour of the mainline stations?

This life was insane . . . but I had to know.

'What's the programme, lads?' I asked after a couple of minutes.

'We're off to Paris, little Allan,' said Sampson, and he leant forwards and grabbed my knee, adding: 'It's an elopement, mate!'

I pictured the wife in her best white dress, fading into the distance and into the past, becoming no larger or more significant than a portrait of a lady that might be found inside a locket. Hopkins did not seem the least surprised at the news of our destination, and I doubted whether it *was* news to him. I imagined that the pair of them might run up to Paris pretty often. I recalled what the *Police Gazette* had said of the man who'd shot the two detectives: 'Will likely be found in hotels.'

He'd shot two detectives in Victoria; would he add a third in Charing Cross to his collection? A new thought came, and not a happier one: wouldn't France be a better killing ground? As the cab rattled along, gaining speed along unknown streets, I hardly cared.

Sampson reached into his sack again to pay the cab driver, and once again he kept me close as we walked into the station. We entered past a kind of little bank, and I turned to look again: 'Bureau de Change'. I wondered how you *said* those words. I thought of the bit of French I could fairly pronounce: 'Au revoir'. They said that every time they said goodbye, two words instead of one. Going round the bloody houses.

There were two coppers in the station: they were standing in the middle of the lobby, and rain made them shine. But seconds after we'd walked in they walked out, and I thought what a dull article the average copper is.

At the bookstall there were foreign newspapers, and I saw a small man in a cut of coat that was out of the common. A Frencher, I thought. The rain thundered down on the glass roof above, and half a dozen trains waited beyond the ticket gates, pressing in on the station, waiting to pluck us away. Like the rain on the roof, they seemed to be saying: why *not* leave this bloody country? Try your luck elsewhere, for God's sake.

Sampson was holding my arm, moving towards the booking office.

'Why must you be always mauling me,' I said. 'Do you think I'm going to do a shit?'

He took his hand off my arm, looked at me: 'Don't lose your hair, boy,' he said, in a tone that stopped a little way short of menace. 'We'll be free and easy in Paris, but just till then . . .'

Hopkins was walking behind, looking about: looking at pockets, perhaps. We were at the ticket window by now.

'Three singles to Paris,' said Sampson.

I did not hear the clerk's response, but Sampson said one further word: 'Deck.' He was an old hand at this boat train business.

We then marched through the station crowd across to the Bureau de Change, where more money was picked from the bag and handed over: tenners again, but some pound notes too, and it looked as though the colours had run on the money that came back. The French currency was the French franc. You read of its doings in the paper – it was always in bother but the notes were pretty enough, I had to admit. I looked on the whole exchange like a holidaymaker in a dream.

Our next call was at the newspaper stall, where Sampson bought a racing paper and Hopkins . . . some London paper. We then all walked to the centre of the concourse, and stood underneath the great clock. Sampson and Hopkins held a conference here, muttering low, so that all I could hear was Sampson saying: 'But the one after's the express', and Hopkins saying, 'You ought to send it by mail.'

At the end, a decision was evidently reached, and Sampson put his arm around me in a more friendly way: 'You wait until we're over the water, little Allan: hot coffee, cognac, roast fowls . . . And pay day. You been to France?'

I shook my head.

'I have not,' I said.

'Thinking about the girl you're leaving behind, are you, lad?'

'Don't you need a paper with a royal stamp on it to quit the country?' I said.

'Passport?' he said. 'Get away. What do you think you're in? A fucking prison?'

I found a little comfort in the signs behind him for 'Telegrams' and 'Telephone' in the knowledge that those methods of communication would be open to me all the way, if I ever got the freedom to use them. Meanwhile, Miles Hopkins was strolling off somewhere.

Sampson walked me over to Left Luggage, where we hung about until Hopkins joined us ten minutes later, carrying two small kitbags. Had he nicked the bloody things or bought 'em? These items you could easily come by in the shops around Charing Cross. Hopkins stood over Sampson as that gentry took bundles from the sack, and stuffed them into the first kitbag; what remained in the sack (a smaller amount) went into the second kitbag, and Sampson then pitched the sack away. The first kitbag was tightly fastened up, and presented to a Left Luggage clerk by Sampson, together with a handful of coins. The clerk gave change and ticket to Sampson while Hopkins looked on closely. We then all went into the gentleman's for a sluice down.

Sampson had not wanted to travel with all the stolen money about him. But I wondered about the gun – where had it got to? Our next call was the station bar, which smelt of cigar smoke and rain-sodden overcoats. There were pictures around the walls of little boats braving high seas, while the blokes in the bar did nothing of the sort, but just supped ale steadily. The boats all looked the same but they were all different, and all belonged to the South Eastern and Chatham Railway. Just inside the door sat a bloke with a greasy brown bowler on his knee, and a suit out at the elbows. At his feet was a box marked 'Haut'. He had no doubt just returned from France. You could go there, and you could come back, and it wasn't so very great an undertaking. This thought, too, brought a small glimpse of hope. Sampson bought three pints and Hopkins, with a little of his former anxiety returning, asked him:

'Reckon you did for those two blokes?'

'Tell you what,' Sampson replied, 'you'd best hope they did take the bloody shots because we're buggered if not. See, mate, I only did what needed to be done. It was the necessary.'

Hopkins asked: 'Why was it necessary to do Roberts?'

(Roberts, I realised, must be – or must have *been* – the clerk.)

'Roberts?' said Sampson, in a thoughtful sort of way, just as though he'd almost forgotten the fellow already. 'Well now let's see . . . because he was a fucking pill? Look, mate, he would've ratted, wouldn't he? And might still if he's not done for. I mean to say, he's taken the tip, but it wouldn't quite cover . . .'

'The knackering of his hands,' said Hopkins. 'He was all right until you pitched the burning metal at him.'

Sampson said nothing to that, but saw off his pint, ordered the second round of drinks and lit a cigar.

'Let's change the subject, mates,' he said . . . which he proceeded to do himself: 'Tim,' he said, blowing out smoke, 'now, he's all right. We'll have no trouble from that quarter, I can promise you. White as they come, that lad.' Sampson now turned to me: 'You n' all, mate. Some blokes . . . they'd take fright having seen what you've seen; have a brainstorm, crack wide open, do you take my meaning?'

He handed me my fresh pint, saying:

'Fact is we've taken the fucking kettle, boys. Not two but more like three grand. None of us will ever have to do a hand's turn again.'

'Not that we ever did,' said Hopkins.

I supped my pint, thinking: I could take my share of that, break free of the wife and the future child, and just give up on normal life as a bad job. I would simply continue to be Allan Appleby – make a real go of lounging about and spectacle-wearing. I looked at Sampson as he drank, and I had to admit that I admired the fellow after a fashion: I couldn't help feeling that he'd treated me better, all in all, than the brass of the Lancashire and Yorkshire Railway and Chief Inspector Weatherill both. I found myself pleased that he did not suspect me of being anything so low (and that was the very word that came to me) as a copper, but rather of being likely to go to the police and confess in hopes of avoiding a charge of accessory to murder.

Sampson also got points with me for the way that all his foul actions seemed to leave no trace upon him. Where Hopkins was bedraggled, his boots still clarted with mud from the Knavesmire and ash from the engine shed, Sampson's were clean and – on account of his kingly grey beard – he never appeared in need of a shave. His great success, now that I came to think of it, was that he was able to kill folks then clean forget about the fact. It also went to his credit that he seemed to have no fear.

And yet he would hurt folk for sport and fly into a paddy when up against it on a job, and I meant to make him pay on all counts.

Chapter Twenty-three

It wasn't until getting on for three o'clock that we boarded the train, and the South East and Chatham did us proud: best bogie coaches with lavatory accommodation; green Morocco chairs, metal reading lamps, dressing case in the compartment. We pulled out at twenty past three, into the roaring rain and the roaring city: London putting on swank – the river below, Parliament to our right. Sampson was leaning forwards, looking between me and the carriage corridor, half grinning.

I had been invigorated somewhat by the station drinks; and I meant to call his bluff.

I stood up.

'Well,' I said, 'I must visit the jakes; there's no help for it.'

I stepped out of the compartment, and was not followed. If the WC hadn't been directly before me as I stepped into the corridor – if we hadn't been in the last compartment, that is – then something different might have happened in that instant. I might have rapped for help. But the door was there, and nature called. When I stepped out again, Hopkins was standing right outside the door.

'Can you speak French?' I asked him, mindful of the notice I'd read above the sink: 'Eau non potable'.

He stared at me for a while, before giving a shrug.

'Sampson?' I asked.

'He's a demon at it,' Hopkins said. 'They loved to hear him. They just lie on their backs and wriggle their legs in the air.'

He gave me one of his smiles, and stepped in to pay his own call.

As I returned to the compartment Sampson was reading his racing paper, the kitbag beside him, and we were just on the edges of London. I sat down over opposite; he did not look up. At the end of it all there'd be a great reckoning: a trial, an inquiry, and I would be judged on whether I made my move or not. Therefore, I had to make it.

Hopkins re-entered the compartment, sat down and closed his eyes. I listened to the engine. It was a noisy bugger, and I tried to work out the speed: the number of rail joints in forty-one seconds gave the miles per hour. Get the answer right and you knew more than the driver himself, but you needed a watch for the business really. At the final reckoning I might be given a medal or I might be stood down; I might, at the outside, be imprisoned but I doubted that I would be hanged. The thought of imprisonment checked me: who knew that I was a police agent in all this apart from the Chief? And the Chief might very well be dead.

When I next thought to look out of the window we were dashing through Ashford, Kent, and Sampson was standing in the corridor, fiddling with . . . well, it had to be the gun. He stood with his broad back to me, but I craned about, and saw that he was once more inspecting the bullets – putting new ones in perhaps, or just admiring the ones already there; I couldn't see which from where I was. I closed my eyes for a space, and when I opened them again, Sampson was grinning at me through the compartment window, making the sleeping sign, with head rested on hands.

Not long after, we were threading in and out of tunnels at Folkestone. The difference between being in and out of the tunnels was not so very great, for, while the rain continued as before, the sky was now quite dark.

But Dover was different, the town all great blue gaslight, as if the whole place served as a beacon for ships: Dover Church, Dover Castle, Dover Prison glowed on one side as we rolled towards the station, all with Union flags flying above. And down below was Dover Harbour. Our train ran through the station, closing quickly on the harbour – a train wandering amongst ships and hard by the cold blackness of the sea, like a stray, until it found out the line that took us along the stone pier where the steam boat waited.

As the train moved slowly along the pier, Sampson was distributing the money from the kitbag about the pockets of his coat. The gun remained in the kitbag, and I thought he meant to leave it in the compartment. But as we climbed down from the train with not more than a couple of dozen others, he picked it up, saying to Hopkins:

'Take it easy, will you? I've done this trip a dozen times and never once been searched, nor *seen* anybody searched.'

Of course, he had to have the gun with him. I'd have been off in a moment otherwise.

The pier was a provocation to the sea, a thorn in its side. The water flew up to left and right of us, and sometimes both at once. Dover glowed above us but the pier had not enough lamps, and those mainly over notices of close type mounted on steel poles. What I took to be the customs shed was before us, and beyond it, the steamer, beating about underneath a signal that controlled its movements and looked like a railway signal.

To get to the boat, you had to cross the customs shed, and it was the thought of doing this that had silenced Sampson and Hopkins, for there was the money, and there was the gun. After a short platform conference with Sampson, Hopkins handed me my ticket. We had to go one by one, of course. Sampson, I was pretty sure, had transferred the revolver to the inside pocket of his coat, for he kept his hand there like Napoleon, and the kitbag looked empty in his hand. 'They ask me about the bulky article I'm carrying,' he said, as we stood in a circle of three before the customs shed, '. . . and I give them a little demonstration.'

'No,' said Hopkins, 'we turn about, and we fucking scarper.'

Sampson smiled at that, but I didn't think his smile was to be taken as agreement.

We broke, and filed into the shed, with Sampson at the head of us. It was a draughty wooden hall, like a village hall, and with that kind of smell, and three swaying gas rings. There was a man on a kind of pulpit, who watched as we fell in with the queue of people filing through between the open door on the train side, and the open door on the boat side. He wore an ordinary suit, no uniform, and did nothing but watch. On a bench at one side sat a man in a uniform: half sailor, half policeman, and this one didn't even watch. Another bloke at the far door, which was pointed towards by signs reading 'Exit' and 'Sortie', wore an ordinary suit, and he was looking at tickets as quickly and lightly as if it was a pleasure boat in the park that we were boarding. As the three of us moved towards him in the queue, I thought: I will speak out now. I looked at the copper, who was looking away. I looked at the man in the pulpit, but it was the wrong look I had back from him. No encouragement there . . . And yet it was possible to end the matter quickly. The crisis would come before you could say Jack Robinson. Maybe I ought to cry out those very words. Any would do Sampson was alongside the ticket inspector, giving him a warning look, as if to say: I dare you to inspect my pockets. The man did not, but simply glanced at the ticket and passed it back.

Yet Sampson did not move on. With the same steely look, he asked the man: 'What's the crossing time today, mate?'

Any words would do, if cried out loudly enough.

'Bank on one hour forty-five minutes,' said the ticket inspector, 'but could be half an hour more or less depending.'

The inspector was on the dead level, but it seemed likely for a moment that Sampson would express dissatisfaction with the answer given, for he still did not move forwards toward the boat. There was no escaping the fact . . . he enjoyed being on the edge of disaster. Hopkins was now nudging me towards the attentions of the inspector, and Sampson had at last moved a few paces towards the boat so that, as my ticket was inspected, I stood with Hopkins right behind me, and Sampson directly in front. Things might be free and easy once we made France, but twenty miles *short* of France they were still very far from that. This was not an elopement but more like a kidnapping, an abduction. My mind was full of words from the shilling novels.

And my chance was now.

But I was like the trees declining into the river at Thorpe-on-Ouse; the blind, rolling bells of the Minster on a Sunday of fog and rain; the drowning man who sees the surface of the water but lacks the will to reach it . . .

On the boat, two minutes later, we sat under an awning next to the wheel. Sampson lit a cigar. The kitbag was on his knee. Had he returned the gun to the bag?

Hopkins looked all-in with anxiety.

'Is it bloody worth it?' he said, over the sound of the engine engaging gear, and the wheel beginning to turn, which took the boat not only backwards away from the pier, but also *up*.

'Want to know the likelihood of 'em sending detectives

after us?' Sampson shouted back. 'Nil. Never known it to happen. They can't run to it. We might as well be on the bloody moon.'

'But there's no custom house on the moon,' said Hopkins.

'Yes,' said Sampson, 'well . . . how do you fucking know, anyway?'

We sat and watched the wheel turn, blue smoke floating over our heads from the funnel. We had a bench and were under a little cover, so were better off than some, who sat about on coils of rope getting the hard word from the crew as and when they got in the way. Again, nobody spoke, and this, I guessed, was because the second customs house lay in wait on the pier side.

'Why do you not pitch the shooter over the side, and buy a new one in France?' I asked.

But Sampson made no reply, or I might have been drowned out by the wheel. I ventured another question, half hiding it, so to speak, behind the screen of the paddle wheel noise:

'Did you never think of doing the Lost Luggage Office at York?' I said – at which Sampson glanced at me but looked away; Hopkins looked at me for a longer time. Evidently, he had heard the question if Sampson had not.

'There's a lot of treasure in there,' I said, 'I've seen it with my own eyes.'

At this, Sampson did give me a proper look, and it was one of his dead-eyed ones. I had been ashamed of myself in the customs shed, and now wanted to make amends with a little boldness. But I looked away first.

It was freezing on the deck, and we began to be soaked, by the sea and the rain flying at us from the side.

Sampson stood up, saying: 'I could do with a nip.'

'Best not to be seen below, though,' said Hopkins.

Sampson was standing before me, hand half in his gun pocket as before, empty bag dangling by his side.

'Come on,' he said, jerking his head. He was still riled over my lost-luggage questions, and could have shot me without the sound being heard, such was the roar of the wheel. It would then have been an easy matter to pitch me over the side, for the deck was emptier than before, most people having paid the little extra to go below, into either the dining room or the bar, which we were now walking towards, looking like drunks already. The entrance to the bar gave directly on to a staircase. Above the doorway, I saw a sign: 'Dover Ales', and at that moment I knew I was seasick. Sampson ordered three pints, and I just looked at mine, for I was coming to hate the rise and fall of the boat, most particularly the way it would rise and then *not* fall for a little while, but boom along at a height as if flying, before crashing back down.

The bar was tiny and bright, and packed, and there was a mass of metal poles, so everybody had something to grip on to, just as all the bottles were fixed in place behind the bar. Sampson paid for our pints, then stood behind me, blocking the doorway. The bar moved like a pendulum, and I watched my glass until half the beer had flown away. Hopkins was pressed up next to me on the other side, along with a bloke in a waterproof who was doing his best to hold on to a spirit glass, and light a cigar. 'Crack boat, is this,' he said, to me.

Even Sampson had had his fill of that place after ten minutes, and we walked back up on the deck, where I saw a low line of muffled whiteness against the dark blue of the night sky.

'Is that France?' I said, as we regained our former perch by the wheel.

'Well spotted, Allan,' said Hopkins, sarcastic-like.

A fourth passenger had come to the bench while we'd

been in the bar. He turned and looked at us as we sat down, which seemed to cause Hopkins to rise immediately to his feet, and move towards the railing of the boat, just to the side of the wheel. I could not make out the reason for this sudden spring, although I did notice that the new fellow on the bench wore wire spectacles in exactly the same style as my own.

Chapter Twenty-four

The boat made some of its biggest bounces as it moved up towards the dock at Calais. Here was the Gare Maritime: I could picture those words in my head, having read them in the *Railway Magazine*. It was not quite a mirror of Dover but a simpler place: customs house and station on the dock like a stage, large hotel behind; the town low, wide and dark in the background with one spire like the hub of a cartwheel. The French shouts came towards us as we moved across the illuminated water.

Sampson, with his kitbag, his gun, and his pockets full of money, was foremost in the queue as the gangplank was dropped. I was behind him; Hopkins was behind me. At a nod from a rough customer in a black guernsey (I could tell he was French, but I couldn't tell *how* I knew), Sampson started walking forwards, and I followed.

I did not trust the steadiness of the ground as I gazed around the customs house. This time there was no pulpit, and the man waiting to look at the tickets sported a uniform, as did half a dozen others sitting about. Two of these were drinking coffee from metal cups, and these two also wore rifles over their shoulders. I looked at these strange, disconnected fellows, who spent their lives killing time half in one country, half in another, and wondered which of them would cop it if Valentine Sampson were to be stopped and asked to turn out his pockets. Sampson would certainly shoot, because he had nowhere to flee to.

He handed his ticket to the French official, who looked it over slowly. Slowly, too, he handed it back, and once again Sampson asked a question or made some remark. It was in French but evidently not carried off quite right, for the official had to lean over and ask for it to be repeated. The official's answer was quite loud, and a lot of pointing went along with it. With Sampson looking back towards me from just before the 'Sortie', Hopkins nudged me forwards, and I thought: I could crown Hopkins, then double back on to the boat and what would Sampson do? Fire across the customs hall and risk all to stop me fleeing? But the thought came once more: if I got away from *them*, they got away from *me*. They were nearer to making their escape now, and I was the only one with power to stop them. I was the sleuth hound; the tables were turned somehow. Or was that the confusion of an exhausted mind?

Very likely; I could not keep my thoughts in a straight line; and the strangeness of France added to the strangeness of all.

We crossed the rails by a walkway, then stepped under the cover of the platform for Paris. Except that there wasn't a platform, so the train, which was in but not ready, stood very high. It was a towering engine; brown inasmuch as it had any colour. Compound cylinders, and a mix-up of gadgets sprouted all over it – it was an engine built inside out. That was for ease of maintenance; it didn't look beautiful . . . but handsome is as handsome does. The tender was massive, overflowing with queer-looking French coal, and I wondered whether it was meant to run to Paris without stop. Hopkins was by my side; Sampson was ten yards off, buying wine and hunches of bread at a stall; beyond him was a promising sign: 'Bureau des Postes et Télégraphes'. Any attempt to telegraph was likely to be a palaver though, with me not knowing the language or the telegraphic address of the Chief, not to mention the likelihood of the Chief being dead. Sampson came up to us, carrying three bottles of wine. They were everyday articles – clear bottles without stoppers, and the loaves which were split with some sort of paste on the top. I bit into the bread, and it was soft and strange and more-ish; I then lifted the wine bottle, and put a load of that in, and when I looked towards Sampson again he was grinning at me.

'They do themselves pretty well this side of the water,' he said.

A thin man was close by, viewing the papers on a circular cabinet outside the book stall. I took this to be Hopkins, but looking again, it was not. A porter was moving towards me with a trolley, setting down little wooden steps at the doors of the train. Imagine doing that every time one came and went. These Frenchers were barmy.

Still no sight of Hopkins . . . Sampson still drinking before me. Dead chuffed, he was. He'd made his breakaway, and he had his ready money. Well, half of it . . . a certain quantity, at any rate, the balance being at the left-luggage place in Charing Cross.

He passed his bottle to me, even though my own was in my hand. I put my own down, and took a drink from his. It was the same but different; and that went for the whole of France. Harbour, sea, night sky . . . the very rain that fell. There was a softness to the place . . . more of a womanly touch to it all.

Things really *were* more free and easy on this side of the water. As Sampson put away the last of his wine I had the freedom to move a little way from him towards the sign, and the door marked 'Bureau des Postes et Télégraphes'. I could

215

see through the window. Electric light. Bank-like inside, with men in starched collars behind polished brass grills . . . All this going off at midnight, or near enough.

There were half a dozen windows: 'Postes', 'Télégraphes' and 'Bureau de Change'. I had about me the twenty quid that Sampson had paid me. I could change it, and use some of it to telegraph the Police Office at York station, or, failing that, the Stationmaster. 'Tell wife all well'. That would be my opener. I set down the wine bottle I was holding . . . and one of the telegraph clerks was eyeing me through the window. The thing about the bloody French . . . *all* the buggers were hoity-toity, not just the toffs. Just then, Miles Hopkins walked out through the door, and I saw an extra word amid all the signs inside: 'Téléphones'.

Seeing me at large, unguarded on the platform, he immediately said: 'Where's Sam?'

And at that very moment, I could not have said.

But a second later Valentine Sampson came into view with more supplies of wine, saying, casual as you like:

'Train's due off in five minutes.'

The three of us walked towards a book stall, where Hopkins picked up an English paper. The crowd was thickening about us now as train time drew near – all French voices.

'Are we in it, mate?' asked Sampson, putting wine bottles into his pockets.

'It's today's paper,' said Miles, 'which means it carries news of what happened *yesterday*.'

He was looking at Sampson in a strange way. Nothing would get Hopkins out of his groove. He was scheming at all times.

Alongside the cabinet from which Hopkins had plucked the paper was a bookshelf – a little library in the rain. I picked up a small red volume called *Paris and its Environs*,

216

with Thirteen Maps and Thirty-Eight Plans. A proper language! And I straightaway saw instructions for telegraphing and telephoning from France. Hopkins was watching me as I said: 'Reckon this might come in useful. It's only marked down as a bob 'n' all . . . Oh no, bugger that. It must be one *franc*.'

Another shout came from the platform guard, and Sampson just lifted the book and put it into my hand, saying, 'For Christ's sake, little Allan, get a shift on.'

The carriage had open seating, no compartments. After a great amount of shouting, the train left the platform at walking pace. To avoid the gaze of Hopkins, I looked down at the first page of my book: 'For those who wish to derive instruction as well as pleasure from a visit to Paris, the most attractive treasury of art and industry in the world, some acquaintance with French is indispensable.'

Hopkins and Sampson were speaking in low voices over the mighty sounds of the engine pulling away. Hopkins had been speaking over the telephone – he made no bones about that. Had he telephoned York? It must have been a pretty fast connection, if so.

I turned to the pages for Paris, and 'Post, Telegraph and Telephone Offices'. The chief telephone offices, I read, were in the Rue du Louvre and at the Bourse. There was a late telegraph office at the Gare du Nord. But telephone was the quickest.

On a later page, I discovered that it was the same time in France as in Britain; Germany and Switzerland had different times. In the section at the back marked 'Language', selected words and phrases were given in English and French, and these were boiled down to the closest necessities such as 'How fond some people are of taking an immense lot of luggage'. Sampson was at his racing paper again. 'Of course, most multiple bets are just guesses,' he was saying to Hopkins, who wasn't listening, but continuing to eyeball me.

Some French words, I saw from the book, were the same as English. 'Omnibus' was 'omnibus'. 'Police' was 'police'. I then looked at some railway speaks: 'Nous allons bien vite.' We are going very fast. 'À quelle heure part le premier train?' At what time does the first train leave?

Having set down his paper, Sampson was saying, in connection with something or other: 'It's always supposed that the big ones are put up.'

Beyond the window, things were floating back fast in the darkness. 'What did your old man do for a living, Allan?' he asked me.

'Butcher,' I said, instantly. 'Yours?'

'Time,' he answered.

'He was a felon?' I asked, and Sampson's eyes went steely again.

I looked through the windows. The French houses were wrong, with the wrong roofs – like a man with a bad hat. We went at a lick through a station: its name began with 'B', and there was sea here too, or a lighthouse at any rate. We were next hurled over a great junction, and Sampson was looking at the other passengers in the carriage.

'Wouldn't mind giving her a shot,' he was saying.

Silence for a space, then Sampson said:

'That French cunt's staring at me.'

I looked up. He might have meant one of twenty. Not that they were all cunts, but they were all French. A woman sitting behind Hopkins was holding a baby, and the sight knocked me. I thought: one of those will be in my way before long, and the second thought came: will I ever see it? The baby was pounding as hard as it could on the shoulder of the woman but that wasn't at all hard. I looked out of the window:

nothing; blackness. I was in the same position as that kid.

By now, I could only tell by my ears when we were in a tunnel. I looked to my left, and Sampson was asleep, an empty wine bottle rolling between his boots. Well, he'd had a long day of it. In slumber, his face lost none of its shape.

'How is it you're so well up on railways?' said Hopkins.

'I did some turns in the goods yard over at Leeds, as I told you.'

Was it Leeds that I'd said? I couldn't recall. Come to that . . . Had I spoken of being employed in the goods yards at all?

'In addition, I used to take the *Railway Magazine*,' I added.

'Take it from others at railway stations, you mean?'

I'd made another bloomer. Hopkins was playing one of his finger games, smiling at me over his hands. I finished off what was left of my own wine, saying, 'I had a hobby in that direction, you know.'

Hopkins leant forwards, and settled himself with his elbows on his knees, giving up his finger exercises. It was a wild night outside, but the carriage was too close and dusty. I wanted to open the window but did not know how, or how to ask one of the Frenchers. I looked down at the book in my hands. The answer lay in there somewhere.

Hopkins raised one of his hands, and pointed at me. I thought this would be the start of a speech, but instead the long pointing finger moved towards me, towards my face, towards my spectacles, and through my spectacles to my eyelash, which he touched, causing me to do the most ridiculous thing. I coloured up; I then tried to laugh.

Hopkins was sitting back, smiling.

'How much did they set you back then, mate?' he asked. 'I would hope they come cheaper than the sort with lenses. See . . . I watched the fellow on the boat with glasses just like yours, and what with the rain and the flying spray they were all misted up.'

'It's a disguise, if you take my meaning,' I said. 'I didn't want to look like I did before because of . . . something . . . something that occurred.'

Hopkins, still smiling, said: 'Who are you, mate?'

And that was the nerve-cracking moment, for I had no answer.

Chapter Twenty-five

'An ordinary working man,' I said to Hopkins as the train thundered on, 'always on the look-out for a spot of . . .'

'What?'

'Adventure.'

'And how do you find *this* adventure?'

The wonder of it was that he had not immediately accused me of being a detective, but then he always went around the houses, this one. He nodded towards Sampson, who was still dead to the world. 'Do you not find him a bit . . . nuts?'

'He gets a little excitable at times,' I said.

'He does that,' said Hopkins.

'In that case why stick with him?' I said, breathing a little easier at this new direction of the conversation.

Hopkins shrugged.

'Keep a cart on a wheel,' he said.

'How are we off for the readies?' I said. 'And when's the share-out?'

'Search me,' he said.

'And what's the plan for Paris?'

He made no answer but, turning towards the black window repeated my earlier words: 'An ordinary working man . . .'

At which Valentine Sampson suddenly started and said: 'It's a pity, but I will *not* work, little Allan. It's hardly any advance on slavery.'

He'd uttered the words while still half asleep, or at the very moment of waking up. He looked at us both with wide eyes, as though waiting to be told something. But Hopkins remained silent and, presently, closed his eyes and fell asleep himself. I wanted to do the same but could not, for fear of what might be said. Instead I removed the spectacles for – at the very least of it – my disguise was all up.

We were now running fast past a spot called Abbeville; then past another starting with 'A'; eighty miles per hour gait. A great church made of darkness and rain; outlines of the weird engines in the rain. Over a maze of lines at somewhere starting with 'L', then we were shooting downhill, into valleys made of tall, rough-looking buildings.

The Gare du Nord, when we came to it, was fitted out like a palace, a freezing-cold palace with high arches, and electric light in great glass globes, and yet even here no platforms to speak of. We climbed down, and . . . We were too early.

The day had not yet begun, and we had caught Paris all unawares. We walked through the ticket gate into a wide hall with a round window like a great white eye opposite the track ends. There were some small offices set into the walls below the window, and we approached one of these marked 'Consigne', which was French for left-luggage office. A clerk stood there with his hands on his hips as we approached. It was Napoleon waiting for Nelson, only lower down the scale of history.

He was eyeing Sampson's kitbag, which of course was all we had to consign. The remaining notes were in there once again, though not the gun. Our boots rattled smartly on the polished stone as we closed on the fellow.

When we were still some distance off, the fellow said, 'Bonjour, Messieurs', which came unexpectedly, for I'd expected surliness from him. Sampson made a go of replying

222

in French and asking to leave the bag, for which he received a ticket on payment of money from his pocketbook. He put the ticket in his right-hand trouser pocket, which, I reckoned, was where he'd put the one given him at Charing Cross. As we walked away from the Consigne, Hopkins said something in an under-breath to Sampson, and I thought: is he telling him of the discovery he'd made about me? But Sampson's answer made me doubt it:

'You'll not catch me taking any quantity of cash into a hotel here,' he said. 'A lot of thieving bastards, these fucking French are.'

A thought struck me: perhaps Hopkins thinks it not worth mentioning after all that my spectacles are false. Perhaps he thinks there's nothing in it. As we walked towards the 'Sortie', I noted the location of the telegraph office.

We stepped out of the Gare du Nord into a cobbled street. Over the road, in the rain and grey light, were cafés and restaurants with the widest fronts I'd ever seen, but all closed up, with seats stacked on tables outside. On the cobbles ahead of us was a mouse – same as an English mouse; no better, no worse. It dashed off as a cart came along the street pulled by a horse that looked high-mettled and restive. There was nothing fancy about this equipage, but that horse knew it was French all right. We began walking across the road, and the cobbles seemed to swim towards us in ripples.

We walked on, turning left, right; I was following Sampson, too done-in to ask questions, or to think about whatever game Hopkins was playing.

The buildings were tall, with windows in their roofs. Lanterns came and went, mounted on swan necks like thin, twisted trees, the gas still burning, though day was coming. We passed two smoke-blackened churches that were more like great theatres – all stacked up like mountains, with peeling posters outside. A blue, round something was stuck on to the front of one of them: sundial or clock? I slowly made out that it was a clock, and that the time shown was a quarter after five. Not two minutes later, the three of us were standing outside the door of a moderately sized hotel. The name was written in gold paint against the blackened stone: Hôtel des Artistes. Three French flags sprouted over the door. I remembered what the *Police Gazette* had said of Joseph Howard Vincent: 'Likely to be found in hotels'.

Well here we were, to the very life.

Sampson pressed a bell, and we waited. Directly opposite the hotel was another great black church, lamps and trees in alternation across its front, but its windows were all bricked up.

The door of the hotel was opened at last by a little fellow dressed in black and white; he was all smiles, so here was another kind of Frencher. We walked through the doorway: red carpet, more gold paint, some giant ferns, and paintings all around the walls of people half hidden in shadowy rooms. The place was quite swanky, or had been once. From the way he was speaking to him, I didn't believe that the little fellow in black and white knew Sampson, but I had the idea that Sampson knew the hotel.

Their chat ran on as the little man indicated that we should follow him up a winding staircase, and Sampson did not lower his voice a bit even though everybody in the hotel must have been asleep. As we walked, I felt my seasickness return on the endless, too-low steps and I wondered in a kind of fury how many of the sleepers in this place were artists. Sampson was quizzing the hotel bloke about something or other, and by my reckoning, the man half understood and half pretended to. What Sampson spoke was French, but it was a little off.

We were taken to the fourth floor, which was the top one. Hopkins took one room, and Sampson and I were to occupy the other . . . which was two rooms: a bedroom and a sitting room; or three, if you counted the privy and bath off to the side of the sitting room. Our quarters were pretty grand but gone to seed somewhat: red carpet a little bumpy; a black smudge beneath the mantel of the white fireplace, which was quite a museum piece, Ancient Greek style. All in all it was a cute arrangement, for I was put into the bedroom (which did give me the bed, whereas Sampson was evidently making do with the couch in the lounge), but I would have to walk past him to quit these chambers.

Well, I would do that if it came to it, and he could fire his revolver and bring the whole fucking house down. For the meanwhile though, I lay on the bed, and while I had resolved not on any account to sleep, my lights were out in a second.

I woke to see Sampson drinking wine from one of those plain bottles in the chair next to my bed. He wore trousers, boots, undershirt.

'What time is it?' I asked him, sitting up.

'Don't know, mate,' he said.

'Those two you shot in the engine shed at York,' I said, rising to a sitting position, '. . . they might be dead; might be mortally injured.'

'Correct,' he said, taking another pull at the bottle.

He passed the bottle over to me, and I took a quick go on it.

'Which would you rather?' I asked, giving it back.

'Me?' he said. 'I'm easy.'

I gained my feet and walked over to the window.

'If it came to court,' Sampson said, 'and they'd only taken injuries, I'd say I was shooting to miss.'

'And if they were killed?'

'Say the same. Can't swing for attempt, you know.'

I opened the window, looked out. French rooftops; French smoke coming out of them, meeting solid white, winter day. As I looked down, my gaze fell further than I'd bargained – down on to a railway valley: a dozen tracks cut between white cliffs of houses. On the wall opposite was written 'Vins', which meant 'wines'; it was like the word 'vine' so you could cotton on to it easily enough. I looked below again, and two trains crossed down in the pit, somehow giving me the idea – by the equality of the exchange – that it was about midday.

'It won't come to that though,' Sampson was saying from his chair. 'Arrest, charge, committal, trial, verdict, sentence, periods of hard labour . . . I can't be fucking doing with it, so I sweep away, little Allan, back and forth . . .'

He was sitting forward in the chair, waving his arm from side to side.

'Sweep away . . . it's like when you're walking through the tall grass with a cane in your hand, and you want the bloody stuff out the way, so on you go slashing to the left and to the right . . .'

'The *clean* sweep,' I said.

'Bingo,' he replied. 'And you'd do it yourself if you could, mate, and so would he.'

He turned to face the door, where Hopkins was standing.

'How are we off for the readies, Sam?' he said, moving his room key between his fingers, as though his hand had a mind of its own. 'I'm in low water, just at present.'

'Hark at the divvy hunter,' said Sampson, now standing up, and with a grin on his face, adding, '. . . Share-out'll come soon enough.' Then he turned to me saying, 'I warn you, Allan, it won't be quite a three-way split.'

I recalled that he'd held back payment to the goods yard clerk, and I thought: he's generous in the tap room – but it

226

was evidently a different matter with larger amounts.

Sampson was putting on his coat, saying, 'Shall we take a turn through Paris, lads?'

I put on my own coat, and walked into the main room. Sampson, following, asked, 'Where's your glasses, Allan?'

'Reckon I'll not bother with 'em,' I said. 'Fact is, I . . .'

Hopkins was in the sitting room, looking out of *its* window, which gave onto the same railway scene as the one in the bedroom. He had not stirred at the mention of the glasses, so no explanation seemed called for on his account, and Sampson had evidently lost interest in the subject, for he said, 'Let's away,' moving towards the door.

———◦———

As we walked, it came on to rain.

Everybody in Paris wore smaller clothes; they were smaller people. It was a proud place: soldiers, flags, stone angels, golden domes. Patriotic-like, even though I recollected from school history that they were always at each other's throats. All the cyclists scorched, all cab drivers shouted, and the sound of Paris – apart from the traffic – was the clash of plates and glasses, and the waves of chatter coming from the restaurants and bars. It was odd to think that all this had been going on all my life without me knowing.

The words over the shops would go along a certain way with English but then they'd take a wrong turning, as with 'Fruiterie'. That or they'd stop some way short of their goal, as for instance 'Tabac'. We passed under a sign in the form of a golden snail.

'They do eat snails, little Allan,' said Sampson, 'and they're proud of it.'

'Less cargo,' said Hopkins, walking along behind, and, when I looked back he gave one of his secret smiles.

227

Had he quite forgotten about the incident of the glasses?

A French dog came by. French dogs were different: nervous and unstrung, and they paid no mind to the food in the streets. Food was everywhere, spilling out of the shops and restaurants. The Frenchers were boiling up soup on street corners, standing guard over barrels of oysters, and it all called for a sight more than three meals a day.

We came to a stand outside some dining rooms.

Inside, it was like a lady's bedroom: mirrors, lace curtains, fancy, tangled lamps. We watched through the window. At a table just inside the door sat a man with big ears and a cigar and from sideways on, he looked like a cannon. Were the faces all different, or was it the difference of the place that made them seem so? At a table further in sat the real prize: a man who was the spit of Napoleon himself, with a beaky nose, puffed-up chest; scant hair pushed over to the side. Sampson said, 'I know this spot', as if the fact was just coming to him. He pushed open the door, we walked in and I looked straightaway at a little sign above a curtain: 'Téléphone'.

We were shown to a table. Sampson said something, and then one of the clear bottles of wine was brought. Sampson knew the word for that, all right. We'd drunk it off before the menus were passed to us, and Sampson asked for another by saying: 'Encore.'

Outside the rain was falling more heavily, but the restaurant was bright and jolly. There was a fireplace to one side of us, with a huge mantelshelf, on which sat giant, empty bottles of champagne which put me in mind somehow of the gas cylinders.

I looked again at the 'Téléphone' sign, and saw that Napoleon was walking towards it, pushing back the curtain, giving me sight of the instrument. It looked nothing like the English ones.

Sampson, smoking a cigar, said: 'If they know you here, they put you in that back room,' and he pointed through to a part of the restaurant where the tablecloths and napkins were even whiter, the red wine redder, the lamps still more jungly and flower-like.

'But they *don't* know you, do they?' asked Hopkins.

'They do not,' said Sampson.

'Thank God for that,' said Hopkins, putting back more wine.

He turned to me and grinned, and I thought: he's going to rat on me now – let on about the glasses. But instead something beyond the window caught his eyes, and he was up and out into the street. He walked away to the left, out of sight, and returned a minute later, grinning fit to bust. At the table once more, he produced a pocketbook – a French one. There was a small paper inside, covered with tiny handwriting, and some of the colour-run notes.

'Bit of all right,' said Sampson.

'Real fag-ender, this was,' said Hopkins proudly, 'side pocket, sitting on top of a handkerchief with just the tip pointing up.'

'You saw that all from here?' I said.

'Lynx-eyed, en't he?' said Sampson, looking at me, and there was silence for a space, so that once again I thought the matter of the spectacles must come up, but instead the food arrived. It was the Plat du Jour (dish of the day) that Sampson had asked for and the turn-up was that it was sausage and onions, albeit of superior flavour. As Sampson called for more wine, Hopkins, who was tipsy by now, sat back in his chair and said: 'Tell you what, mates, I do miss the Garden Gate though.'

He just sat there grinning for a while, and I knew he'd made a plan of some sort.

Chapter Twenty-six

Half an hour later, we were walking by the river which came through the city in a stone channel. There were lines of flat barges, all covered up with tarpaulins as if to say: this is all French business, none of yours. We walked on into a park, where indoor chairs were placed outside. A man sat at one of them with an easel before him and an umbrella over his head; he was painting a fountain with stone horses set all around the edge. The design made it look as if the horses were trying to run away but were trapped by their hind legs; trapped by being painted. We sat on the chairs underneath a dripping tree, and I fished out of my pocket *Paris and its Environs*.

'Can I have a look at that, mate?' said Hopkins. He seemed in better spirits now. I handed him the book, and he fell to reading in the 'Language' section. 'Only two things you really need,' he said after a while: "Une bière, s'il vous plait", then "Où sont les toilettes?"'

'What's "Would you like a fuck?"' said Sampson, who was watching a young woman sauntering under the trees. But Hopkins was now looking at some other part of the book.

'I tell you, I mean to have a ride tonight,' said Sampson.

There were many baby carriages being pushed about in the park, all going in different directions, each carrying a new human who would do the same in time. I could not bear to think of the wife. Had she decided that I'd skipped, taken fright at the thought of fatherhood? I dragged my thoughts in the direction of the seated artist, but his umbrella reminded me of Lund, the fellow who'd put me in this fix – it was all his doing.

I looked to my right, and Sampson was asleep.

Hopkins was looking at me:

'It must be done with the tread of a cat,' he was saying, and there was a new look to him: electrified.

'What must?'

'You are to take the left-luggage tickets from his pocket.'

He was looking towards the area of Sampson's privates.

'No fear,' I said.

'But you must,' he said.

'That calls for your skill,' I said, 'you're born to it. You said yourself I'd never make a dip.'

'Don't argue,' he said, giving me one of his grins. 'I'm down to your game.'

'What game?'

'You don't do it . . . I tell him who you are.'

'And who am I?'

Hopkins just stared at me.

'The name's Appleby,' I said, 'Allan Appleby.'

'Is it fuck,' said Hopkins, and still the smile was there. 'It doesn't want doing just now,' he said, 'but later on, when he's had one or two more gallons of wine.'

'Later on,' I said, '. . . he'll take his trews off in any case, won't he?'

Hopkins shook his head.

'He'll not,' he said. 'Not with tickets to nearly three grand in his pocket, and me hanging about.'

The artist was packing up, defeated by the rain, or maybe the fading of light.

'See, you *must* do it,' Hopkins went on, 'because one word from me to him, and you're finished. You might think you can get up now and walk off, but no. I'll give him a poke in the ribs, and I'll let on, and he'll take out that gun of his and he'll fucking have you, right here in this fucking *shar-dan*.'

'You'll let on to what?' I said.

'What you are.'

'And what am I?'

I wanted him to say it, and he did:

'You're a fucking copper, en't you?'

Chapter Twenty-seven

Night was coming down fast, along with the rain, and full dark found us wondering through empty streets. We were somewhat returned – having visited plenty of bars – in the direction of our hotel. There were big, blank churches about us, and trains running out of sight behind ranks of tall crumbling houses.

Now we were in another bar; it was the colour of illness, bright white and green. Another bottle was coming towards us; we were all smoking Sampson's cigars, and that gentry could by now barely speak English leave alone French. He had finally found his limit, but then I was at least half-cut too. As for being a copper, I'd denied it to the hilt until Sampson had woken in the park; and the question had not come up since. A train of ideas kept starting in my mind but I couldn't follow it out. One thing seemed pretty certain: the cart was about to come off the wheel, somehow or other.

I turned about at our table, and the wife was standing at the bar.

No.

It was a woman who looked like her but blonde – like Lydia in a photograph with too much light. Sampson was chatting to a woman in a blue dress. She was chubby, rather monkey-looking but pretty with it. The dress showed all of her arms, and was low at the front. Her hair was curly and loose. She looked as though she was practically in bed already.

'Monsieur Allan Appleby,' Sampson was trying to say, indicating me.

Hopkins looked on, smoking and grinning. This was all quite fine by him.

'Encore,' said Sampson, calling over to the barman.

'It's the wrong word is that,' said Hopkins, turning to me, 'but don't mind me.'

Sampson paid no heed. He was kissing the woman, his beard at a stretch as he worked his mouth. Hopkins was leaning towards me, and I thought for a horrible moment that he was making to give *me* a kiss. Instead he was saying:

'It must be done tonight, before midnight.'

'You're crackers,' I said.

'I'll take no slavver from you, copper.'

'He'll divvy up the money soon enough,' I said.

The doxy was half sitting, half lying over Sampson's knees, as though dropped there from a great height. They were whispering things to each other: she to him, him to her, on and on in strict alternation.

Meanwhile Hopkins was holding me with his eyes, saying, 'You're Stringer, detective on the railway force. You live at number 16A Thorpe-on-Ouse Main Street.'

'What?' I said.

'Look, do you want me to spin the whole bloody works? I had it all at Calais last night from Mike.'

'How?'

'He was speaking over the telephone line from the Black Swan Hotel. I called him to see what's what in York.'

'And who did *he* have it from?'

Hopkins was grinning at me, and it felt as though this grin of his might go on for ever, so I twisted away from him, looking behind me and towards the barkeeper, who stood with his arms folded. Behind him was a great poster for 'Bières . . .' Bières . . . something. A proud French soldier was shown holding up a glass. They were full of pride, these Frenchers, and yet this chap behind the bar had to throw open his parlour (for that's what the bar was really) to all sorts from anywhere to make a living. He was trying to look away from the lot of us, pretend we weren't there.

My gaze fell on Sampson and the doxy, still playing their drunken whispering game.

Following my gaze, Hopkins said, '. . . You've no need to worry on that score. He knows I spoke to Mike, but he has no idea about what . . . And he'll never find out either, just as long as you lift those tickets of his . . . Only you must do it before midnight, because I've asked Mike to take a look in at 16A . . .'

I stood up, and swung my fist at Hopkins, who dodged back easily enough, saying something I could not hear for the sound of the barkeeper, who'd now been set chattering – whether to us or to himself I could not have said – blathering away like a complaining engine that couldn't be turned off. Sampson was so busy with his doxy that he barely noticed. He just took his left hand off her bosom, and made a calming gesture, saying, 'Easy, lads, easy.'

I asked Hopkins:

'*When* is he going there?'

'Never you mind. I've asked him to pay a call, that's all.'

'If I'm Stringer,' I said . . .

Hopkins was grinning at me.

'If I am,' I carried on, 'and I'm *here* . . .'

'Oh, I think we can take it as read that you're here . . .'

'Then there'll be nobody in at 16A, will there . . .'

'I've seen your fucking wedding ring,' said Hopkins, 'so

you needn't come that one. I've asked Mike to pay a visit. Only it's conditional-like. If you do the job tonight I'll telephone again, tell him to stay put.'

The barkeeper was still spouting, and now he was coming towards us. It was clear enough that he wanted us out. Hopkins had been suspicious of me since the night of the Garden Gate, and he had learned my identity from Mike as soon as we arrived in France. He'd kept silent since then, revolving the information in his mind, designing away . . .

I looked back at Hopkins, thinking whether to try another swing, and he was grinning at me, saying, '. . . I'll telephone the big fucking lummox again; his place of work is right by the instrument, you know. They can make a quick connection from here . . . I'll stop him in his tracks . . . honour bright!'

The barman talked on, standing over us now. I glimpsed Sampson's gun, in the waistband of his trousers. Sampson and the doxy were rising to their feet. They had their own pressing reason for wanting to quit the little bar. Hopkins stood too, leaning closer to me again, saying: 'If I don't have those tickets in my hand by midnight, then Mike'll be round there, and it'll be . . . It'll be the fucking clean sweep, matey . . .'

He had overheard the expression from Sampson. In my mind's eye, I saw Lydia in the parlour; I saw her at the typewriter; I saw the Opopanax and Parma Violets standing beside the machine . . . I saw the copies of the investigation reports, freshly typed. She would not be able to plead ignorance of my work.

—◇—

The bill had been paid – somehow, by someone – and we were now heading back to the Hôtel des Artistes. I was walking next to Hopkins in silence; Sampson was just behind, one arm around the woman in a courtly way (yet also a drunken one), the other hanging loose in the vicinity of his gun. The churches, temples, abandoned theatres came and went until we entered the hotel, and the black and white man was not there, but the paintings were. I peered at the gloomy people shown in them, but they had retreated still further into the shadows.

We climbed the long staircase, and my mind went back to my first meeting with Lund at the Lost Luggage Office. I saw myself writing my name in the ledger. It was there for any-one to see.

On the silent and evidently empty fourth floor, Hopkins had somehow faded away into his own quarters, while I stepped into the opposite room with Sampson and the French doxy. I tumbled through into the bedroom on the far side of those quarters, with wine Sampson had given me in a bathroom glass. I closed the door behind me while Sampson and the doxy fell to in the main room. At first the pair of them were quiet . . . and then they weren't.

I sat staring at nothing for a space. I could hear a train run-ning along the lines below. It was timetabled, but at the same time free. A good minute after it had gone from earshot, its black smoke finally ascended to the level of my window.

In the room beyond, the French tart was giving way still further to Valentine Sampson or Joseph Howard Vincent as the case may have been. I picked out of my pocket *Paris and its Environs*. Christianity, I read, had been introduced to France by St Denis. Visitors to the Louvre who had only a short time to devote to the galleries were recommended to begin with the antique sculptures.

In the room beyond, matters reached the screaming stage just as a train went rumbling below, making a contest of it for loudest noise. It was a wonder that Sampson could perform at all, given the amount of red wine he'd put away. Hopkins, alone of the three of us, was *not* blotto, and he would hold to his plan, I knew.

A couple of minutes later, Sampson opened the door, and beckoned me through into the sitting room. He wore his trousers and his undershirt.

I could see the doxy through the open door of the bathroom: she was painting on rouge.

'Did you hear any of that goings-on, little Allan?' Sampson asked, picking up the wine, which he'd not quite seen off.

'Maybe a bit,' I said.

'You'll have learnt something if so,' he said, and he sat down on the couch with the wine, as the doxy stepped out of the bathroom.

'You look nice,' he said.

'I 'aven't fineeshed,' she said.

'Well you should do,' said Sampson. 'Pack it in while the going's good.'

She left in the next few minutes, following a short conference that took place just beyond the outer door.

'Silly cat,' Sampson said, when he walked back in.

He eyed me for a while before saying:

'Sorry, mate, did you want a ride yourself?'

Not looking for an answer – I believe he'd asked only for form's sake – he walked over to the window, lifting the sash and gazing down at the tracks.

'Where does Mike work?' I asked.

'Black Swan,' said Sampson, scratching his beard.

Coney Street. The stone swan held out over the door looked burnt, and its blackness had somehow smudged the front of the building, making *it* look burnt in turn.

'And I suppose they have a telephone there.'

No reply from Sampson, who was walking over towards the couch, as I enquired, casual as you like, 'You thinking of having a kip?'

Sampson turned and gave me one of his looks; no life, nothing in the eyes.

'Why are you asking these cuntish questions?'

'What?' I said.

'You're getting up my *fucking* arse,' said Sampson.

Was it Lund who'd given word to Mike? Was he trying to check the investigation he'd begun for fear of being run in over the lost-luggage theft? I could not believe so.

Sampson caught up a wine bottle from the floor beside the couch. He then drifted towards the bathroom, where he pissed for what seemed about half an hour. He walked towards the mantelshelf and I saw, too late, that the gun was there. Sampson picked it up.

Of course, another man might very well have seen my name in that ledger: Parkinson, the lost-luggage superintendent. What did he know? And who else could've passed on my address to Mike?

Sampson moved back to the couch, where he put the gun underneath a cushion, of which he made a pillow. He pulled the coverlet from the back of the sofa – and that became his over-blanket. He lay down, taking a few short pulls on the wine . . . which seemed to see him off. But he stirred again, reaching once more for the bottle, and saying to me, friendly once more: 'We'll be all right over here, little Allan . . . Live shallow for six months if need be.'

A few more quick wine goes, then he rolled over on his side and looked at me with his violet eyes. It was very strange to see him lying down; unnatural somehow.

'Why d'you kill the Camerons, mate?' I asked him.

But his eyes shut at that moment.

I waited a quarter of an hour, then made straight for the door, opened it. Hopkins was there, with a knife in his hand.

Well, he had me three ways. He could wake Sampson, crying copper. He could do me with the knife (although I didn't think that was in him). And the third way he voiced directly: 'Think of Mike,' he said in an under-breath, pressing me back into the room. 'He'll be on his way soon, unless I give the word.'

I whispered back: 'Why the fuck don't you lift the tickets yourself?'

He said nothing, but twirled the knife in his long right hand.

I tried another tack, saying: 'He'll shoot anybody he catches at it.'

'That's your lookout, copper,' he said.

I looked at Hopkins; at his curly hair stuck down at intervals by sweat. I turned and watched Sampson sleeping. I screwed myself up to it, and moved towards him.

'Right pocket,' Hopkins was saying from the doorway as I peeled back the coverlet, '. . . right pocket. The two chits are in there, I fucking swear it. London ticket is the principle one. The larger amount was stowed there.'

Sampson was flat on his back. I had to lean across him to get to the right pocket.

'Fingers only,' Hopkins was saying, 'fingers only; don't stick your fucking fist in.'

If Sampson woke, Hopkins would dart back to his own quarters. And I'd catch it. My finger ends were creeping into the pocket now. It was all in folds, my fingers approaching mountains and valleys of silk. From beyond the window and below, I heard a train approaching. As its rocking grew louder, Sampson, too, rocked in his sleep. Back and forth he went, back and forth; but it was only a small disturbance. I leant into my work again; into the sharp wine smell that was rising off Sampson; my fingers creeping further into the mountains and valleys. The shaming thought came to me that I was like the doxy, with my hand moving ever further towards Sampson's privates.

I gave a glance back towards the window, and saw the rising of steam and smoke from the lately passed train. I was Jack in the Giant's Castle, high in the clouds, and making away the Giant's gold.

The thought came that I could wake Sampson and tell him I'd been put up to this by his confederate – the designing fellow skulking in the doorway. It would be my word against Hopkins's. Might Sampson believe me, and then order Mike not to make his call? Mike's true governor was Sampson, after all, and he would have believed that the orders he'd had from Miles Hopkins were given on the say-so of Sampson.

My finger ends met paper, and I said out loud: 'I have my fingers on one of the bloody things.'

'Collect the tickets scissor-like,' said Hopkins from the doorway.

Sampson slept on, silent and quite still as my fingers closed over the paper, dragging it into the light. The left-luggage ticket was blue, and the words upon it were in English. It was the one from Charing Cross, and the colour of it gave me the beginnings of an idea.

I stood back from the couch and, looking directly across the room at Hopkins, folded the blue ticket several times over, and lowered it into my own right trouser pocket.

'Give it here,' he whispered from the doorway.

'Hold on, mate,' I said. 'I'm going in for the other. I know it's there.'

I was sweating like a bull as I started on my second finger

creep. But just as my fingertips had reached the pocket entrance for the second time, another train came rattling along the line below. Its rapid approach seemed to send a secret message to Sampson's right arm, which began to rise – a snake being charmed to the tune of a train. It wavered in the air, making as if to swipe at me. I drew back, and the thick arm landed heavily on top of the right pocket entrance, sealing it up, preventing any further attempts and deciding me upon my idea.

As the train rattled away I turned to Hopkins, saying, 'We must give it up now.'

He nodded. He could see the sense of that.

'Hand over the blue one,' said Miles. 'It's the English one, en't it?'

I did not have Hopkins down as a violent man, but I knew in that instant that he would never let me go even if I gave over the ticket. Why would he, knowing I was a copper? He would guess that the moment I was free, I would ask for men to be sent to the left-luggage offices, to prevent the money being taken, and to arrest anyone trying to claim it. As he looked on, I reached into my trouser pocket, where lay *two* blue left-luggage tickets. One unfolded, the other folded tightly. I took out the first. It was the ticket I'd been given at York in return for the good suit after my hotel breakfast with the Chief. I placed it on Sampson's belly, and retreated from the couch, making towards the door, and Hopkins.

'You must take it yourself,' I said, drawing level with him.

The ticket rose and fell with Sampson's belly, stirring somewhat in the breeze from the open window. Hopkins did not look at me but, cursing in an under-breath, moved rapidly towards the fluttering blue paper with knife in hand. As he reached out to take it I gave a cry, something that was not even a word. But it was loud, and I saw Sampson rise in the moment before I turned and fled, screaming out with rapid rising glee. I was the brilliant sleuth hound after all. I had recovered half the stolen money, and I'd fixed Hopkins, Sampson, or the two bastards both . . . But most likely Hopkins, for he only had the blade where Sampson had the shooter. I saw in my mind's eye – as I crashed down those red-carpeted stairs – the bookstall at York station, with the glowing covers of the shilling novels, and all the detective heroes there depicted . . . But in the next instant the bookstall of my mind combusted in my rage at my own stupidity, and a terrible coldness came over me. I had won out over the ticket, and I had set the two at each other's throats, but Hopkins would not now be able to take back the order he had given. I had condemned the wife to the revenge of Mike.

I flew on, and at one mid-air moment – as I bounded the final three steps of the second or third landing – I thought I heard the crack of a gun – or was it a cry? – from the floors above.

I pounded on down the red-carpeted stairs, past the doors of all the sleeping artists, until I was at the front door of the hotel, and out of it and away, flying along shuttered streets, boots rattling crazily on the cobbles, with two cabs rushing along beside me. I tried to gaze through the windows as I ran, half expecting to see Sampson in there, taking aim with his shooter. The two cabs both turned left at the end of the street, so that was a direction leading . . . somewhere.

I took that turning myself, and was galloping alone in a wide street with thin trees on either side. I had to believe that Hopkins had been spinning a yarn; that no order had been given to Mike, for it was a queer sort of thing to ask: do such and such a thing unless you hear from me. Or that Mike would not obey. Or then again, I might be able to *beat* Mike to Thorpe-

243

on-Ouse. Would he go out in the middle of the night? If not, there was hope, for I might be able to return by morning.

But this was all a gamble, with Lydia's life as the stake.

I ran on. Why was Sampson not giving chase? (For I was taking for granted that he'd won the scrap.) Perhaps he was, but in the wrong direction. Had I thrown him off already, by taking just one turning? He must know I'd be making for the station. This street was all signs. Without slackening my pace at all, I read 'Boulangerie', 'Glaces', 'Dentiste', 'Pharmacie' . . . but everything was closed, it being so late.

The only thing moving in my line of sight was a clock on an archway but there at the end of the street I saw my goal: the mighty window of the Gare du Nord, the eye looking outwards this time. I ran into the station, clattering on to the circulating area where three men in uniform looked at me, as if to say: 'What do you mean by running inside this palace of ours?' One train was leaving as I looked towards the platforms; the others in the station looked dead, stabled for the night.

Feeling the weight of the guide book in my coat pocket, I took it out, and scrabbled through the pages, finally looking up and asking the three: 'À quelle heure part la premier train . . . for London?'

No answer. You'd have thought one of the bastards would have stirred. I turned about and a lady of middling years in a very broad white hat was standing a little way off and saying, in the most beautiful of voices (meaning an English voice): 'The next boat train for London is in half an hour's time, but it goes from Saint-Lazare. There isn't another from here until 4.30.'

One of the men said a single word, and it sank in slowly with me: 'Métro'. The Métropolitain. The underground railway. They had understood her English better than mine. The human angel was still standing behind the men, still smiling, and not speaking now but pointing with a gloved hand to a spot on the station wall. I ran over, and saw a plan showing . . . a tangle. I looked behind me at the station clock: midnight. I looked again at the map, which was called a plan. The three guards had gone now and so had the lady, but that meant I would be able to work it out for myself. The glass globes stretched away along the empty platforms, and they lit the way north to Calais. I turned again to the map. At the top, at the *north* was 'G. du Nord', but it was joined only to a thin pencil stroke of a Métro line. This was a line not yet existing. But the thick black lines were different. They were more useful, for they *existed*.

Saint-Lazare must also be somewhere to the north if it sent trains to London. I roved immediately right, then left from the spot marked G. du Nord, and there was Saint-Lazare. It was to the left, and connected to a thick black line. The nearest station on the thick black line to Gare du Nord was called . . . well, it began with 'B', and it was the longest French word I'd so far struck.

I was running again through empty streets, heading left from Gare du Nord. I had twenty-five minutes remaining at the outside. I was checked by the sight of two men walking towards me under a metal bridge: one was broad, the other thin. I watched them, putting my hand into my pocket, and touching the folded left-luggage ticket. It seemed a very poor sort of prize. I ought not to have gambled with Lydia's life, but with my own. I had not been gentlemanly.

The two men moved towards me, becoming by degrees ordinary Frenchmen; behind them, an electrical train went over the metal bridge.

I ran towards the bridge – and in fact it was a station, with the ticket offices below. Electrical train, electrical station. All bright lights and a smiling Frencher at the ticket window. 'Saint-Lazare,' I said, reaching into my pocket . . . all my pockets . . . but there were only the two ten-pound notes. I had no French money. I looked around, and I believe that I was searching for the Angel-lady in the broad white hat, but the ticket was there waiting on the window ledge, pushed out by the clerk.

I held up a ten-pound note.

'Just remembered,' I said, 'only English money.'

What he made of that I don't know, because I took the ticket and ran for the stairs that led to the platform. It was the Underground but you went *up* to reach it. The train came in: a line of boxes. It stopped in a heap, the doors flew open with a sneezing sound, and an official walked slowly out from one of the carriages. He watched me carefully as I climbed aboard into a carriage containing four men, all smoking. The train ran along level with the rooftops for a little way, before dipping down into a tunnel. At a station called Villiers I climbed down to look for another line, as I knew I must according to the plan I had seen.

After charging along white tunnels following blue arrows that I didn't understand, I came onto a platform where an electrical train waited. I climbed aboard without any notion of where it was going. One station later, its doors opened on the words 'Saint-Lazare'. I ran up into the mainline station passing a ticket gate with no checker. Into the station: few people, low roof, smoke everywhere. A clock dangled in the smoke: 12.25 – five minutes remaining. I looked at the signs: 'Bar', 'Consigne', 'Billets Internationaux', 'Télégrammes'. I could send a telegram. Who to? The Chief. But he would be in bed asleep, or he might just be dead. It came to me then: the Chief knew my address.

I looked at the signs again: 'Téléphone'. I could not telephone. I was not up to it; did not know how. I looked again at the clock: 12.27. There were some electrical trains in the bays; but smoke floated over from somewhere beyond. I saw the ticket windows. Would they accept English money? 12.28. I could not see the money-changing place. I dashed to the ticket window – Billets Internationaux – and slammed down one of the tenners. 'London,' I gasped out, 'boat train, second-class', and then I added for good measure, 'deck', which I'd heard Sampson say at Charing Cross. The man was writing out the ticket before I'd finished. But this writing out took an age. I looked at the clock. Dead on half past.

The ticket was pushed across to me, and the man began counting out the change. But he stopped half way because he was short of English money; he had to go off into some back room to fetch more. I was gone, flying past the ends of the electrical trains, looking for the source of the smoke and steam. It came from an engine on the furthest platform – an engine that was leaving. I ran after the last carriage; it was moving slowly, and soon I was level with the buffers. I ran on, so that I was level with the rear windows, but now it was all I could do to keep up. The passengers inside were all looking dead ahead. I yelled out, but now I was only level with the back of the rear carriage once again, and then I was staring at the strange looking red lamp on the retreating back of the train.

I came to a stop, and drew a long breath. I looked to the right, and there was the whole business over again: a long train, steam locomotive at the front, pulling forwards. I ran across the platform, and was up and inside in no time. I found a seat next to a woman in Victorian black, who said: 'You're in a rare hurry.'

'This *is* the boat train for England, en't it?' I asked, but it was a daft question, for the very fact we were speaking English proved that it was.

Chapter Twenty-eight

The journey passed in a daze of questions. Was Mike up to making a clean sweep? What was the character of the man? And who was the splitter? If Lund was the culprit . . . why would he try to check an investigation he'd started? Could it be his governor, Parkinson? Could it be the Chief . . . if he'd been left alive after the shooting? I thought of the little clerk: Roberts. Had he worked out that I was a policeman? He'd certainly made me jumpy with his questioning. And was he still somehow in with the gang, despite having the skin of his hands flayed off with burning metal and then being shot at? No, he was finished; he'd been too free of his patter; had talked himself into an early grave. He was shot – I was quite sure of it.

We had now entered a great ravine five times higher than the train. A giant white arrow painted on the left-hand wall showed the way out. Off to the right was an illuminated shed lifted up on piers, so that the engines could go in from underneath. I saw a white, shining church on a hill far above it, and shortly afterwards we were into blackness. I looked down at the Métropolitain ticket that I'd not given in. It said 'Aller et Retour', but I never meant to make the return journey.

I thought of Edwin Lund. All that religious blather, forever talking goody-goody, and going round the houses. He would never act for himself but do all his work by an agent, with little insinuations here and there . . . But to what purpose?

To think of the wife in the same room as Mike was impossible . . . and with all the copies of the reports to hand. How was Mike described in those? Not favourably. The wife had thought she was only marking time by her typewriting: it was something to be going on with before her brain could be really put to some good use. She'd talked at times of turning schoolmistress, which was possible, at a stretch. There were courses to be taken, dragging on for years.

I thought again of the wife, now walking towards me along a sunlit empty street in Halifax . . . only she'd spied me too early, and didn't know where to look, and there hadn't been a great deal else to look *at* in that street, so she'd been in a fix. Well, she had coloured up beautifully by the time we'd come close to.

Whatever had gone on in that hotel room, Sampson would be heading back to the homeland now; coming after me. The gracious white-hatted lady in Gare du Nord had said there was no further boat train until . . . four o'clock was it? I had stolen a march on *him* at least. But just then the train stopped, hard.

I looked at the Victorian party, and she said: 'Strange.'

There was nothing at all to be seen beyond the windows.

After five minutes, I made out a man walking slowly along the tracks with a pipe in his mouth. He carried a lamp, and rain whirled around him. I pointed him out to the lady, who called down something in French, to which he shouted up a reply.

I asked: 'What's the cause of the delay?'

'Oh . . . *France*,' she said with a sigh.

'The boat'll have to wait though, won't it?'

'It will not,' she said. 'They've passengers to collect on the other side . . . Not that they care for those any more than they do for us.'

The train waited, and when half an hour had passed I began to think of Sampson beating me to Thorpe-on-Ouse, leave alone Mike. After three quarters of an hour I began pacing the carriage. I could not sleep, think, stop thinking. Presently, a whistle came from the engine, and the train began to roll forwards, and it continued making twenty miles an hour at the most until a great railway works came in sight, with ranks of half-made engines illuminated by little fires burning about the place. This seemed to give heart to our train, for it at last picked up speed for the run to a spot called Rouen, which was sunk into a stonewalled cutting between two long tunnels. The train stopped here to change engines, and I could see nothing of Rouen but a clock: quarter to four in the morning. The deadest time of all. Within forty-five minutes, Sampson would be able to begin his journey to England if he was so minded.

I believe I slept during the next stretch, and when I woke we were crawling through the town of Dieppe, making for the sound of seagulls in a thin grey light. It took an age but we reached the harbour where a single steamer waited. I climbed down on to a platform that said 'Dieppe – Gare Maritime' and smelt of fish. There was a fish market to the right. I watched a motor taxi crawl through it as I took my place in the queue for the customs house. Nobody ahead of me was being searched, but I was sure I would be stopped, and some contraband found causing new delay.

I came out of the customs house ten minutes later, walking underneath a sign reading: 'Aux Paquebots'. I was quickly aboard. After an hour at sea in clearing light and what might have been moderate rain or spray, I began looking out for the coast of England, and sat there doing so for a further three hours. The crossing was much longer by this route.

I may have slept again, lulled by the thunder of the paddle – in which case I was woken by the snap of a triangular sail unfurled at the bow to bring the boat into what proved to be Newhaven Harbour station, which was entirely made of wood, and in want of a roof.

The London Brighton and South Coast Railway took me, in a dream, to Victoria where, if I'd been feeling brighter, and thinking better, I would have sent a telegram to the post office at Thorpe-on-Ouse, telling the wife to leave the house and not return; instead, I rode the inner Circle to King's Cross where, at midday, I boarded the Scotch Express for York and Edinburgh. Every mile, the swooping telegraph wires told me of the course I ought to have taken. At 3.30, I glimpsed a finger post by the line reading 'York', and just then the first spatterings of rain fell against the window glass, as if the very word had brought it on.

PART SIX

The Hat Box

Chapter Twenty-nine

Rain blew softly at the windows as the train rocked on. The Cathedral of Peterborough came; the red brick of Retford, red brick of Doncaster; the normal world returning by degrees.

And York was still there. We passed under Holgate Bridge, where the mass of points made the train thunder until the right line was found, and then all was peacefulness, rain, the gliding of the train as steam was shut off . . . and Platform Fourteen. I was down long before the train had come to rest, and it was still moving as I pounded over the footbridge. I was the only man running in York station, and I felt foolish – heavy-booted and red-faced like some oaf of a boy, but still I kept on, past the ticket barrier, shouting something about a warrant card, in answer to which I fancied I heard from within the box a low muttering.

I thought: I ought to go back directly to the Police Office, and ask after the Chief. Instead, I ran through the ticket hall, and beyond where there were new posters on either side: 'Spring: Conducted Rambles in Yorkshire'. The Humber – that loyal article – remained at the bicycle stand hung with a thousand raindrops. I yanked it free, leapt on the saddle.

The last two miles of distance . . .

There had been no developments in the gardens of Thorpe-on-Ouse Road. All those householders lived in happy ignorance of the low hotels surrounding the Gare du Nord, the underwater greenness of that Sunday's last bar, the fearful black canyon in which lay the Gare Saint-Lazare. I left the city lamps behind, and on the dark road that ran past the race course, my worst imaginings immediately doubled. The clean sweep was what I had to prevent; the killing of two for the price of one. It could not happen. By picturing the event in my mind's eye I was seeking to make sure of that, because it is known that we are not able to predict the future. What is predicted does not occur.

I stood on the pedals to increase speed, and towards Thorpe-on-Ouse the darkness deepened. A man stood in shadow beneath the clock on the gatehouse of the Archbishop's Palace. He stood quite still as I rattled towards him on the Humber. He wore a bowler with a curled brim; did not look a religious type. I thought of the man I had seen outside the bootmakers, standing in between Scott and William Johnson. Had he been sent to keep a watch? I was now bringing all possibilities across the circle of my imagination.

I turned into the main street, and there were two men in the road, standing as far apart in the darkness as if they were about to fight a duel. I rode between them knowing that something would happen, and it did: one of the two shouted something and began to give chase. I had gone from the beginnings of hope to desperation in a minute. The men were coming fast, I knew as I dropped the Humber at the gate of 16A. The door was ajar and the lights blazing. I stopped for a moment, and waited for the next thing. A scream. It was my worst imaginings and it was fact. Another scream. Bootsteps on the ground beyond the gate; another shout from that direction, another scream from inside the house. I burst through the door, and the question and answer came at once: the typewriter stood on the strong table, but the report copies were not by its side. The room was empty. One loud bang from upstairs, and the wife screaming again as I set foot on the stairs. There may have come a disturbance from the kitchen, but I ignored it, climbing the stairs towards the scream.

I opened the bedroom door and a woman was saying, 'Now I want his shoulder, love, so when I tell you, scream for your life.'

But the wife's scream had come long before the midwife had finished . . . and the room was full of candles. The wife, the midwife, Lillian Backhouse . . . all at their different positions (Lillian holding the wife's right hand), like participants in a religious ceremony as they brought a life into the world.

Hold on a minute: *his* shoulder!

The midwife moved aside, and I saw him come tumbling out of the wife, looking for revenge it seemed to me, as though somebody had played a low trick on him by keeping him cooped up for so long in those cramped quarters.

Lillian Backhouse, who had been holding the wife's hand, was staring at me, and Lydia was looking – *not* staring – across the top of the baby, which was being brought up towards her.

'Jim,' she said, and it was the shortest utterance I ever heard her make.

'The father's here,' said Lillian Backhouse to the midwife, who spun around, looked at me, and turned back towards the baby; she was wiping him down with white towelling. He had a lot of hair at the side, and it seemed to have been combed. I went to the wife, and Lillian Backhouse, indicating me to the midwife with a nod of the head, said, 'We've not seen *this* one since Sunday.'

As the baby was cleaned and turned, I saw him full-face for a moment, and I thought: good; I like him.

'I've been in France,' I said.

'Jesus Christ,' said Lillian Backhouse.

The baby was lying quiet on top of the wife now; they seemed to have been acquainted for years.

'The Chief Inspector came,' said the wife. 'He said not to worry – that you were haring about York after those burglars.'

'You can't hare about a little place like York,' I said.

'Well,' said the wife, '*you* can.'

'So you weren't too worried . . . Did he mention any shooting?'

'What shooting?'

'Just *any*.'

'I'm sure he didn't . . . How do things stand now? Are you clear of these men?'

'That's just it. I don't believe so. We must all remove, right this minute, to Lillian's house.'

I looked at Lillian Backhouse.

'Fine,' she said instantly, no doubt having quickly rejected a lot of other possible remarks. The midwife was staring at me, but the situation cracked when I clapped my hands.

A relay was created on the staircase, with Peter Backhouse and Bill Dixon, keeper of the Fortune (they'd been the two blokes out in the road) at the end of the chain. They went off through the rain with the crib, layette, blankets, shawls and other baby goods; Lillian Backhouse went next carrying the baby in any number of shawls, and I walked the wife around to the Backhouses' place, which was next to the church.

On the way, she said, 'I think we'll call him Harrison.'

'That's Dad's name,' I said.

'I'm quite well aware of that,' she replied.

Half an hour later, with the wife settled at the Backhouse place, I was standing with Peter Backhouse before 16A, to which I had returned for no very good reason beyond feeling I ought not to abandon my house for anything. Over the road, the Fortune of War glowed softly, and Peter Backhouse was anxious to be in there.

He said: 'You ought to fetch Turnbull; he has a gun, you know.' But I didn't want the complication of a toff about the place, and having to speak mannerly when I didn't much feel like doing so.

'Are you coming in for one?' he said, nodding towards the pub. 'You ought to by rights, today of all days.'

'Don't know,' I said. 'Reckon I ought to guard the house.'

'But you're running away from it, en't you?'

'It's all a bit of a tangle,' I said. 'I don't know what's for best.'

Silence for a space.

'Bonny kid, any road,' said Backhouse.

'Bit of all right, he is.'

'Did you see him coming out?' said Backhouse.

I nodded, and Backhouse pulled a face.

I looked along the length of the dark garden. The door of the house had been left ajar, I noticed. 'I think I'll go in for a tick,' I said. 'I might take a pint later on.'

'Just as you like,' said Backhouse, but he was delaying crossing the road.

'I saw a bloke earlier on,' he said, '. . . hanging about near the gateway to the Archbishop's house.'

'OK,' I said, presently.

'Lot of workmen come and go from there,' said Backhouse, '. . . dozens of the buggers, some days.'

I gave him 'Good evening', and he walked over the road.

Chapter Thirty

I walked back to the house, and pushed the door further open. The gas was still up; the typewriter remained on its table, the fire burning low. I tipped on some more coal, picked up the poker, and thrust its end into the heart of the fire, leaving it resting there so that in time it might come in as a weapon. I walked fast into the kitchen and gave a sudden shout, 'Hey!' while watching the back door. I moved towards it, bolted it, stepped back into the parlour. Parting the lace curtains, I looked across the road toward the Fortune of War, and something about the name of the pub made me reach into my pocket for the Charing Cross left-luggage ticket that was worth the thick end of two thousand pounds.

It was not there.

I hunted through every pocket in my suit, looked across the floor, but the thought kept coming back of my scramble for money at the bright, high-level Métropolitain station. It must have tumbled from my pocket then, but the fact didn't seem to signify. The wife was all right – wife *and* baby – and that was all that mattered for the present.

I returned to the parlour, which was too dark or too bright, and no longer at all homely but more like a waiting room, and I sat down in the rocking chair. Outside, the wind was getting up. I could hear trees moving. Half a mile away, I heard a Leeds train going south, fleeing the scene. Over the road, I saw the lights die in the Fortune of War, heard the parting shouts of the drinkers.

I sat on, staring through the window, though it was too dark to see anything. When the knock on the door came it must have been past midnight, and I fancy that it woke me up. The knock came again.

I sat still and counted my heartbeats: one . . . two . . . three.

The knock came once more. I caught up the poker, and turned the handle of the door with it raised above my head.

Standing in the doorway, with the rain blowing into the parlour from behind him, stood the white, maggoty man, Edwin Lund. He wore his porter's suit, the cap without a badge. Over his shoulder was the usual small valise. As he stood in the doorway, he opened the flap and removed from the bag a bundle of muslin.

'The Blocker was about,' he said.

'Mike?' I said. 'Where?'

'Don't fret – I've seen him off.'

'Come again?'

I showed him into the parlour, and he was unwinding the muslin as he walked. Closing the door, I turned towards him.

It was a revolver that lay in his hands, as I may have guessed it would be.

'Take it,' he said.

I lifted the gun still in the muslin, stepped back. I put the poker down on the hearth and placed the gun on the strong table. It was bigger than Sampson's, and the letters 'D.A.' were stamped into it. I nodded at the sofa, and Lund sat down on it. His face glowed like gaslight, and he coughed a little as he settled.

'Did you rat on me, mate?' I said.

He shook his head, coughed a little more. His tunic was dark with rain all about the chest.

'You'd best take that off,' I said.

'Never mind,' he said, shaking his head.

My mind was full of thoughts of death, which was partly the strange effect of the baby coming – for birth makes you think of its opposite.

'You did for the Camerons, didn't you? Out on the cinder track?'

He looked straight ahead, frowning, as though trying to recollect; then he suddenly sat forwards, looking into the fire.

'I daresay there was some mistake . . .' I began, but could not think how to continue.

'It was the trial of my life,' Lund said, after a space, '. . . and I was found wanting.'

What had Sampson said of the Cameron killing? 'I enjoyed that business', or something very like. He had not laid claim to having done it.

'. . . Parable of the Talents,' said Lund, into the fire. 'What do you suppose is the right reading of that Scripture?'

'I wouldn't have the foggiest bloody notion,' I said.

'Would you not?' said Lund, eyeing me now. 'I was just thinking on, because when I first saw this . . .'

He nodded towards the gun on the table.

'. . . It brought to mind that text.'

'And where was that? Where did you first clap eyes on it?'

'Wolverhampton train; first-class compartment. Tucked down a seat back.'

'It just would be in first,' I said.

'St Matthew 25,' said Lund, '"I reap where I sowed not." Six bullets inside, too. I'd have given it over, had anyone come to claim it . . . but nobody ever did.'

'The trick would have been not to *use* it,' I said. 'Why d'you turn it on the Camerons?'

'I was afflicted, and that was God's will . . . but I prayed for relief and it was then that . . .'

'Afflicted? Don't get you.'

He sighed, looked away, saying:

'I must go a little way around the houses.'

'All right,' I said, 'but start now.'

'There was the robbery at our place – Lost Luggage Office. You know of it.'

'You didn't want to speak of it directly . . . but you meant that I should find out, didn't you?'

'After a fashion.'

'Who was behind it?'

'Don't know, but I should think the Brains and the Blocker. They're a bad lot; they haunt the railway, and there've been other robberies similar.'

'Well, I reckon it *was* them,' I said, 'but they're not independent units, those blokes. Their names are Miles Hopkins and Mike . . . summat . . . And they have a governor.'

'Big fellow? Well turned-out?'

'That's it.'

'I've seen him. He must be smarter than the Brains, even.'

'No. He leads by force of character . . . And he works by buying blokes off. Servants of the railway; put-up jobs, do you see? If you didn't have a hand in the lost-luggage theft, then it must have been your governor, Parkinson.'

Lund shook his head again.

'He was all out to find who had done it, because he knew he was suspected of the business himself . . . Parkinson's God-fearing. He wouldn't have done it.'

'You're God-fearing,' I said, 'and you did worse.'

Lund looked keenly at the fire, searching there.

'Parkinson takes a drink,' I said.

'He's church, not chapel. They have a freer hand there.'

'And he's not over-friendly to you.'

'We haven't passed a word since the robbery.'

'You're just trying not to throw blame. Parkinson's crooked, and that's all about it; otherwise how would they have opened the safe?'

'That safe came to us six month back from another place.'

'Where?'

Lund looked at me once again.

'Station Hotel.'

I thought of Mariner, the suicide. Perhaps he had a different connection to Sampson, another reason to regret his own actions.

Lund sat further forwards, watching the action of the wind on the fire. Did he suppose I lived here alone? He'd never asked after my wife, leave alone any child. But wives and children were nothing in his way. The wind was increasing outside, and I thought: we might be in for another windrush, and I knew that somehow all of this – the rising wind and the story that Lund was telling – was all the baby's doing.

Lund was saying to the fire:

'Parkinson knew me for a watchful sort; knew I had by heart the numbers that open the safe. He put word out that I'd done it; told all comers, and he honestly believed it, too.'

'And the Camerons got wind?'

'They let on they thought that I'd been involved somehow . . . And they would ask me for money; said they would go to the Company brass or to the police if I didn't pay it over.'

'How much did you give them?'

'A good deal. They would follow me home after work, and they would have ten bob off me every time . . . I couldn't risk losing my position.'

I looked at the cap beside him, at the space where the

badge ought to have been. He'd be on rather less than a pound a week wages.

'That night, 26 January, I went down Leeman Road – try and throw them off. But they came after me, and at last I said I would give no more money.'

'And what did they say to that?'

'It was the straight-haired one did the talking. The other was . . . queer. The straight-haired one said, "Well then, it comes down to a fight." The other one, the mental-case . . . he grabbed me, started fairly strangling me, and the other pitched in. I reached into the bag, and the gun was in my hand. I saw the flash in the sky.'

'It was the planet Mercury,' I said, 'what did you think? Star in the bloody East?'

That checked him.

'You're over-keen on tales from the Scriptures,' I said. 'Have you ever thought that you might find an argument for owt in the Bible . . . I mean, it *is* rather a jumble.'

'It is God's book,' said Lund, looking directly at me once more. '. . . It's the word of God, and if you want to call that a jumble, that's your look-out. I fired once, and that was the weird one settled, but then the other was at me with a knife.'

'You fired again?'

He nodded.

Half a mile off, another train went past but in the opposite direction, York-bound; the wind in reverse.

'Well,' I said, 'what do you reckon on doing now?'

'I must atone, and bear all the consequences.'

'You mean to own up?'

'Mean to?' he said. 'I've just done it.'

I shook my head.

'I'd best talk to the Chief about it. Chief Inspector Weather-ill, who's my governor . . . Have you spoken with a minister?'

'We don't hold with confession,' he said. 'You should know that,' and for the first time since I'd known him, he seemed angry.

'I'm not chapel,' I said. 'I'm not anything in particular.'

'The minister would say I must admit to it. He could do nothing but.'

'You may very well swing for it.'

'I dare say. That's part of the penalty.'

'I'd have thought it was the whole of it.'

He shook his head.

'Only part – and the least part.'

'Why did you take me along to see the pick-pocketing on the London Express . . . It would have been the Monday after, wouldn't it?'

'It was a start, but only half measures – because I could not quite see the way to go.'

'You knew I'd come to the lost-luggage business, and you knew I'd come to the Camerons' murder. You were setting me to trace out a crime that you'd committed.'

'Well,' he said. 'I thought you might get to it in time, but in the end, I've brought you to it myself.'

Silence for a space.

'Listen,' I said. 'You'll have heard about the robbery in the roundhouse. That was more of their doing. I fled to Paris with Sampson and Hopkins – had to do it to keep cover. While I was over there, Mike – the Blocker – spoke by telephone to Miles Hopkins, giving me away as a copper. Now who let on to Mike?'

'Parkinson.'

Silence again.

'He *must* be a wrong 'un,' I said.

'He saw me talking to you outside the Central Chapel. His church is St Saviour's, a little further along in the same street. He already knew you for a detective . . .'

'How?'

'Not sure of that. Did they know in the Institute?'

'The barmaid knew; I'd just had a set-to with the Camerons myself in there . . . ended by cautioning the pair of 'em.'

Lund stood up from the sofa, cap in hand.

'Parkinson believed I was making complaints to you against him, letting on that he'd been behind it all. Monday last, he thought I was out on the platforms, but I was in the back of the office. I heard him telephoning the police station.'

'Tower Street?'

Lund nodded.

'"The proper lot", as he thinks. He wanted to know if he was being investigated, asked to speak to Constable . . . can't recall the name. He's the copper who patrols past the police station.'

'That's the Five Pound Man . . . and he's fucking bent.'

'Aye,' said Lund. 'I know he's not right.'

'That's why you're here,' I said.

'Later that day,' Lund went on, 'Parkinson had a confab with him. I reckon that's how your name was given out.'

'Name *and* address.'

'That's in the lost-property ledger as well. Parkinson would've seen no harm in passing it on.'

I tried to reason it out. On Sunday, Parkinson had seen me talking to Lund in St Saviourgate, and he knew I was a detective. On Monday, he telephoned Mr Five Pounds, the bent copper (although Parkinson did not know he was bent), in order to ask outright whether he was being hunted up for the lost-luggage burglary. Mr Five Pounds would then have asked him for all details of the detective mentioned – meaning myself. He must then have spoken to the one member of the band left in York, namely Mike, who in turn spoke over the telephone to Miles Hopkins, when Hopkins was in Calais.

Hopkins had then kept back from Valentine Sampson what Mike had told him. I wondered whether Mike and Hopkins had immediately connected the name Stringer with Allan Appleby. Perhaps not. Any description of me passed on by Parkinson would not have included the eye-glasses, for Parkinson had to my knowledge never seen me in them. Perhaps there had remained in Hopkins's mind a little doubt about the identity of Appleby and Stringer. He was not sure of this until he put his long finger clean through the spectacle frames on the train to Paris, and by then he had decided to somehow make use of me.

I looked again at Lund; he was staring at me with bright eyes.

'Your missus is quite safe, is she? And the bairn? I saw you all trooping off to the house near the church.'

He missed nothing. Had he placed my *Railway Magazines* beside my bicycle to keep me away from Parkinson – the man ever on the lookout for treachery?

A thought came to me.

'Did Mike see where we all went?

Lund shook his head.

'Reckon he was long gone by then.'

Mike's heart had not been in the business. He was not one to act alone, in any case.

We waited, listening to the wind, neither with the energy to speak.

At last, Lund said: 'Is there a divinity shaping life?'

'Well, you ought to know, mate.'

Silence in the parlour; wind running on outside.

'. . . Hold on a tick,' I said, and I darted into the kitchen to fetch the bottle of beer I'd been in need of for some little while past. When I returned, Lund was gone, and the gun with him.

Chapter Thirty-one

When I came to the station at eight the next morning (after my usual hour) I shot the Humber hard into the bicycle rack, for I had seen the Chief heading past the booking halls in his long coat. He looked, all of a sudden, like a music-hall turn: two men under a single giant coat, the one on the shoulders of the other.

We quickly fell in step together without any greeting, although I might have said, 'Sir', and the Chief might have said, 'You'll have had a time of it, then.' I started directly in on my story, having sat awake all night in the Backhouses' parlour (with the baby crying overhead, like a new variation on the sound of the wind), there working out a version that excluded Lund and his confession, because I had decided I would not see him hanged for the killing of the Camerons.

'The job happened directly, sir,' I said, as we went on to Platform Four, the Chief showing his warrant card to the ticket man, '. . . straightaway on the Sunday night with no further plotting.'

'Don't I bloody know it,' said the Chief, turning left, so that we were approaching the Police Office. The Chief's big, prizefighting face looked raw. His nose was *not* the same as when I'd seen him last, although his 'tache was perfect as ever – the one part of his features to have been drawn with a ruler.

'You were sent for, I know. I saw you shooting at us.'

'What about the bastard shooting at *me*? He has it coming, I bloody tell you. Where is he this bloody *minute*?'

The Chief walked on fast, and we were now passing the Police Office. The bay platform, number Three, was empty in front of it, the Fish Special having long since come and gone.

'The one firing was Valentine Sampson.'

'Joseph Howard Vincent,' said the Chief, striding on, not at all surprised. Evidently the two were one, as far as he was concerned.

'I never knew you were passed to use a gun, sir,' I said. 'Do you have a special certificate?'

'What I have is the key to the bloody armoury cupboard.'

'I saw you lying down in the four-foot, sir – thought you were done for.'

No reply to that from the Chief, for of course he'd lost dignity by playing dead in the soot and muck that lay between the rails. I wondered what had become of his moustache during that episode. We walked on. Beyond the south end of the platform stood the roundhouse, where the whole thing had gone off two days before. An engine in steam stood outside, like a peaceful cottage with a fire in the grate, and it was as though nothing that had happened there mattered in the least.

'What became of the goods clerk? Roberts?'

'He's said a little.'

'Rum is that,' I said, 'because he did nothing *but* talk beforehand . . . How are his hands?'

'Burnt,' said the Chief. 'What happened there?'

We had changed course to the left, and were now going down the stone staircase next to the Left Luggage Office.

'Sampson pitched hot metal at him,' I said as the weak light of the station left us, '. . . from the cut safe.'

'Right,' said the Chief. It was just another occurrence to him.

The sound of our boots changed as we came off the stairs and began walking along the rough, dark passage that led to the underneath of Platform Fourteen, the furthest limit of the station. Only three gas lamps lit the way, and they were for some reason numbered 1, 2 and 3.

'Why are we down here, sir?' I asked, as we began walking between lamps number one and two.

'Because no bugger else is,' said the Chief.

He still wanted me kept out of sight.

I asked: 'Who uses this, now the footbridge is built?'

'Gloomy sorts,' said the Chief.

In that tunnel, the station sounds came to us in a strange way – like one mighty, never-ending disturbance. We walked up and down, and I told the Chief all about what had happened in the roundhouse. When I'd about got to the end of that episode, he said, 'Then, I expect you were drawn half over York as they looked for hiding places.'

'Half over France, more like,' I said, and then I gave him *that* part of the story. He was surprised at none of it, and when I came to speak of the Hôtel des Artistes, I half expected him to say, 'I know that place pretty well', and to make some remark on the breakfast.

When I got on to how someone – not named, because the question of Parkinson was too close to the question of Lund – had given me away to Mike, we were under gas lamp number three, and there we stayed as I raced on, trying to get it all done with, but worried by the strange expressions that would fly across the Chief's face, which seemed to suggest that I'd done things wrong, or just described things in not quite the right way, or, worse still, that I was missing things out. Partly out of guilt at holding back Lund's confession, I was anxious to give the Chief all the other information I could. I told him all about the business with the tickets – admitting losing the Charing Cross one (at which he might have given a sort of sigh) – and said he should have men sent immediately to the left-luggage place there, just in case Sampson or Hopkins should try to get the kitbag by persuasion or main force. I gave an account of the sighting of a mysterious stranger in Thorpe-on-Ouse; and went along with the truth so far as to say that I was certain it had been Mike. I ended by asking for a police guard to be put outside the Backhouse place in Thorpe-on-Ouse.

The Chief looked at me carefully for a moment. Then he said:

'As I told you, Roberts, the goods clerk, has not been entirely silent.'

'Right,' I said. 'Good. What does he think of me? Allan Appleby. Worst villain that ever stepped.'

'He couldn't make you out, though he never said much on that score. One thing he was most anxious to get over . . . Sampson, alias John Howard Vincent, admitted to killing the Camerons in his hearing. Now did you hear the same, because it'll go hard with him if we ever lay hands on the bugger?'

'He gave the impression he'd done for the pair of 'em,' I said, and I coloured up as I said it. I knew I was in queer.

'I had the idea you weren't that bothered about the Cameron murders, sir,' I added. 'Tower Street matter, you said.'

'Aye, it was, but now they've made us a present of it, having seen they've no earthly chance of solving it.'

I cursed myself for being so foolish as to think that I might cut what Lund had said the night before out of my story; and I went a little way towards repeating what he'd told me.

'I have my suspicions of the constable who walks by the station,' I said. 'It's only an inkling, so I left it out of my account just now, but I believe I saw him talking to the bad blokes over in the Grapes just before the roundhouse job.'

The Chief was silent.

'What are you going to do, sir?' I said, at which the Chief asked in turn: 'What day is it today?'

'Tuesday,' I said.

'First things first . . .' he said, and he produced a brandy flask that I'd always somehow known would be lodged in his inside pocket.

'. . . What're you going to call the boy?'

'The wife's after calling him Harrison, which is my dad's name.'

I took a belt on the brandy.

'Then he'll be Harry,' said the Chief.

'Yes,' I said.

So we were agreed on that.

The Chief took another brandy go, and said, 'I'll have a watch put on the house at Thorpe – that will be done direct-ly. It will be lads from Fulford.'

Fulford was just across the river from Thorpe-on-Ouse. I was glad it would not be Tower Street men.

'There'll be a guard posted at the Left Luggage Office in Charing Cross . . . and bulletins'll be sent to all Channel ports,' the Chief added, just as if the drink had given him the idea, which it might well have. 'There'll be new notices put in the *Police Gazette*, and I'll have a quiet word at Tower Street about the copper you mentioned.'

'I would have Mike run in while you're at it . . . before he comes looking for me again. He works at the Black Swan, Coney Street . . . outdoor porter, I think.'

'Right you are,' said the Chief.

'Can I start to book in at the office as normal?'

'Best not,' said the Chief, '. . . not with the bad lads still at large, but I'll see you there at the usual time tomorrow. Meanwhile start your report.'

He leant back against the tunnel wall, breathing heavily through his moustache before taking another couple of brandy goes. He looked ill.

'I'll give you this: you've stuck with it, lad,' he said, which made me feel worse about my secrecy over Lund.

There came at that moment a scuffle of boots at the far end of the tunnel. The figure approached in the gloom, with all the strange, station sounds overhead. They might have been underwater. As he came by lamp number one, I saw that it was the Lad, the telegraph boy, grinning all around his head as usual, and carrying telegram forms. When he was passing under lamp number two, the Chief called to him, 'Know all the dodges, don't you?'

The Lad said: 'Have you seen the weather, sir? Tippling down, it is.'

'There's a roof on this station, you might have noticed,' said the Chief.

'There is,' said the Lad, 'but it leaks.'

Chapter Thirty-two

Walking back towards the Humber, I caught sight of Lund walking between the booking offices, carrying a tiger-skin trunk. Was I looking at a killer? It was very hard to credit, but I believed so. Ought I to risk a word? I wore my bad suit, but not the glasses. I said his name in an under-breath while walking a little way to the right-hand side of him. He looked towards me, sad as before.

'You spoken to your governor yet?' he said.

'Aye,' I said. 'He'll call you in for an interview.'

He stopped dead. Behind him was another new Company poster: 'North Eastern Railway to the Yorkshire Coast: Breezy, Bracing.' There was a picture of a ship, half sunk, as it seemed, in rough seas.

'But what proof is there that you did it?' I said.

'I have the gun,' said Lund, although he did not have the valise with him, 'and the bullets will be shown to match.'

'You might need the bloody thing again if Mike comes after you.'

'I'll never lay hands on it again, though I have it stowed away safely.'

'Does Mike know where you live?'

He shrugged.

'Reckon not. I en't bothered either way.'

I read the label on the tiger-skin trunk: 'Dawkins, New

Malden'. What earthly fucking use was that? Some folk deserved to lose things.

Lund said: 'The Chief Inspector means to come over to the office, does he?'

'Aye,' I said.

'When?'

'Today,' I said. 'Today or tomorrow.'

He frowned, as well he might've.

I said: 'It's a queer going-on, you know . . . ?'

'I must seek my peace,' said Lund, walking on with the trunk, and leaving me behind. I drifted over towards the Humber, revolving the now familiar questions: did I believe Lund's confession to be true? Yes. Did I think he ought to swing for the murder of the Camerons? No. Would I be in the shit if it came out that I had kept from the Chief knowledge of Lund and his doings? Yes. Was Lund determined to carry on with his confession, taking it out of my hands if necessary? Yes. Was not Sampson, rather than God, the true cause of all Lund's affliction and the true cause, besides, of the Cameron killings? He was.

I biked about York in aimless fashion, passing the Big Coach in Nessgate, passing along Clifford Street with the Tower Street copper shop to the right, slowly skirting the twenty-foot black wall that bounded Clifford's Tower, the Castle, Court House and Prison. It seemed a cheek to ride such a comical machine as a bicycle in the shadow of that wall, although the Yorkies rattled back and forth quite happily in their traps and wagonettes. The sky was white, and the brown river was up. It wasn't raining at that moment but it would do soon. I had every confidence that it would do soon.

I biked over Skeldergate Bridge watching the smoke coming out of the glass-works chimneys and falling away to the right. Then I doubled back over the bridge, hitting Clemen-thorpe, and the smell of Terry's, the second confectionery works after Rowntree's: they might make sweets in there, but it was a factory all right, with its due allowance of red brick and smoke.

I pedalled into Thorpe-on-Ouse keeping my eyes skinned, but I could tell that this was how the village looked when all was well: empty. I was at the Backhouses' place in time for dinner – not that there was any dinner. Two coppers sat in the scullery, and they'd finished the lot. They were playing cards; looked decent sorts. Peter wasn't at home, so I had Lillian to contend with. She said the wife was asleep with the baby upstairs, and I looked in on them even though Lillian had said I mustn't.

Returning to the scullery, I asked the general company, 'No one's seen any strange men about, I take it?' and Lillian Backhouse said, 'Not 'til you pitched up.'

I was not sure whether she believed I stood in any danger at all, and I wondered whether the coppers did either. What did they know of my adventures? They took pride in not letting on.

I walked out of the house, and climbed back on the Humber. I dawdled about near the gateway to the Archbishop's Palace, turning the bike in ever tighter circles, thinking, until I locked the front wheel, and came off. I picked myself up – no harm done – and pedalled off to the Fortune of War.

Peter Backhouse was in there, and he stood me a pint. Beyond the window, one of the masters at the village school was leading a class out towards a river ramble; they were meant to be walking sober-sided crocodile fashion, but it was a little cavalcade going past. I chatted to Backhouse for a while, and as I did so, I worked out that Dixon was exchanging a few words from behind the bar with a bloke drinking in the parlour. I stood up, pushed through the door of the smoking room, and looked hard at the stranger in the parlour. He had a spirit glass in his hand; he was nobody I knew.

I sat on with Backhouse, drinking Smith's, and the beer did its work of lessening my nervousness by degrees. Backhouse then returned to his graft in the churchyard, and I to his home – where the coppers were now roaming about the garden, each in a world of his own – and the wife let me pick up the baby. Little Harry cried as soon as I did so, and I wondered whether I would be out with him for ever, having missed his first hours. He was small, as Dad had feared, and this was on account of him coming early, but that didn't bother me. To my mind the trouble with most babies was that they were a sight too *big*. I watched his hands; you'd think that somebody had paired and polished his nails, they were so dainty.

I slept a little in the afternoon, patrolled the village come nightfall in the soft rain with my cap pulled low, keeping on the kee-vee, and feeling a confounded twit, before returning to the Fortune with Backhouse. That night, I hardly slept again, what with the worry of all, the night-time movements of the many Backhouse children, the baby refusing to settle, and the coming and going of the police guards, who changed shifts in the small hours.

At four in the morning I dressed and walked back to 16A. Opening the front door, I whispered 'Sampson? Hopkins?' For I was now of a mind that they might have reached an accommodation, and remained together. If so, would they bother travelling hundreds of miles to settle my hash? And as for their confederate, Mike . . . I was not quite so vexed about him. I had him down as a man for a nasty assault, but killing was not his line.

The thing was the left-luggage ticket though. They would come for the ticket, which I would not be able to hand over.

Feeling like a burglar in my own home, I put on my good suit, collected up the Swan pen that Dad had given me, some of the blank papers I'd had from the Chief, and the book I'd lifted in Calais: *Paris and its Environs*. In the low gaslight, I opened a page haphazardly: 'The stranger visiting Paris for the first time, and anxious that his first impression of the city should be as striking as possible, cannot do better than a walk from the Louvre to the Place de la Concorde.' I closed the book and looked at the gold lettering on the cover. It was like a souvenir from a dream.

I stepped out of the house, locking the door behind me, and rode the Humber through the blue darkness to the station. There was nobody at the barrier. A long black coal train was rolling through, and when it had passed, I saw the Night Station Manager across the way on Platform Five, holding his black top hat in his hands like a mourner at a funeral. He turned away as I made for the Police Office.

Inside, I turned up the gas, lit the stove, put the kettle on to boil. I fished out some carbons from the drawer of Shilli-to's desk, took up the Swan pen and, beginning 'Special Report' and 'Persons Wanted', set about my account of the roundhouse robbery and the flight to Paris.

I had brought along *Paris and its Environs* so as to get the spellings of some of the French words right, but after the best part of an hour I was still describing events in the round-house. Knowing the young Company man who'd come along with us only as 'Tim', I did my best to describe his looks, with a funny feeling of digging the man's grave as I went about it. Did I want them to see him run-in? Yes and no. I'd liked him in a way, and he hadn't seemed a violent sort.

I had a second hesitation as I came to recall just what

Sampson had said in the roundhouse about the killing of the Camerons. The Chief wanted Sampson charged with their murder, should he ever be found. This was because Sampson had shot at the Chief and made him lie down between the tracks. It was one thing to keep back Lund's confession, but it would be another again to lie in writing about what I'd heard, with the words repeated on the carbon beneath . . . And then stand to it all in court.

Roberts, the Clerk, had it wrong. Sampson had said 'I enjoyed that business', meaning he enjoyed hearing of it or reading of it – at least so I believed, and I would write my account accordingly, letting people make what they would of his words. But in fact I wrote nothing. Instead, I sat back and thought again of all the crimes of Sampson, beginning with the ones I suspected him of (he had somehow caused the hotel man, Mariner, to make away with himself; he had very likely killed the two detectives at Victoria), and then running on to the ones I was witness to, which included railway trespass at the lowest, attempted murder of the Chief Inspector at the highest. But you could not swing for attempt. Why should that concern me either way? Was my goal the execution of Valentine Sampson? It would have been nearer the mark to say that my goal was the saving of Lund, but unfortunately the two could not go together.

I stood up and made another pot of tea. I looked at what I now knew to be the armoury cupboard, tried the door – locked, of course. I wandered over to the mantel, looking at the photograph of the Grimsby Dock Police Football team of 1905. Did every man in that team suffer the same vexation as me over police work? You would not have thought it from their faces. I went back to the desk and picked up *Paris and its Environs*. On the second page, I read 'A Railway Map of France will be found at the end of the book', and I turned to the map, where the English Channel was put down as 'La Manche'. The lines shown extended a good way beyond France, and the sea routes to England from Belgium and Holland were also drawn in. As I looked at the map with an idea dawning, a mighty noise rose within the Police Office, the sound of a wind or a great wave rolling into shore.

I stepped through the outer door as the sound rose to its highest pitch, and there, ten feet away and leaking steam, stood the engine that had brought in the fish special from Hull. Four doors opened along the three carriages, and half a dozen unimportant people walked away to fade into the city of York. After a space, another passenger climbed down in a Homburg hat and Norfolk jacket; he placed a portmanteau on the ground as another man approached him. The gentry in from Hull was Sampson, and he was being met by Mike. Of Hopkins there was no sign, and that was because Sampson had put his lights out.

Mike stood before Sampson; I was looking at Mike's wide back. He was up to his old tricks: blocking . . . although he didn't know that he was standing between me and his governor. At the very moment that I stepped back towards the Police Office, Mike turned aside, great head dipped low under his low, wide cap, and Sampson was looking directly at me, revolver in hand.

He advanced upon me, gun in one hand, portmanteau in the other. A long article, half muffled in rags rested on top of the portmanteau. Beyond him, at the far end of the train, the fish boxes were down, but not attended to on the platform, which was quite deserted. The engine was now retreating beside the train it had brought in a moment before; it would be coupled at the opposite end presently. An engine going backwards . . . It was a crazy spectacle, like time itself in reverse.

Sampson, still walking forwards, said: 'You know what

I've come looking for, little Allan.'

'The left-luggage ticket?' I said, sounding as if I was trying to be helpful, and so sounding daft.

He continued to advance. He had travelled to Hull by steamer, crossing the North Sea, and missing the Channel ports.

'Hopkins said you had it. Whether he put you up to it, I don't know. But he came at me with a fucking cutter in his hand . . .'

His voice went high as he said those final words. Even now, he couldn't credit it. But of course . . . the knife had been meant only to put the wind up me. I was backing towards the door of the Police Office.

'Where's Miles?' I said, for some reason.

Sampson shook his head.

'Gone case, little Allan,' he said.

I thought of the tracks running below the window of the hotel room in Paris, the word 'Vins' painted on the wall of that great French hole.

Sampson said: 'One hour I sat there looking down, little Allan . . . Waiting for a train to roll over him . . . Waited in vain, too.'

'Well, it was late on,' I said.

My back was against the door of the Police Office.

Sampson was shaking his head once more.

'Long time to wait for nothing to happen,' he said.

'Oh, I don't know,' I said. 'I reckon it's about average.'

'Hopkins told me you were a copper, in which case the ticket may be out of your hands, resting in a box marked "Evidence". Or then again, little Allan, you might just have held on to it, knowing you'd touch for a fortune just by taking a trip to London . . . And do you know something, little Allan? I'm having difficulty trying to decide which of those two actions would be the most cuntish?'

It was only then the light fell from his eyes.

'I don't have the ticket,' I said.

I made my breakaway at that moment, having realised that the article in the portmanteau was an axe. How he had put his hands on such a thing on the way in from Hull, I could not have said. Perhaps Mike had handed it to him as he stepped from the train. At any rate, it meant there might be worse in store than a bullet in the brain.

I was running as I had these thoughts, and I was not my present self as I ran, but a young boy caught in a thunder-storm on the beach at Baytown, fleeing the one lightning bolt that would do me, while the lugger I'd been watching out to sea rocked on the waves and waited.

The bullet came into my back, pushing me forward, so that I flew a little way before landing in darkness.

Chapter Thirty-three

It was the rumbling boots of the railway clerks that brought me back to the world. They were coming down off the footbridge, and swerving away as they caught sight of me. I was lying on the hardest of beds: Platform Four, but with half a dozen blankets placed over me. And I was shivering. A train came in over the way on Platform Five, and I had the notion that *it* was shivering too. The sky was bright blue, spring-like beyond the roof glass miles above me, but my teeth were chattering.

Some of the clerks looked sidelong at me as they raced towards the ticket gates. What were they thinking? Passenger in bother? Company man in bother? Either way, the Company would deal with it. The right side of me, I realised, wasn't somehow keeping up with the left.

The Stationmaster was standing a little way off talking to a station official I did not know. I noticed him before I saw the Chief, even though the Chief was closer. He was talking to another stranger, and all these men were different from me, for they were all *standing*. I put my hand under the blanket towards my chest, feeling as if they must have placed a hot bottle or hot brick there, but there was none to be found and when I removed my hand, I saw and tasted blood at the same time; I turned my head to try to spit away the blood, and that brought the second stranger kneeling down beside me. I tried to look again at my hand, for it had been whiter than I had ever known it before, and I wanted to marvel again at the colour. I knew there was a bullet in me, and I badly wanted it out.

Somebody, another upright person I didn't know, was coming forwards from the refreshment rooms, carrying a glass; it was handed to the man kneeling beside me, who lifted my head and made me drink; it was warm wine, which mixed with the warm blood in my mouth. Other people came racing forwards now, ambulance attendants, carrying a stretcher. As they lifted me, and the blankets slid away, a great commotion broke out in my body, and I was shaking rather than shivering; it took them all aback, I could tell, and I tried to apologise for it, but could not control my speech, so that the word 'sorry' was more like 'surround'. I also tried to ask for immediate extra-special protection for the wife – for yet more men to be posted outside the house near the church at Thorpe-on-Ouse, and I believed that the message got through. At the moment they hoisted me, a train came in on Platform Four, and I caught a glimpse of my reflection – head bandaged, I had not bargained on that – and the mortified faces streaming by at the carriage windows.

I was taken by fast-trotting horse to the County Hospital; I tried to say to one of the attendants that I had never expected to go so fast along Monkgate while flat on my back, but that was quite beyond me. It bothered me that nobody spoke back, even so. I was about to try again as we flew along the hospital drive but it suddenly came to me that I'd done a great piss in my trousers, and that silenced me.

I was whirled about the whiteness of the hospital on a trolley, catching some of the words passed between the people moving about me: 'gunshot', 'concussion of the brain', 'fixity of the chest' and 'heart' and 'great vessels'. In a tiny, crowded room a needle came towards me, and somebody was good enough to say 'ether' as they put it in. It put me into a daze, not right out, and I was quite aware of my head being shaved by a very fast woman barber, and then painted, while at the same time my suit was removed, and my under-shirt cut by mighty shears that moved from my waist to my neck in three great bites. A man entered the room whom I knew straightaway to be the top man, for he moved a little slower than all of the others. He was looking at my ribs, and I thought I was supposed to be looking too, and I raised my head like an idiot to see an open eye there on my chest. The man pushed my head down, and ordered me to be turned over, where he looked at my back, saying some words I did not care for, like 'lodged bullet', 'traversed the whole thick-ness of the chest'. Then the bandage was unwound from my head, and I don't believe that he liked the look of that either. I saw the Chief in the room, in his long coat as ever. But not for long, and soon a pair of fat India rubber lips came towards me and put an evil-smelling kiss on my whole face that sent me sinking into the bed below with all the voices roundabout becoming bent out of true.

The top medical man appeared out of nowhere some time later; he was carrying something small and silvery. I was in a long dark room, and there were other people there, all in beds and at the head of each bed was a shuttered window. The man sat on my bed, and his name came out: Kenneth Munroe; we had a conversation, but I cannot recall it, except that he made it clear the wife was quite safe. He returned again some time later, when I was still in the same place, with all the beds, and the closed shutters as before, but this time sunlight was fighting to come through them. He carried the silver object, also as before, and he placed it in my hand. He was smiling a very beautiful sort of smile, but there was a better one behind him: the wife, without the baby . . . free of the baby. She watched me as Kenneth Munroe said, 'These are for you', in words as clear as a bell. I raised my hand and saw a pair of forceps. His speech ran on just as clearly, like a stream, but he spoke a little faster than I could understand.

'Bullet forceps,' he said, '. . . they grip the bullet with great force . . . seize it, you know, with no entanglement of the soft parts . . . smoothly rounded blades as you see . . . It is the extractor of preference for the British army.'

Everybody – for there were some more people around the bed by now – waited as I said, 'It is a very pretty instrument.'

'Thank you,' said Kenneth Munroe, 'they are constructed to my own design.'

He said that I might keep them, adding, as he rose from the bed, and the wife replaced him there, that he had many more besides.

'Where's the baby?' I said, and the wife said, 'Oh, he's . . .'

But I had fallen back to sleep already.

When I woke I had my hand to my head, feeling the bandage. I saw the bullet extractors on the cabinet beside me, and there was a thing like a metal tooth beside them: their trophy, the bullet itself. Kenneth Munroe was there again, and now the shutters had won their fight against the light outside; it was night time, the gas low in the long room. He explained that I had taken a bullet to a lung; it had gone clean through without causing over-much damage.

'If you *must* be shot,' he said, 'be shot in a lung.'

But there had been worse bother higher up. I had fractured my skull on falling and a fragment of bone had become lodged in the crack, like a penny in a 'Try Your Weight' machine, and Kenneth Munroe proudly told me that he had fished it out with his little fingernail. There had been no compression of the brain, and after telling me this he walked away into the darkness once again.

The bullet had notched a rib, and my chest was strapped. I was put on a low diet, and the next little while was all gruel, beef tea, and darkness followed by the swelling light at the shuttered windows. I would cough some blood from time to time, but it was always quickly wiped away by the nurse, as though it was an embarrassment over dinner and nothing more. I was in the room for head cases rather than lung cases, and here the rules were darkness, perfect quiet and regular dreams of Paris and babies.

After a while, I became more aware of York beyond the shutters: trotting horses in the far distance, faint cries of the drivers and church bells. The Chief came with two cigars, a bottle of John Smith's, a pen – the Swan – and with my report, which he said I might finish in due course. He would not speak about the manhunt that was going on across the city. It would agitate me too much. When he went away, the cigars were removed without a word by the nurse, although she opened the beer for me.

. . . But I couldn't face it.

A little while later, I drank it, flat, while sitting up and continuing with the report, writing at a lick, and setting down all of Sampson's words just as I remembered them, and putting the confession of Lund quite out of my mind, except to wonder whether he had perhaps made it to The Chief himself by now . . . But the matter did not seem very pressing for it was now all in the same category as the dreams.

The wife returned at some point. She kissed me, and I gave her the report. She read it on my bed, the press of her body making me realise I needed a fuck.

'Firstly,' she said, when she'd finished, 'you can't spell.'

'Can't spell what?'

'Anything.'

'Can't spell *hardly* anything, you mean.'

'Second of all,' she continued, 'you must send the London police to the left-luggage place in Charing Cross Station because I'm sure he means to collect the money he left there.'

'We've already done that,' I said with a grin.

'Well then . . .' said the wife, '. . . I thought you would've.'

She coloured up (for she'd thought nothing of the sort).

It was night time, no light at the shutter edges, when the Chief came again. He looked sad, and placed a large brown paper sleeve on my bed. Inside was a photograph. I began to pull it free, and stopped halfway, but he nodded at me to continue.

The photograph showed a long white head sleeping in a hat box. It was turned a little to one side, just as if resting between the long spells of hard work that might be the lot of a head trying to make its way in the world without benefit of a body. Around it was blood, but not the *colour* of blood.

I sat upright, and stared at the Chief, who said, 'Three of his fingers were found in the hat box besides', at which the quantity of beef tea that had been set whirling within me sprang from my mouth. I had done this to Lund. As far as Sampson and Mike were concerned, he and I were in league. What had they asked and not been told three times? Had they, even with a manhunt going on, come by 16A and, finding it empty, tried to discover the house to which I had removed – the place where the ticket might be? Or where, failing that, the clean sweep might be made as a settling of accounts?

The nurse came and took away the stained top cover as the Chief waited with hands in his pockets.

'Can we get a nip of something?' he said.

She shook her head, walking away, adding that if we were to talk, we must do it in whispers.

As she moved off, the Chief muttered, 'I have my hip flask about me . . .' before nodding at the photograph and continuing more loudly, 'The box was found on Platform Six yesterday, and carried over to the Lost Luggage Office by a porter.'

'Just as it was meant to be,' I said.

'Lund had been missing for three days,' said the Chief. 'Whether they came upon him at his home, about the station or somewhere in between, I couldn't say.'

'He put me on to the whole investigation,' I said, 'out of conscience at what he'd done.'

The Chief said nothing.

'. . . He killed the Camerons,' I went on. 'He let on to me, but I kept it back because I didn't want to see him swing.'

I repeated all of Lund's confession to the Chief, and he lost interest by degrees as I did so. He was looking down at his boots as I added: 'There ought to have been a guard for Lund, but I wanted him kept out of the whole . . .'

The Chief looked up.

'Sampson, or Joseph Howard Vincent, was taken this morning at the Charing Cross Left Luggage office. The arresting officers found the pistol on him that shot the bullets into the Camerons.'

'That's because he took it off Lund,' I said.

'The Sureté in Paris,' continued the Chief, 'have found a body, believed from the pocketbook to be an Englishman, on the railway lines by a spot called . . . Boulevard de la Chapelle.'

He could not say it right.

'That was Hopkins,' I said.

'No face left on him,' said the Chief, 'all smashed away. What'll happen over that I don't know, but I daresay it'll come to naught because you can't hang a man twice. Sampson is to be sent back to us. We'll charge him for this . . .'

He indicated the photograph.

'. . . But if you ask me the magistrates will not commit. There was not a spot of blood on him when he was run in; we have nothing to connect the bastard to it.'

'You'll have the evidence of Parkinson,' I said. 'He knew what Lund was about.'

No reply from the Chief.

'And Mike,' I said. 'He makes a connection.'

'That bugger's scarpered,' said the Chief. 'But I en't bothered because what will get past the committal is the charge of murdering the Camerons. We have the gun, we have the evidence of the goods clerk, Roberts; we have yours. They were vagabonds, that pair; they had a lot to say about any bad business – we have that from the Institute staff – and they'd turned copper in the past . . .'

I had twisted my body away from the Chief as he added, 'I mean to say . . . they'd *inform* from time to time.'

The Chief sighed, out of sight.

'There's Sampson's motive, do you not see?'

He rose to his feet.

'Sampson'll swing for killing the Camerons,' he said, picking up the photograph, 'and you'll be commended to the Super at headquarters.'

By killing Lund, Sampson had removed the one obstacle between himself and a capital charge. It was another new thought; another new sickness. And everything marched in the direction of death. As I closed my eyes in an attempt to go directly to sleep, the Chief chucked something heavy onto my bed.

'Here, lad,' he said. 'Medicine.'

Chapter Thirty-four

Dad shut the door of his house at the top of Baytown, after a good deal of palaver over closing all the curtains in the front room.

'I always close the curtains so as not to fade the dining room carpet,' he'd said to the wife, who had immediately turned and whispered to me, 'I swear he has that from the "Ladies' Column".'

But the sun *was* strong as Dad came up to us, and we all turned to face the sea. The wife was carrying little Harry, for the steep cobbled streets didn't suit the baby carriage that Lillian Backhouse had given us.

A ship was heading north on the sparkling blue water, moving over small, friendly waves of the sort you see painted in a seaside theatre. Dad took the baby off the wife – which he did at every opportunity, even going so far as to walk without his cane in the hopes of having a carry. He pointed young Harry out to face the sea and the ship, saying to him: 'That's ballast for Hartlepool,' at which the wife burst out laughing.

She was walking on ahead, making towards the little row of houses at upper Bay that were always called 'Two Houses', even though there were three of them. We were twisting and turning down the little streets – not so much streets as steps – that led on to Main Street, where the first shop was the sweet shop, the window half blocked out with advertisements for 'Cleeves Toffee'. Dad showed the baby the sweetmeats in the window, saying, 'Thee and me'll be going in there regular, Harry.'

'When he gets his teeth,' called the wife from up ahead.

'. . . When you get your teeth,' said Dad, 'we'll be calling in for . . .'

'Hard Spanish!' called the wife, and she stood waiting for me as I walked slowly down the cobbles. She put out an arm for me, because I was still a semi-invalid, given to shortness of breath, and a ticklish cough at nights.

Bob Langan, son of the Baytown Stationmaster was coming up as we went down.

'How do, Jim?' he said, as I nodded at him. I knew him from my schooldays in Bay, just as I knew half the town for the same reason. He'd learnt all about my adventures in the *Whitby Gazette*, and from Dad too, of course.

'Afternoon, Mr Stringer,' he said, as he went past my dad.

I turned and looked at Bob Langan, and saw that he was looking back at me. A gunshot case was a new thing at Bay, where a lifeboat rescue was the more common run of heroics.

We were going past Barraclough's now; this was the bottom Bay butcher, whereas Dad had kept the top Bay butcher's shop. As usual, he had a long hard look in the window, reading out one of the advertisements in a doubtful tone: 'Prize-Winning Beef from Ruswarp'. Didn't think much of Barraclough's, didn't Dad, and it had been noticed in Bay that if he wanted a nice tongue – which he was particularly partial to – then he went to Whitby on the train to get it rather than call in at Barraclough's and strain to be pleasant.

A cart was coming up, bringing fish for the afternoon train, and we all had to stand aside. As we did so, I thought how Baytown put me in mind of the number one courthouse at York assizes: the 'Two Houses' . . . that was where the judge sat; the dock was the Independent Chapel, tallest of the buildings on Main Street, while the witness box was the post office over opposite. The sea, low, wide and changeable . . . that was the jury box, and the public gallery was the drying ground out along the cliffs, where a dozen white sheets leapt away in the summer sea breeze. The next thing to do was to picture Sampson in the dock, making him bigger than the Independent Chapel, making a giant of the man. The real courthouse had been sunlit too, just as Baytown presently was, with the sunbeams streaming down from the high windows for – what with all the many remands – the trial had not begun until a fortnight after Easter.

Sampson had been arraigned for the murder of the Camerons only, the evidence not being up to the mark regarding the killing of Lund, although the Chief had done his best to bring it about. Parkinson, the lost-luggage superintendent, had given evidence before the magistrates to show that Lund had found himself in the way of harm from the Sampson lot through his (Parkinson's) own actions. It was quite white of him, I thought, to make no bones of the fact that he'd spoken to Mr Five Pounds, the bent copper of Tower Street, who was now awaiting his own trial.

We were walking past the Independent Chapel now, and I saw Smith, the organist darting in, followed by the little fellow who was the organ blower. We were at the lowest level of Bay within another half-minute, directly outside the Bay Hotel.

'The Sunday dinners in there have a very good name, you know,' Dad was saying to the wife.

'A good name where?' said the wife.

'Why, here in Bay,' said Dad.

I was the chief prosecution witness at the trial of Valentine

Sampson, although Roberts, the goods clerk, had run me close. His hands had been made small by the burning metal, like an old maid's and he had been brought to court every day from the infirmary at Armley Gaol.

Looking on from the police seats at the Assizes, I had generally avoided Sampson's eyes, but had snatched a few glances, as for example on the opening day, when he turned in the dock to face the falling sunlight, as though to take strength, and – later – as he smoothed his beard and shook the hands of his brief after the verdict we in the police seats had all been banking on was given.

We went down the steps to the beach, where the wife spread out a blanket, and Dad lowered the baby onto it. We all watched the sea, but little Harry was trying to raise himself and so, taking pity on the lad (I remembered being the only one not able to stand on Platform Four) I picked him up. As usual when I did this he looked set fair for a cry, so I put him down again sharpish, recalling as I did so that there had been one further eye-connection during the judge's summing up, when Sampson had smiled across to me, and made the sleeping sign: two hands together as in prayer, head rested against hands. He had done the same on the train to Dover.

From the Independent Chapel I could hear choir practice, and a hymn I knew: 'Now The Day is Ended', the sound sent out across the sea from the chapel door. I stood a while and listened, then turned sharply to my right – the wife was bringing the baby to me once again.

And now read on for . . .

Murder at
Deviation Junction

The next 'Jim Stringer, Steam Detective' novel

Chapter One

'Cut you in half, it will!' shouted the bloke.

He was talking about the wind coming in from the river.

He called to me again: 'Step over here, lad,' and I walked into the lee of the five great blast furnaces. They were as big as railway tunnels set on end, and joined by gantries at the top along which ironstone tubs ran. In between stood banks of coke, which made the sound of the wind different on this side, but just as loud. Men worked at the hearths set into the bottom of the furnaces – on this freezing day, men without shirts.

'I'm looking for a bloke!' I shouted to the bloke. He grinned and looked up; there came a fast upwards roaring, and the sky above the furnaces turned red. The redness held – like a man-made sunset – and when I looked down again, the bloke was closer to me.

'Name?' he shouted.

I couldn't bring to mind the name of my quarry, although it was set down on the arrest warrant in my pocket, and I carried a photograph of the bloke there too. I knew him as 'Number Nine'; and I knew his place of work.

'Hudson Ironworks!' I bawled at the bloke, and he pointed with his right hand, an action that came easily to him, for he had only one finger attached there. He began to smile, letting me see he had no teeth either. Eighty feet above our heads, I could feel the heat descending, and the wind rising again. I looked at that lonely finger, and the bloke shook it, as if to unfasten my gaze, and get it fixed where it ought to have been: upon the roaring Ironopolis of Middlesbrough.

I began crossing the railway lines half buried in hot cinders, making towards the centre of this city of blast furnaces. Strange trains criss-crossed in front of me, like black curtains being drawn and redrawn, all towed by short tank engines that looked as though they'd been run hard into a wall and made taller than they were long by the smash.

Some of the lines were operated by the company that employed me – the North Eastern Railway Company, I mean – and some were not. Over towards the black River Tees, I watched a line of small hopper wagons move forward, and then it was taken *up*, a little mineral train rising through the sky towards the top of a line of furnaces, brought by the turning of the endless iron rope. The inclined line was mounted on steel struts, and they were shaking in the wind, but the little train kept on. The tops of the blast furnaces were fifty feet high, and the track was – what? one in fifteen for five hundred yards? Men waited for it on the high gantry.

And then I saw giant Hs painted on a row of three. That would have to be Hudson's furnaces. I moved across the ashfield with my coat wrapped round me blanket-wise. I had entered the iron district directly from the Whitby train, without having fastened the buttons, and now my hands were too cold to do them up. I was in want of a decent pair of leather gloves.

As I made towards the Hs, I opened my coat to reach in for my pocket book, and the wind came at me. That's pneumonia right there in that single stab, I thought. I fished out the arrest warrant, and my warrant card. The arrest warrant was inside an envelope, and my hands wouldn't work to open it. I thought again of the bloke's name, but no, it wouldn't come.

I was supposed to lay my hands on Number Nine – orders from Detective Sergeant Shillito, the bastard who breathed beer fumes at me all day long across the floor of the Railway Police office in the station at York. Number Nine was evidently inclined to rowdiness, and Shillito had promised there'd be a Middlesbrough constable to help with the arrest. But no man could be spared, as Shillito had told me with satisfaction just before I'd set off.

Number Nine was a centre forward; turned out for Middlesbrough Vulcan Athletic (Vulcan being the name of the road that skirted the west side of the iron district). At a game played at York on Saturday last he'd crowned Shillito in a football rush. As well as being my governor, Shillito was captain of Holgate United. But I wasn't being sent after Number Nine on account of that first assault. No, I was to arrest him because he'd then laid out the Holgate United goalie during an argument over a penalty kick. The goalie was called Crowder, and his skull had been split. He was at death's door in the York Infirmary, if Shillito was to be believed.

I walked on with head down, thinking again that the affair was not, rightly speaking, a railway police matter at all. Yes, Holgate was the railway ground, but neither of the teams had been Company teams. It was Shillito's personal war that I'd been sent to fight.

I was now directly before the Hudson furnaces. Red molten iron was flowing away from their bases, just as if they were bleeding. Men wearing undershirts or no shirts at all attended the streams with long steel poles as they flowed away into a great building near by.

I began trying to work my hands. I took the warrant from

its envelope. Clegg – *that* was the footballer's name: Donald Clegg. Nickname 'Cruncher'. I felt in my pocket for the photograph Shillito had given me. Middlesbrough Vulcan Athletic played in a strip that made them look like a pack of playing cards: shirts dark-coloured on one side, light on the other, and a crest over the heart. Clegg, the biggest of the lot, stood in the centre of the back row.

'You there!' one of the blokes was calling to me from the bank.

I looked up.

'Step away!' he shouted.

'I'm looking for Clegg!' I called up, but he didn't hear. I held up the photograph and my warrants.

The bloke was striding down the bank now, stepping over the flowing iron channels as he came crosswise towards me.

'Put your boot in one of these and you'll know about it,' he said when he was level with me. He wore a coat over his bare chest, as if he couldn't decide whether it was hot or cold: and the queer thing was that, this close to the furnaces, it was *both*.

'I'm looking for Clegg,' I said, showing him the photograph. 'Works here; turns out for this lot Saturday afternoons. There's been a complaint of assault made against him . . .'

'Clegg's a bloody good player; marvellous at dribbling.'

'What?' I said.

'Dribbling. He's brilliant at it.'

I just looked at the bloke; I did not follow football.

'I know Clegg,' the bloke continued. 'He's a good lad.'

'Well, there's a man lying half-dead in the York Infirmary.'

'Shamming, I expect,' said the bloke.

'Twenty bloody stitches,' I said, 'and you call that shamming.'

'An artist, is young Clegg,' said the bloke. 'An artist and a *poet*.'

'"Cruncher" Clegg, I believe they call him,' I said.

The bloke kept silence.

'Where does he work, mate?' I asked, and the bloke craned his head up towards the over-world at the top of the furnaces, where tiny men moved silently along gantries amid the snow. What was put into blast furnaces to make iron? I tried to think. Ironstone, coke and . . . something else. Limestone.

I joined the bloke in looking again at the high gantries. Had this been Shillito's programme all along? To get me sent up there? But the bloke tipped his head down again, his gaze now roving between the roaring sheds behind us.

'You'll find him over yonder,' he said.

I nodded thanks and turned on my heel.

In the heart of the shed, four men were pacing about in front of a strange and mighty vessel. It looked like a forty-foot-high brick head that pivoted on its own ears, these being formed of two mighty steel wheels held in place by giant iron stays. As I approached, the head tipped upwards, as if to say, 'Who is this come to visit?' And the men stepped back from it.

A bloke came at me from the darkness. 'Look out, mister,' he said, indicating behind. I turned around and a huge ladle of molten iron was rattling towards me, suspended from a moving crane. I tore my eyes away directly, for the sight burnt them. I stood aside as the ladle passed. It was like a piece of the sun put into a bucket, and it was approaching the great swivelling head, which was turning again, ready to receive its drink of hot iron. This was steelmaking.

The roof had been cut away above the thing's head, and some snowflakes that fell through the gap escaped melting, and swirled towards the watching blokes. I fixed my eye on a particular one of the four: the tallest. His right hand was bandaged. He was Clegg, I was sure of it, but the only light I had to go on was that from the iron in the ladle, which had now stopped short of the blokes. It swung in the cold wind that came through the open roof, making weird shadows.

I turned to the bloke who'd warned me of its coming.

'Is that fellow Clegg?' I said, pointing to the one I'd been eyeing.

The man's glance travelled from my warrant card to the four blokes. He said nothing, but I could tell I'd hit the mark. I stepped over towards the blokes and the head somersaulted so rapidly that I thought it might leave its moorings. At that moment, the one behind called:

'Look out, Don – he's a copper!'

I turned about to see the man sprinting to the mouth of the shed. I started after him, running hard over the hot cinders. At the shed mouth, the bloke turned left. I did the same, and one of the red iron streams was right before me. I leapt it and, in the middle of the air, saw another just where I was about to land. I tried to make my leap into a dive, and cleared the second stream with inches to spare. I rolled away from it and lay still for a moment, feeling its warmth all along my left side. I stood up and looked across the territory of Ironopolis. The men who worked in it were made tiny by the size of the blast furnaces; and Clegg could have been any one of the hundreds of tiny blokes in view. I stood up, and tried to brush the red dust off me. One false move in this bloody place, and you were done for. I had no chance of running in an ironworker in the ironmen's own stronghold. If Shillito wanted the job done, he could bloody well ride the train north and do it himself.

I walked back towards the bloke who'd warned Clegg.

'What's your game?' I asked him.

'You could have been anyone, walking to him. He'd have jumped out of his skin if he'd turned round to see you – and that's not safe in a spot like this.'

He looked me up and down

' . . . big fellow like you.'

I was half his size, and getting on for a quarter of his thickness.

'It's obstructing a police officer, that's what.'

'I don't think so.'

'Look, I'm *telling* you. Don't make an argument of it or I'll run you in as well.'

'As well as what?' he said, and a slow grin spread across his blackened face.

Mastering myself for the cold, I headed back towards the mouth of the mill, where snowflakes were swooping about in confusion. I picked my way back through the towers and smoking ore rivers of the iron district, presently hitting Vulcan Road where once again things were human-sized: snow floating down on motor cars, carts and traps; people pushing on grimly, heads down. This was the town that iron had made. I saw a woman at some factory gates over opposite. She was all folded in on herself, quite motionless under accumulating snow. She looked like Lot's wife, and I thought: this party is frozen solid, I must *do* something – but as I approached, she lifted up her head and smiled, as though it was quite a lark to be snow-coated.

Chapter Two

In the middle of town, Queen's Square was a white ploughed field, the ruts made by the cartwheels stretching away towards the railway station, where I saw the wife waiting in her woollen cape and best winter hat. She held her basket with one hand, and young Harry's hand with the other. She'd come up to Middlesbrough with me, and she'd told me she would be at the station for the mid-afternoon York train, should I be able to finish my business with Clegg earlier than expected. (The plan had been for me to take him into the Middlesbrough Railway Police office, for questioning and possible charge.)

'It's snowing, our dad!' young Harry bawled out, as soon as he saw me.

Lydia stooped down and said something to the boy – 'our dad' being a vulgar expression he was forever being told not to use. I looked again at the wife's hat, and I was glad to see that it was the same one as she'd been wearing that morning. She'd come up to Middlesbrough because she'd fancied a look at the new millinery department in the town Co-operative Store, and I'd been fretting that she might have gone on a bit of a spree.

'You've got a bit frozen, Jim,' she said, when I walked up.

Harry asked, 'Where's tha bin, dad?' and Lydia corrected the boy: 'Where have you been, *father*?' She was a kind of echo to Harry, who generally paid her no mind at all.

'I've been to see a man about a dog,' I said.

It was something when your business was unmentionable to your own son.

'We had spice cake,' Harry said.

'As if your father couldn't guess,' said the wife, leaning down to brush a scattering of crumbs off Harry's coat.

'And was it nice?'

'It was *expensive*,' he said.

The wife laughed, looking for my reaction as she did so. The topic of money had been a delicate one between us of late.

'And what else did your mother tell you?'

'Eh?'

'To keep your muffler up to your chin.'

I tried to make from his muffler and coat a seal against the snow. Then we turned and made towards the station, which was a curious mix-up: made of about four churches by the looks of it, with one great hump in the middle. Steam and smoke leaked out from the seams and rose upwards.

'You didn't lay hands on the man then?' said the wife.

'He scarpered.'

She sighed.

'He's a footballer, isn't he?'

'Aye,' I said, 'amateur.'

'And you know which team he plays for?'

'We do.'

'It's pretty easy to track down football teams, you know. They're generally to be found on football *pitches*.'

'His lot dodge about a fair bit.'

'Give over. It's all league and cup, league and cup.'

'There's friendlies as well,' I said. 'That's where he split the goalie's skull – in a friendly.'

'It's a queer town, is this,' said the wife as we walked on towards the station. 'There's red dust everywhere . . . especially on you.'

She lifted her hand up towards my bowler hat.

'It's iron,' I said. 'The air's full of iron. Puts most of the populace into an early grave.'

'I *like* it!' said Harry from behind.

'Get *in*!' Lydia called, stamping her boot, and holding open the booking office door. But Harry had stopped in the snow for a good cough.

'Connection's gone,' Lydia said, shaking her head. That was her expression for when Harry was off into his own world, which was a good deal of the time. She walked out into the snow again, and fairly dragged him in through the station door, where the air was a little warmer from the unseen engines waiting. He was a funny, forward little lad, our Harry, but a very good speaker, considering he was just two months short of his fourth birthday.

Lydia took from her basket the cough cure and spoon she'd carried with her to Middlesbrough, and fed it to the boy amid the swirl and bustle of the ticket hall – for now the evening rush was starting.

We found the Whitby train waiting on the main 'up' platform, and then . . . well, Harry would have to have a look at the engine. He never missed. I led him along to the front, and there stood an M1 Class 4-4-0. 'Outside steam chest – good runner,' I said to Harry, although of course that went over his head. 'It's eeeee-normous,' he said, which is what he almost always said. He then removed his mitten, threw it down on to the snowy platform, and there in his palm was a tiny tin engine.

'I got this today,' he said. 'I keep it in my hand.'

'Where did you get it from?'

'Monster lucky tub,' he said.

'Which shop?'

'Don't know.'

'It's a bobby-dazzler, that is,' I said.

I was glad he'd fished a locomotive out of the bran tub, even if he ought not to be getting presents so close to Christmas. I fancied Harry might make an engineman one day – succeed where I'd failed. But the wife wanted him educated to the hilt, make an intellect of him. Even at a little under four years old, she swore he had all the makings.

Harry was coughing again, so I whisked him back along the platform to where the wife waited, and we climbed up. The steam heat was working in the carriage, but Harry still coughed. He was on the mend from his latest bad go, but he had a weak chest: at age two he'd had pneumonia. Three months in the York Infirmary, pulse at a fever rate for days on end. Our sick club didn't cover the cost, and most of our savings were gone.

We settled ourselves in an empty compartment, and I took out from my pocket the *Middlesbrough Gazette* for Monday 13 December 1909. A succession of polar lows were moving south in an Arctic airstream. There had been much freezing of water taps and gas mains, and now widespread snow was forecast for the district.

The train was being quickly boarded: it was the main service of the evening down the coast to Whitby. You could go by the country way, but I wanted to see the sea. People clattered along the corridor, carrying snow on their shoulders, shouting about the weather: 'Bad weather for thin boots, this is!'

Harry settled eventually, and the wife took out her library book – something on the women's movement, probably with a dash of religion. She always had something like that on the go.

The whistle blew and we were fast away. A moment later, a man and a woman walked into the compartment, and Harry immediately fell to staring at them, which I couldn't stop without drawing attention to the fact that he was doing it.

They were both small. The woman carried a big basket stuffed with parcels. As she pulled the white fur mantle off her shoulders, I caught sight of Lydia's flashing eye. It meant this was the fashionable kind of mantle, worthy of notice. The woman sat down quickly, but took a long time settling herself. The man wore wire-rimmed spectacles, a flat, snow-topped sporting cap, black suit and a green topcoat of decent quality. The cap didn't belong, for he did not look the sporting type.

He carried a valise and a canvas case about a foot and a half square. He looked twice at the notice on the string rack over the seats: 'Light articles only'. He took off his specs and blew on them, as though thinking about that sign. Then he stowed the case on the rack anyway. He put his topcoat up there, and whipped off the cap; he was bald, except for a line of hair that ran round the perimeter of his scalp. It was just a memory of hair, marking the boundary of where the stuff had been. His nose was queer as well. It was an arrow, coming out sharply and going in again quite as fast. It was just right for supporting his specs, though.

Sitting down, he gave me a quick nod, which made his red face turn redder still.

As we rocked away from Middlesbrough station he took some papers from the valise and began leafing through them at a great rate, while occasionally making jottings in a notebook. I looked out of the window. The iron district was to my left, the mighty furnaces burning under the snow. The woman was reading a picture paper – Household Words or some such. I caught sight of the question: 'A lemon cake for Christmas?'

The man lifted his feet and rested them on the seat over opposite, at which Harry's mouth opened wide. I knew what was coming, but could see no way of stopping it.

'It's not allowed!' said Harry, pointing at the boots.

Lydia shook her head, though she was almost laughing at the same time. The man coloured up and – continuing with his note-making – took his feet off the seat.

'Don't bother on our account,' I said to this clerk-on-the-move, who acknowledged me once again with a nod.

Harry was now looking out of the window.

'The boy's quite right though, isn't he?' the woman was saying. 'Where would we be if everyone put their boots on the seats?'

She looked at the man.

'Where would we be, Stephen?'

'I'm sure I don't know, Violet,' he said, hardly looking up from his scribbling.

(She did not look like a Violet – too pale.)

'I think it comes from his being a policeman's son,' said Lydia, at which the clerk looked up over his glasses at me.

'The man two doors down from us in Wimbledon is on the force,' said the woman. 'He's quite high up – an inspector, I think.'

She was pretty but, like her husband, small in scale – like a child playing at being an adult. Whenever she spoke, she caused a commotion, or so she seemed to think, for she rearranged herself afterwards, refolding the gloves that rested on top of her basket and patting down her skirts.

'He's only been in the street for a year,' she went on. 'Well, we all have. But the milkman for the area, who was known to give short measure . . . he doesn't try it in Lumley Road.'

She looked at us all.

' . . . that's because of the Inspector.'

'James is on the North Eastern Railway force,' said the wife, after a moment. 'Detective grade. He's going for his promotion on Christmas Eve.'

And because we were in company, she left off the words: 'He'd better get it as well.'

Lydia had spent the past two years fretting about our futures – mine and hers both. Would she end up at the kitchen sink? That was her leading anxiety. She was a New Woman, forward thinking. There was to be a sex revolution, and you knew it was coming by the speed at which Lydia went at her typewriting. Whenever Harry slept, or was at school, she would be at the machine in the parlour by which she got her living, writing letters for the Co-operative Movement or the women's cause in general or the Co-operative Women's movement, which was a frightening combination of the two. She got a little money by this, and now she'd been offered a position in the Northern Division of the Co-operative Movement: half-time secretary to Mrs Somebody-or-other. Three days a week, ten bob a day. Very fair wages, all considered. Lydia was to give her answer by the first week of the New Year, and she would only be able to say yes if I achieved promotion to detective sergeant. That would be a big leap, for it would all but double my pay, letting us take on a girl who could do the weekly wash and mind Harry for the three days.

My interview was to be with the chief of the force himself, Captain Fairclough, and it was fixed for twelve noon in the spot we were now leaving behind: Middlesbrough, to which the headquarters of the North Eastern Railway Police had lately removed, having been first at Newcastle.

We rolled through Redcar station, for we were semi-fast to

314

Whitby, where we would change for York. I caught a glimpse of the beach as we rocked through Redcar station. It was snow-covered. A torn white flag planted in the sand flew the word 'TEAS'.

The ladies in the compartment were developing a conversation.

'Do you wash at home?'

'Some,' the wife said, very cautiously. 'Only handkerchiefs and the like.'

That was a fib (we washed everything at home), and I flashed the wife a sideways glance, which she avoided.

The woman started in with another question: 'Do you wash the – ?' But she broke off at the sight of three rough-looking blokes whisking along the corridor, shouting at each other as they went. Iron-getters most likely, I thought, and half-canned at the end of a turn. Harry was kicking his feet, looking out of the window at more furnaces – set high on a hill in the weird light.

'Everything's on fire, dad,' said Harry, and it was evidently fine by him, for he spoke the words calmly.

'Wimbledon's home to us,' the woman was saying. 'Lumley Road.'

She would keep on mentioning it.

'It's well away from the railway,' she said.

Was that good or bad? She found the railway noisy, I supposed. But there'd be no Wimbledon without it. I remembered the place from my days on the London and South Western company – a medium class of houses, and seemingly more of them every week you rode by them.

I looked again through the window. A little light left in the day; lonely cottages here and there; snow landing slantwise on the sea beyond.

'Do you know London?' the woman was saying.

'I'm from there myself,' said the wife.

'Oh, where?'

She was cornered now.

'Waterloo,' she said, and that was the end of the conversation for the moment. You could not say the lodging house the wife had kept there had been well away from the station; it had been almost in it. Lydia frowned at the gas lamp over Harry's seat. He suddenly smiled and waved at her with the full length of his arm, as though she sat half a mile away, but she did not respond. She was fighting for the sisterhood, but that didn't mean she had to like all individual women, or even very many of them, and it was ridiculous of me to think so, as I had often been told upon raising the point.

Harry was keeping rhythm with the train, repeating over and over, 'Rattly ride, rattly ride, rattly ride,' until Lydia, ever so gently, kicked him on the knee, after which he fell to whispering the words.

I turned to the boy, saying, 'Those hills are full of miners, Harry – getting the ironstone from which the iron and steel is made. There's a whole world underground: miles of tunnels, workshops, storerooms, even horses and stables.'

'Have you been doing your marketing in Middlesbrough?' Lydia asked the woman.

'I did a little shopping,' said the woman. She was not the sort for marketing.

The village of Marske was to our left – a big house on a hill stood guard over it, but snow fell on village and mansion alike.

'We had tea at Hinton's,' the woman was saying. 'The main dining room, you know.'

We crashed over some points and there was a winding gear suddenly hard by us, all lit up.

'We had lovely macaroons,' the woman was saying, 'and then Stephen smoked a cigar in what they call the More-ish Room. It's rather select.'

At this, the man was finally provoked into speaking.

'The Moorish room,' he said. 'After the Moors, who come from North Africa or wherever it might be . . .'

'Or the Yorkshire Moors,' said the wife, grinning, and the Wimbledon pair both laughed at this: the man quite briefly, the woman for longer. It surprised me that she should have laughed, and made me better disposed towards her.

I turned to Harry. 'Have you seen that we've been passing wagons full of the stuff? They're taking it to Middlesbrough, but must wait for the passenger trains to go by.'

'Why?' said Harry.

'Because,' I said, 'people come before lumps of stone.'

'You reckon,' he said, and Lydia touched his knee with her elastic-sided boot again. This was another of his regular expressions she considered coarse. I looked at the wife, and she grinned. I liked those boots of hers. I wanted to see what she looked like standing in them with nothing else on, but had not quite had the brass neck to ask. I would do, though – I would do it come Christmas Eve if everything had gone all right in Middlesbrough, and we had more money in view.

We were now winding our way towards the new seaside town of Saltburn. The black sea was to our left; a slag break-water stretched out like the black hand of a clock. More shouts came from along the corridor, and the Wimbledon man had stopped work to listen. Harry was coughing again.

We began rolling past tall houses. The cornerstones of some did duty as telegraph poles, and the wires between were thick with snow. Too heavy a coating and they'd come down. Was the blackness I could make out beyond them the sea or the sky? We stopped against the station name: 'Saltburn'. It hung on chains, restless in the sea wind, and I imagined the sea as vertical beyond the houses, like a great wall.

'Want a turn along the platform, son?' I said to Harry.

'Don't be daft,' said the wife. 'He'll catch his death.'

So I went out alone.

As I stepped down, a gang of big, raggedy, snow-covered blokes climbed up. They carried long articles in sacks, and they were not Saltburn types at all. It was rum. There were more like them already aboard.

Saltburn was a terminus – you left by the same direction you arrived. Beyond the buffer bars towered the Zetland Hotel, facing out to sea, which meant views in summer and a terrible battering from the wind come winter. I looked up. A bit of the fancy wooden edging of the platform canopy was coming away in the wind. I stared as it rocked back and forth, thinking: this might come down on the carriage roof at any moment.

I heard the bell before I expected, and was back up in an instant. As I returned to the compartment, Stephen the clerk-on-the-move was coming the other way along the corridor. There was something in his hand, which he put behind his back somewhat as I looked on.

He stepped into the compartment after me, and whatever had been in his hand was now gone. We rumbled backwards, then forwards again; more shouting from along the corridor. Skelton came; Brotton; Huntcliffe – a tiny spot, with no station, but we stopped there anyway. I looked to the left and saw only blackness. But I knew it to be the sea.

Harry was asleep, and the ladies were nodding off too.

The train went on its slow, jerky way for another minute, then came to rest again. At once the gleaming whiteness of snow began to build up against the window frames to the left. There was a sound far off like a war, but it was only the rumbling and booming of the sea. And still the shouts came from along the corridor.

'Irregular, is it?' the man said after a space. 'To come to a stand here?'

'Just a little,' I said, and I couldn't resist adding in an under-breath, 'We're not more than six foot off the cliff edge.'

The clerk moved his boots in a way that made me think he didn't like that idea, so I added, 'Should be away shortly.'

I ought to have introduced myself to the fellow, but something told me he didn't want that. The sharp scream of the train whistle came, and we rolled slowly on. Stephen the clerk said, 'There's some strange working on this line, I'll say that much.'

The train motion sent the ladies' heads rocking, and Household Words slipped to the floor between them, but we hadn't made more than another half-mile before we stopped again. The banks of a cutting enclosed us on either side, and I was ready for the jerk of the applied brake, for something was certainly amiss. We creaked on past a lineside cottage that looked tumbledown, and with a badly smoking fire. Then came a high signal box followed by brighter lights rising to meet us, and we were into a station. There came more shouts, the sound of running boots along the platform.

The Wimbledon woman was awake.

'Where is this?' she said, just as we came to rest with the station sign conveniently filling our compartment window: Stone Farm.

The snow was flying at the words as Harry said, 'It's like Christmas here.'

He always woke up just as though he'd never been asleep.

'Are we booked to stop here?' asked Lydia.

'No,' I said, 'and not much ever is.'

I'd suddenly had enough of the compartment, and all the

319

uncertainty brought on by the weather.

'I'm off for a scout about,' I said. 'See what's going on.'

The rough-looking blokes were moving along the corridor.

'We mustn't be stuck here for all hours,' said the wife. 'Harry wants his bed.'

'Do not,' he said, but he said it quietly, which proved he did. The mysterious Stephen watched me go as I pulled the door closed behind me. The fellow hadn't put pen to paper since Saltburn.